P9-BVG-594

BLOOD ON THE ROCKS

A Selection of Recent Titles from Priscilla Masters

The Martha Gunn Mystery Series

RIVER DEEP
SLIP KNOT
FROZEN CHARLOTTE *
SMOKE ALARM *
THE DEVIL'S CHAIR *
RECALLED TO DEATH *
BRIDGE OF SIGHS *

The Joanna Piercy Mysteries

WINDING UP THE SERPENT
CATCH THE FALLEN SPARROW
A WREATH FOR MY SISTER
AND NONE SHALL SLEEP
SCARING CROWS
EMBROIDERING SHROUDS
ENDANGERING INNOCENTS
WINGS OVER THE WATCHER
GRAVE STONES
A VELVET SCREAM *
THE FINAL CURTAIN *
GUILTY WATERS *
CROOKED STREET *
BLOOD ON THE ROCKS *

The Claire Roget Mystery Series

DANGEROUS MINDS *
THE DECEIVER *

* *available from Severn House*

BLOOD ON THE ROCKS

Priscilla Masters

This first world edition published 2019
in Great Britain and the USA by
SEVERN HOUSE PUBLISHERS LTD of
Eardley House, 4 Uxbridge Street, London W8 7SY.
Trade paperback edition first published
in Great Britain and the USA 2019 by
SEVERN HOUSE PUBLISHERS LTD.

British Library Cataloguing in Publication Data
A CIP catalogue record for this title is available from the British Library.

ISBN-13: 978-0-7278-8940-9 (cased)
ISBN-13: 978-1-78029-605-0 (trade paper)
ISBN-13: 978-1-4483-0222-2 (e-book)

All Severn House titles are printed on acid-free paper.

Severn House Publishers support the Forest Stewardship Council™ [FSC™],
the leading international forest certification organisation.
All our titles that are printed on FSC certified paper carry the FSC logo.

MIX
Paper from
responsible sources
FSC
www.fsc.org   FSC® C013056

Typeset by Palimpsest Book Production Ltd.,
Falkirk, Stirlingshire, Scotland.
Printed and bound in Great Britain by
TJ International, Padstow, Cornwall.

ONE

Monday 22 October, 8.20 a.m.

'Still get in through the door, can you?'

Joanna shot him a baleful glare. 'Bugger off, Korpanski.'

He simply grinned, knowing he had another jibe up his sleeve. Joanna dropped into her chair and Korpanski took in her outfit with some surprise. 'You still cycling in, Jo?'

'It's the only thing that still makes me feel half human and less a dumper truck.'

He looked dubious. 'I don't think I'd have been very keen on Fran cycling through a pregnancy.'

'I'm not Fran, am I?'

Korpanski opened his mouth to respond but quickly shut it again without asking what Matthew thought about her cycling at this time.

She'd picked up on something. 'You got something up your sleeve, Korpanski?'

'Yeah, I have.'

'Well, spit it out.'

But DS Mike Korpanski was taking his time. He was going to get maximum satisfaction out of this one. 'Something right in your line.'

'Go on.'

'Old man gone AWOL from a residential home.'

Her head whipped round. 'And you think I should be investigating this, do you?'

He'd picked up on her dangerous tone all right but DS Korpanski enjoyed sailing close to the wind. He nodded, not even trying to suppress a smile.

Detective Inspector Joanna Piercy glared at her detective sergeant. 'You're kidding me, right?'

Korpanski didn't respond to the furious demand as she continued her rant. 'You really want me to investigate an old man who's wandered away from a residential home? Mike,' she appealed, 'I know I'm pregnant and have the belly of a blue whale and the brain of a flea but, bloody hell, I haven't sunk that low. Haven't you got uniforms looking out for him? He can't have gone far.'

'The uniforms haven't come up with anything, Jo.'

'Well, get them to look harder then. It's hardly something for us.'

He was grinning at her as he leaned back in his seat, tempted to spin it around, peer into his computer screen and avoid seeing the fire that was burning in her eyes. 'As he hasn't turned up so far, Chief Superintendent Gabriel Rush, your favourite CS ever, says we should be asking questions and getting involved.'

'And you think it's one for me.'

'The sooner he's found, Jo, the sooner we can all get on with some real work.'

He followed that up with, 'Besides, a nice easy task like this. I thought it'd be right up your street.'

She almost ground her teeth before realizing that was exactly the response he'd been counting on, so modified it to, 'You,' she said, finger pointing, 'are trying your bloody luck, Mike. I don't even give birth for a couple of months. I can't do crap like this until then. I'm an inspector, for goodness' sake. Matthew already wants to wrap me up in cotton wool, ban me from riding my bike. He wants us to spend our time off together looking at prams and cribs and . . .' And then it was all too much for her and she dropped her face into her hands, almost sinking her head on to the desk. 'Mike,' she appealed again, 'how on earth am I going to cope with all that? Matthew's parents simply can't wait to become acting grandparents though . . .' Mercurial as ever, she smothered a grin herself now. 'I can't say *my* mum is quite so keen. In fact, she's keeping her distance, as is my sister and her pair of brats.'

Korpanski bit back the retort, *don't blame them*, contenting himself with a long sigh which could have meant anything and smirked into his computer screen as she continued with her rant.

'This whole role – it's not me. I'm not some earth mother.'

He turned around then, studied her face and read only apprehension. And he felt an unexpected wash of sympathy for her misgivings, realizing they were all centred on her doubts about the approaching 'happy event'. 'Jo,' he said, wanting to reassure her, 'you'll love it. Take to it like a duck to water. It's a piece of cake. Nothing to it being a mum. It'll all come naturally, I promise you.'

She was unconvinced, her doubt failing to melt away but staying, a block of ice inside her heart. 'I'm not so sure,' she confessed. 'Unlike Matthew who just can't wait to cuddle it. He's so convinced it's a boy, Mike, he's even chosen a name.'

Korpanski chuckled. 'So what is it?'

Shoulders up in exasperation. 'He won't tell me.'

Korpanski smiled. He and his wife had had a pact. He could choose his daughter's name, Jocelyn, while his wife had chosen their son's: Richard, who was never ever called anything but Ricky.

'And just think of his disappointment if it's another girl.' She gulped. 'Another Eloise.'

'He'll get used to it.' And as she still looked unconvinced he added, 'Well, at least he's not Henry VIII and won't be chopping your head off for a child of the wrong sex.'

They both laughed at this and the atmosphere melted while the surrounding officers looked up from their desks and thanked their lucky stars for the way DS Korpanski could deflect their inspector's growing irritability which was only matched by her increasing girth.

When they'd stopped laughing Mike couldn't resist tacking on, 'You *can* find out the sex of the child before it's born, you know. You don't have to wait, Jo. Maybe it'll take some of the stress out of it?'

'No, thanks.' She held up her hand. 'Heaven forbid. I wouldn't exactly be enamoured at the thought of another Eloise growing like a tumour inside me.'

Korpanski looked over, dark eyes concerned. 'I'd keep that particular thought to yourself.'

And even she realized she'd crossed a line. 'Yeah. You're right. I guess so. I'll cross that bridge when I meet it.'

Korpanski rested his large, meaty paw on her shoulder. 'It'll all be worth it, Jo, I promise.'

And she nodded, thinking, maybe, maybe not. Too late now.

If Matthew had the son he so fiercely desired, it would be worth it all – the sickness, the nausea, the tiredness, the *huge* waistline, the horrible clothes and *big* knickers. It would all be worth it just to see that wondrous look on his face again – the very same look that had lit his face when she had first told him she was pregnant. A look she hadn't seen since they'd first become lovers – a sort of amazed disbelief at his good fortune. The realization of a dream which was coming true, the fulfilment of his ambition.

Mike brought her back to the present. 'I tell you, Jo. When you have your baby, be it son or daughter, you will love it more than life itself. They become everything to you. More important than career or ambition or anything else. They become your life. Your future.'

She looked at her sergeant, at his dark eyes and tall, burly form and felt a wave of affection matched only by her interest in these foreign emotions he was describing. 'You really feel that strongly about Ricky and Jossie?'

'Yeah,' he said. 'I do. I'd give my life for them, Jo.' But even as he spoke the words he sensed the vulnerability this confession exposed, which for a moment knocked him silent and made him thoughtful, dark eyes clouded even at the thought.

'And you really think I'll feel like that . . .' she rested her hands on her bump, 'when this child is born?'

He nodded.

'Matthew already does.'

Korpanski simply nodded again and she held out her hand for the notes she'd spied on his desk. 'OK, then,' she said. 'I give in. Tell me about the case?'

Sensing the storm was now abating, Korpanski tossed the few papers across the desk. 'Here it is, Inspector Piercy,' he said, smothering his grin. 'Old guy with dementia missing from a residential home. We've already alerted the local lads but he hasn't turned up so far. And that's about it.'

She took the notes from him. Read the top line.

Zachary Foster, age ninety-six, missing some time during the night from Ryland's Residential Home. Absence noted seven a.m. Suffers from dementia. Stroke two years ago. Speech impaired. She looked up.

'Hardly a major case,' she said wryly. 'How are the mighty fallen.'

And to that even Korpanski couldn't produce an answer.

TWO

They wouldn't exactly be using the blue light to drive to Ryland's. There was no hurry. The longer they left it, the likelier it was that the old boy would turn up of his own accord. Joanna had googled the home and read only glowing reviews.

'Cared for my dad like one of their own.'

'A pleasant, welcoming atmosphere.'

'Wonderful, kind staff.'

'They even made Mum a birthday cake.'

And so on. By the time they got there, she guessed, the old guy would have wandered back. They'd be met at the door by an apologetic matron and sent on their way, back to the station and Korpanski's jibes.

She'd elected to bring PC Bridget Anderton with her. Besides the fact that she would do well interviewing confused elderly people, Joanna had an ulterior motive.

Bridget had three children. That meant three pregnancies and, presumably, three labours. If anyone knew about childbirth it was Bridget Anderton. As the time approached, Joanna was becoming increasingly anxious about this inevitability. Considering her husband had done three months' obstetrics in his medical student days, Matthew had not been very helpful on this subject. He'd ummed and aahed and said, 'They just get on with it.' She'd wanted more details. A personal view from someone who had actually experienced labour and giving birth. At the back of her mind she was curious and increasingly concerned. The baby was growing and somehow, in the not too distant future, it was going to have to make an appearance, which meant being pushed out of her nether regions by her – unless, of course, she opted for or needed a caesarean section. She wanted Bridget's story straight from the horse's . . . she smirked. Not exactly the mouth.

She glanced at her watch. It was now ten a.m. Mr Zachary Foster had been missing for anything up to eight hours. Even so the chances were that he was still not too far away, probably cowering in a shop doorway or trying to buy a coffee in the Red Cross charity shop on the Butter Market. But no one had rung in so far.

She and Bridget made their way to the car, walking through chilly sunshine, anticipating the simple case ahead.

When, later on, she returned to that moment, she found herself again in that comfortable place where this disappearance was nothing more than a confused old man who had wandered out of a residential home which probably had next-to-no security measures. Later on she might wish herself back there.

Somehow Bridget, with her sensitive and intuitive nature, had already sussed out the reason for her being chosen to accompany her and was doing her best to respond to the DI's questions. 'It's not that bad, Jo.'

Joanna kept her eyes on the road. What did that mean: It's not *that* bad?

PC Bridget Anderton tried again. 'It's like period pains.'

'Ugh.'

Bridget tried again, a bit harder. 'Just a bit more fierce.'

'And what about . . .?'

'When you push – oh my goodness. That's an urge like you've never felt before. It is all consuming.'

Joanna frowned. 'Not sure I like the sound of that.'

Bridget sat back in her seat, a smile lighting her plain face. 'You haven't got much choice, Joanna.'

That drew a scowl.

Bridget tried for a third time. 'But then they put the baby in your arms and, oh, Jo,' she turned to look at her inspector. 'It's heaven. You feel this warm glaze of honey all over you. It's magic and you feel powerful.' She echoed Korpanski's words. 'You feel you would die for this tiny, vulnerable being that you've just produced.'

Joanna wrinkled up her nose and turned to look at the PC. 'I'm really not sure about this.'

At which point Bridget burst out laughing. 'That baby's got to come out and that's the way it'll be. Head first – usually.'

'Was Steve there with you?'

'For Katie and Sollie but not for Troy. He came too quick.' She turned to look at her. 'But Matthew's a doctor, Joanna. He'll *want* to be there to see his child's birth and make certain everything's done right.'

'Oh, he'll want to be there all right. Make sure everything's done properly.' Was it a consolation that he would be there, witnessing the moment she gave birth to his son – or daughter – or would it inhibit her? Was being together at such a personal moment a good or a bad thing? She didn't know . . . yet. Something else she would learn.

A sign, black with gold lettering, swinging in a light breeze, told them they were there and put paid to their conversation. Joanna turned the car into the drive.

Ryland's was one of the last houses before the town gave way to empty moorland. It was a large Victorian house, set back from the A53, a road that climbed and climbed up to Ramshaw Rocks and the Winking Man, crossing miles of bleak moorland, empty apart from scattered smallholdings, finally dropping into the spa town of Buxton. Before they petered out, giving way to the deserted moors, the houses along this road were huge. Plenty big enough for a good-sized residential home. The sign moving in a cool autumn breeze read: *Ryland's Residential Home for elderly folk.*

It sounded friendly. Safe. Reassuring. Inviting. As they travelled up the drive, Joanna's thoughts were that this was the civilized way to care for the frail, the vulnerable, the elderly. Already she was piecing together a narrative. The guy had wandered out, too confused to find his way back. He would soon be found. The fact that he hadn't yet been spotted could be an indication that he was somewhere near, perhaps paranoiac, hiding from what he would perceive as a hostile, alien environment and people who might harm him.

She inched the car along the drive, eyes alert to any sign of movement. Two squad cars told her a search was already under-foot. So why drag me in? she wondered, still irritated. Any time now there would be a shout and she could return to the station.

The grounds were neatly lawned with a few mature trees lining the driveway, already sprinkled with freshly fallen leaves which made it look like a brightly patterned carpet against the brilliant green of the grass. A sign pointed to a large car park at the rear but Joanna pulled up in front and parked at the side of the police cars, taking in tall bay windows either side of a panelled front door, shiny with black gloss paint, which was now firmly closed. Shutting the stable door? All looked neat, quiet, well-ordered and civilized, the squad cars the only sign of drama. She and Bridget climbed out of the car and locked it behind them.

Now Joanna had reached the scene her narrative was finding colour and movement. An old man creeping out of that door, standing on the step, looking around him, already tense, nervous and completely lost. He would step down, getting even more lost and confused as he reached the grounds. So had he headed down the drive, out into the long, unfamiliar street where he would either turn right, towards the town, a slight decline, or left, climbing up to Blackshaw Moor, stepping into the dangerous void that was the moorlands, where he might suffer exposure, an accident, and where there was less chance of him being found by a passer-by. And already she was working through something else. This end of the road wasn't actually in the town but a good half-mile outside, and at night was lit only by lampposts. To his left the road would have been black and bare, the lampposts finishing in a hundred yards or so. To the right the road sloped gently down towards the town and civilization. But, depending on what time he had made his escape, Leek is hardly a town of late-night bustle, bright lights and noisy bars. It is a rural market town, the native folk, in general, more likely to keep to their homes on a cold night in late October.

So . . . she stood for a moment trying to put herself in his place. A confused old man. What would he be most likely to do? Surely he would have headed down the hill towards the lights? But there was always the possibility that he had turned left out of the gates and been swallowed up in the dark. It seemed unlikely but would their man have had the power of reason? Did he think he was heading somewhere? Had he a plan? A trigger for leaving – perhaps staff cruelty? Confusion? A misapprehension? The trouble was, unlike a person suffering from depression or a rebellious teenager, she had absolutely no idea how a person suffering from dementia would reason; whether they were capable of rational thought, a structured plan. She recalled the description of the missing man's medical condition. They had described his mental state with the word dementia. A stroke two years ago. Surely that must have affected his mobility? And speech impaired, so if anyone did find him he might be unable to describe where he had come from. This didn't look good. But surely he was nearby? He must be, hampered by that collection of medical stumbling blocks. She frowned.

Had he headed into the darkness, they would have a logistical problem – the need to sweep the moors to search. It would be very difficult to achieve this on foot or by car which meant the police helicopter. There were tracts of land that roads couldn't penetrate. The ground was soft and peaty but she couldn't see Chief Superintendent Gabriel Rush authorizing a search with the police helicopter. Not in today's straitened economic climate.

But if their missing man was in the town, she would have thought the locals would have found him already. And if he was in the grounds, likewise the uniforms would have stumbled across him. It was only if he had, for some unfathomable reason, headed out towards the moorland that he might have escaped attention.

Still, in her mind, this was a case which should soon solve itself.

All she had to do was to play the game for a few hours, speak her lines and wait for the inevitable to happen, i.e., for Mr Zachary Foster, aged ninety-six, to turn up.

Alive. Someone would find him. But for now she needed to act the professional, ask the right questions, home in on the detail. Privately she gave the case one day at most.

PC Bridget Anderton was standing on the doorstep at her side, waiting for her to knock or ring the bell. Bridget wasn't one of the world's beauties – her face was pale and plain, the skin slightly doughy. The transformation happened when she smiled. It was as though all the love and joy in the world was contained in that smile. It actually seemed to radiate happiness. Added to that she was genuine and loyal and Joanna trusted her. She was one of the world's good people who, unusually for a policewoman, rarely saw harm in anyone.

Before knocking, Joanna eyed the solid-looking door. Unless this had been left open or unlocked, her missing man would have had no chance of getting through it. But then, surely in a well-run establishment which catered for elderly gentlefolk, *all* doors should have been secured so residents could *not* wander off. So what had gone wrong last night? Her first thought was how had he left without anyone noticing? There were surely watchful night staff? Had one door been left open and that had been enough for Mr Foster to abscond? Had he watched and waited for his chance? Plotted and planned? So her first questions to them had to be when exactly had he gone and when had his absence been noticed?

Again her questions turned full circle back to Mr Foster's state of mind and his ability to form a plan. She tried the front door. Locked. As it should be.

She pressed the button and heard a satisfying ring reverberate inside.

After a minute or two the door was pulled open by a pleasant-looking woman of about fifty wearing black trousers and a pale blue sweater. A pair of glasses sat on the top of her head. She looked questioningly at them, blinking shrewd grey eyes.

'Detective Inspector Joanna Piercy.' Joanna flashed her ID and Bridget did the same.

The woman bent forward slightly to read them. 'Have you found him?'

'I'm sorry. No. Not yet. And I take it he's not turned up here either?'

Yeah, that was a little too hopeful.

The woman shook her head and put her hands to her cheeks, sighing, 'Oh, I do hope he's all right. He's a nice old man. I wouldn't want any harm to come . . .' Her voice trailed away as she realized how inadequate her words were. She gathered herself, stood upright.

'Come in. Come in.' She held out her hand. 'I'm Sandie Golding.'

'You're the owner of Ryland's?'

'No, no. I'm just the manager. The owner is Sadiq Haldar. He's based in the Potteries. He owns quite a few . . .' an ingratiating smile, '. . . establishments. I just see to the day-to-day running. That is—'

Joanna interrupted her. 'Can we go into your office and speak privately, please?'

'Yes. Of course.' Embarrassment surfaced. 'Umm, I'll have to get you to sign in, I'm afraid.' And the usual explanation. 'Health and safety.'

Which hadn't worked for the missing man. But to release that comment wouldn't exactly move the case forward.

They obliged, Joanna in a flourishing signature, Bridget's childish and square lettered. Then they followed Ms Golding along a cream-painted corridor lined with sepia prints of ancient Leek, passing a room of residents sitting in high-backed chairs.

Joanna peeped in. The television was on in the corner but most weren't watching it. Though many of the residents, mainly women, were simply sitting, staring, doing nothing, she noticed one woman fiercely knitting and was immediately transported back to the pink-washed cottage in Shropshire and her grandmother's knitting needles similarly flying and clacking, the air of total absorption identical. The woman looked up from her knitting, met her eyes and smiled.

The manager led them into a small, snug office, pale green walls lined with rows of certificates. From a quick glance it looked as though all the staff had passed the appropriate training which must, in turn, have inspired potential clients to park their elderly relatives here with confidence. For the first time Joanna saw this disappearance of one of their residents from another angle. It would result in bad publicity for the home. Next time a potential user Googled it the reviews would not be all so good.

Sandie Golding sat behind a desk and Joanna and Bridget took their seats. Joanna's instinct was to ascertain the hard facts as soon as possible, a description, the when and where of the last sighting. 'So . . .' She pulled out a notebook. 'First of all, let's start with a description.'

'About five foot ten. Brown eyes, sparse . . .' The first glimmer of humour. 'Very sparse white hair.'

'His eyesight?'

'He wore glasses. Like most elderly people he had limited sight.'

Bridget Anderton interrupted. 'Registered blind?'

'Oh, no. Nothing like that. Not that bad.'

Joanna took over. 'And his hearing?'

'He wore a deaf aid.'

'Is that in his room or is he wearing it?'

For the first time Ms Golding faltered. 'I'm sorry,' she said. 'I don't know. I should have checked.'

'No worries. We'll search for it when we look around his room.'

That provoked a smile.

'So . . .' Joanna moved on to less tangible matters. 'Tell me about Mr Foster. What was he like?'

On safer ground here, Sandie Golding smiled. 'He was a sweet old man with dementia.'

'And what form did that take?'

'He lived in the past.' She smiled again. 'He'd lived in Leek all his life. Worked for the Staffordshire Moorlands District Council – as a clerk, I think. He'd lived with his mother but when she died years ago he just lived alone – in the very same house he'd been born in.' She smiled. 'I can see him now, wandering around, always looking a bit bemused, clutching a battered old teddy bear he'd had since he was a child, dragging it behind him like Christopher Robin.' She paused, lost in the memory.

Though it was a sweet picture, it described someone suffering from dementia quite graphically. But when you superimposed this image of a ninety-six-year-old man clutching his teddy like a six-year-old, possibly wandering the moorlands on a chilly October night, the smile was soon wiped from your face.

'Was he prone to wandering?'

'No. He wasn't.' A thoughtful smile. 'He wasn't one of our wanderers. He was a contented sort. He's never done this before.'

'OK.' Joanna continued writing. 'His full name?'

'Zachary Foster.' She gave an ingratiating smile. 'No middle name.'

Joanna didn't smile back. 'Can I confirm his age?'

'He's ninety-six.'

'And you say he's never absconded before?'

'No.'

'Does he have family in Leek?'

'No. He was never married and his mother died years ago. He was quiet and self-contained. A shy man who said little.'

'The stroke. How did that affect him?'

'He dragged his leg a bit but – considering his age – he'd made a pretty good recovery.'

'And his speech – how bad was that?'

'His speech was slurred. Deliberate and slow. Sometimes he just couldn't find a word. That could make him upset and a little frustrated but in general he was a quiet, contented man.'

'I see.' Now for the nitty-gritty. 'How did he get out, Miss Golding?' (No wedding ring.)

'I don't know.' Hesitation before the infill. 'We're reviewing our safety policy.'

Of course they would. Joanna was finding it hard not to sigh. 'Do you have CCTV?'

Sandie looked even more embarrassed. 'No – Mr Haldar . . .' Her voice trailed away with misery and embarrassment.

Joanna could guess. Saving money. Cutting costs. Privacy.

'How many entrances are there to Ryland's?'

'Three main ones plus two fire exits.'

'We'll take a look at those in a minute. Do you know which exit he used?'

Ms Golding shook her head miserably. 'No,' she said. 'The front and back doors into the kitchen are both deadlocked. The keys are locked in my office and the spares stay with whoever is in charge. He couldn't have got out through either the front or the back doors.'

'And the third exit?'

'The French windows open from the day room. The keys hang on a hook to the side. The night sister is responsible for locking up after the evening staff have left. The French windows were locked and bolted this morning when they were checked. We take security very seriously here.'

The irony of her statement was obviously eluding her.

Joanna bit back her words. *So, this old guy with dementia is a reincarnation of Harry Houdini, able to exit through locked, bolted doors, hanging keys back on the hook, shooting the bolts across behind him. Either that or he magically pickpocketed the nurse in charge, relieved her of the keys to either the front or the back door, locked it behind him and equally skilfully replaced them. Without her knowing.*

Possibly sensing the flaw in her account, Ms Golding frowned, and Joanna knew someone would be getting into big trouble over this. She had to go through the motions – the public expected this from their police service. But already she could see holes. Someone was lying here. Probably to cover their back. Someone had broken the rules and Mr Foster had walked.

'The fire exits?'

'They were both secured and closed.'

Joanna absorbed this. 'So back to the day room. The French windows, you say, were locked and bolted?'

There was a touch of asperity in the manager's reply. 'The key hangs on a hook, the bolts shot across.'

'Could he have reached the key, shot back the bolts, opened it himself and maybe the staff secured it after he'd gone not realizing he was outside?'

Sandie Golding gave a miserable shake of her head. 'No,' she said, reluctantly. 'I don't think he could have let himself out. The bolts are stiff, the top bolt right on the top of the door, halfway across, only reached by standing on a chair,' She smiled. 'Even by the staff. We did that deliberately to stop anyone reaching them. The key is hidden behind the curtain and quite high up. I don't think Zachary could have reached it.'

'How tall is he?'

'Oh, around five ten. I'm not absolutely sure.' Her eyes grew hard and challenging.

But Joanna sensed hesitation. 'So had he exited that way, somebody would have had to let him out and then locked and bolted the door behind him?'

The manager shook her head, hung it miserably, focusing on the parquet floor. 'I was wondering whether the night staff forgot to lock it in the first place and he wandered outside then later, one of them realized the door wasn't properly secured and locked it, and he couldn't get back in.'

'Has that happened before?'

Sandie shook her head and, more confident of her ground now, looked up again. 'Not to my knowledge. They're generally pretty thorough and careful. And he would have shouted.'

'Have you checked with them?'

'Of course. They insist they followed correct procedure.'

Joanna looked up. 'And you say you don't think Mr Foster would have been capable of unbolting and unlocking the door by himself?'

Sandie Golding tried to retrieve her previous comments. 'Well . . .' She looked flustered and changed her story. 'Well, yes. Perhaps he was *physically* capable. I think he *could* have . . .' She gave in. 'Oh, I don't know,' she said.

Bridget Anderton spoke. 'What was Mr Foster's mobility like?'

Perhaps sensing a softer persona, Sandie Golding's attention turned to the PC. 'He could get around,' she said cautiously, as though anticipating a trap.

Bridget persisted. 'Was he unsteady on his feet?'

'Not particularly. It was only the effects of the stroke that made him drag his foot.'

Bridget wasn't giving up. 'How far could he walk?'

'I don't know. It's hard to say.' Sandie Golding was hedging.

Joanna pressed her. 'Roughly?'

She ducked the question. 'You'd better ask the nursing staff.'

'Could he have climbed on the chair to let himself out?'

'I don't know.'

Joanna reverted to the subject of Mr Foster's point of exit. 'You say the day-room key hangs on a hook right by the door?'

'In case of fire.'

Joanna remembered the fire certificate. 'How high up?'

'About shoulder level.' Her eyes were evasive. But Joanna was trying to puzzle out this initial part of the investigation. If the missing man was only a couple of inches short of six feet, he could easily have reached the key. Climbing on a chair and shooting back stiff bolts, though, might have proved more of a challenge. Looking at the manager's face, Joanna sensed she could already see the negative reviews and dwindling list of prospective residents. For the home this could prove a disaster.

But . . . Joanna's mind moved along. If Mr Foster been accidentally locked out, surely when they had realized he was missing they would have found a cold, shivering old man sitting on the doorstep. Or else a corpse.

She glanced at Bridget Anderton. Her face was a picture of sympathy and understanding. But, mirroring Joanna's thoughts, there was a touch of accusation against the manager. In their opinion this case was one neither of them should have been involved in. Joanna breathed in the scent of elderly people, something fusty and confusing. She was resentful at being here at all. And the humiliation was making her mood scratchy.

'And he was last seen . . .?'

'They checked on him around two a.m. He was fast asleep. The staff had given him his evening medication.'

'At what time?'

'Around nine. Sometimes earlier.'

'The medication consisted of . . .?'

'Zopiclone.' Sandie Golding shifted her glasses down from the top of her head to cover her eyes. She was embarrassed that the staff medicated their way to a quiet night. But that wasn't Joanna's concern.

'And he took it?'

'Oh, yes. There was never any trouble with Mr . . .' Her voice trailed away as she acknowledged she'd just, inadvertently, used the past tense.

Joanna glanced at the notes she'd already made. 'Can you think of a reason why Mr Foster might have wanted to go outside?'

That drew a deep breath, hesitation and a flicker in her eyes. 'I mentioned he always carried an old teddy bear, dragged it around like Christopher Robin. He'd mislaid it.' There was a certain tinge of contempt creeping into both her voice and her facial expression.

Bridget spoke up again. 'So what happened to it?'

'Oh, I don't know.' It was a throwaway remark. 'Perhaps one of the other residents "borrowed" it. It's possible it was accidentally thrown away. It was a horrible old thing his mother had given him years ago when he'd been a child. But he was very attached to it. Took it to bed every night. Carried it everywhere, got in a panic if he couldn't find it.' She smiled, for an instant forgetting the story behind this interview and to whom she was speaking. 'In a way, many of our residents are children.' Her face hardened. 'The teddy went missing last week and he was upset.'

Joanna felt an expletive bubble up inside her, imagining the leg-pulling at the station. Not only searching for a missing geriatric but his teddy bear too. Great!

Out loud she meliorated her response, managing to make her tone if not concerned at least neutral. 'His teddy bear's gone missing before?' She avoided Bridget's eyes. The pair of them would have exploded.

'No. He kept it very close.' Ms Golding's tone was severe. No mirth there. Joanna reminded herself this was a vulnerable adult, their responsibility, who was missing – on a quest for his beloved teddy bear or not.

'When exactly did it go missing?'

'I don't know – exactly.' She seemed irritated by the question. 'I only know some time last Wednesday he couldn't seem to find it and spent the day searching for it. Half the staff helped him look.'

Bridget's quiet voice broke in again. 'But you didn't find it?'

'No.'

Joanna took over. 'And you think that would have been reason enough for him to get up in the night, sometime after the night staff had, presumably, observed him sleeping, and search for it outside? When he'd been dosed up with sleeping tablets?' Somehow she'd made it sound almost impossible.

'I can't think of any other reason,' Ms Golding responded sharply, still defensive. 'Some of our patients do wander. But not Zac. He always seemed perfectly content with his daily life.'

'Until his teddy bear went missing,' Bridget put in again. Joanna's head flicked round to look at the PC and Bridget gave her a cheeky smile in response.

Sandie Golding appeared not to have noticed, simply adding, 'It did upset him.' She gave a little huff of a laugh. 'The strange thing is that he seemed to have found another one from somewhere. Or maybe one of the staff took pity on him and got hold of another one.'

Joanna didn't even know why she picked up on this. 'Did anyone *say* they had?'

Ms Golding looked even more irritated. 'Had what?'

'Substituted another bear?'

'No.' Said curtly, it shut the avenue down.

Joanna looked at Bridget and raised her eyebrows. Was this what pregnancy had reduced her to? Investigating the theft and substitution of an old man's teddy bear?

'I think somehow,' Ms Golding continued, 'that he must have slipped out and gone to look for it and then got lost.'

While someone locked the doors behind him?

'The grounds are currently being searched,' Joanna said, 'by a team of uniformed officers, but so far they haven't found him.' She couldn't resist tacking on with cruel irony, 'Or, apparently, a teddy bear. If your patient did wander, it seems he left the grounds and has wandered further afield.' She made a mental note-to-self to make sure the search of the home had been thorough. Maybe they should look again *inside* the home.

Ms Golding continued trying to find an explanation. 'He was quite disturbed. I'm sorry, but it's the only reason I can give you for his absconding.' But something had changed in her expression. Doubt. She was doubting her own version. All three of them could hazard a guess as to what had gone on. If Zachary Foster had not managed to unlock the door himself, the door must have been left unlocked by a member of staff. So it appeared that the befuddled elderly gent, possibly in a quest for his missing teddy, had simply wandered out and been unable to get back in, possibly accidentally or as a result of his confused state of mind. Either that or someone had deliberately let him out and locked the door behind him. There seemed no logical reason for that, unless a member of staff had malicious or psychopathic tendencies. And that seemed unlikely. Joanna recalled the glowing tributes to Ryland's.

Looking at the guarded expression on Ms Golding's face, if he had managed to open the doors himself and accidentally been locked out, at the very least Ryland's needed to review their safety and security policy. And judging by Sandie Golding's face, her mind was tracking along the same route, displaying wariness slowly morphing into damage limitation.

There was an uneasy silence until Sandie Golding spoke again, confessing more to herself than to the two officers. 'This'll be bad publicity.'

We all have our own perspective.

Joanna looked out of the window to a large patio which stretched the entire side of the home and a patchy lawn beyond. As in many Victorian houses, the grounds were extensive. The

5

likelihood was that if the missing man was nowhere in the home, he was somewhere in the undergrowth and would soon be found. She could see the team of officers moving forward in a line. They would have divided up the grounds into a grid and would cover every single inch of lawn, flowerbeds, bushes, trees.

Bridget followed her glance. 'Shall I go outside to talk to them?'

'Yeah. That'd be good.'

Bridget left.

Minutes later Joanna saw her outside the window, approaching a couple of fellow officers who were poking through the bushes with long sticks. From their demeanour the old man was still missing.

Joanna watched.

Bridget was wrapping her arms around herself against the cold. The weather had turned bitter, as it could in a town which was high and bordered miles of moorland. Leek, in times gone by, could easily be cut off even in autumn. The sky was a heavy, luminous grey and threatening enough to herald a storm which could even bring snow. The wind was rising, the leaves swirling around on the trees which bordered the lawn, branches jerking in an increasingly frenetic, mad dance. Soon they would be stripped bare, wearing winter's nudity. If a ninety-six-year-old man was out there, he would be unused to such cold after the oppressive heat of the home. It was no weather for him to be wandering around searching for a lost teddy bear. He would die of exposure if he hadn't already.

Unless.

'What would Mr Foster have been wearing?'

'I – I don't know. I'm not sure.'

'Slippers? Pyjamas? A coat? A dressing gown?'

'I don't know. I really don't know.' The manager was flustered. 'You'll have to ask the nurses. They'll know what clothes he had.' She hesitated, adding, 'What's missing.'

'Right. I shall need a list as soon as possible, please. As well as a list and contact details of the staff who were on duty last night.'

'Of course.'

Afterwards Joanna would deliberate over questions she could have asked, focused more on points she was now discarding like unwanted cards in a poker game, expecting all the time for there to be a shout from outside.

'Excuse me one moment.' She pulled her mobile phone from her pocket and located Korpanski. 'I take it the uniforms have done a thorough search of the premises?'

'Yes. They're still there, aren't they?'

'Yes. I'll speak to them and see if they've come across a teddy bear.'

Korpanski's splutter was as eloquent as a comment. When he spoke his voice was low and still full of humour. 'You are kidding me, aren't you, Jo?'

'Unfortunately,' she responded drily, 'no.' She wanted to add so much but Sandie Golding's grey eyes were taking everything in and her ears practically flapping.

I'm now reduced to finding a fucking teddy.

She knew Korpanski was having trouble suppressing his laughter as he said formally, his voice mocking and saturated with humour, 'Description of the said Edward Bear?'

And now even she was having trouble concealing her smile.

'I'll see if I can get one, Mike.' And returned to the point of her call. 'So our missing man hasn't turned up yet?'

'Sorry, Jo. Not yet.' And he couldn't resist tacking on, 'Nor his teddy bear.'

'Not even any sightings from our ever-vigilant public?'

'Not so far.'

'Only – the weather's turning.'

'Yeah, I know. Forecast is bad. Below freezing tonight. You got any useful leads from the home?'

'Not so far.'

In front of the manager she couldn't share the fact that there was little likelihood of there being any logical plan in the missing man's mind. He would simply wander at random, so the police search could not be structured around a 'plan' or delving into the missing geriatric's confused state of mind. Apart from what their missing man was wearing – dressing gown? Striped pyjamas? Slippers? The thing she was most curious about was how he had got out. If he'd let himself out that spoke of memory – where the key was held, purpose – a hunt for a lost toy, and forward planning if he had dressed for the outside in a dressing gown or coat. Ryland's itself was very warm, almost stifling, the heat hitting the moment you stepped inside the front door. He would not be acclimatized or prepared for the bitter outside weather.

And she still hadn't worked out how he'd got out in the first place.

Unless one of the staff had opened the door for him or the night staff had lied that they'd locked it, it seemed, on the surface, impossible. The most likely explanation was that they'd forgotten to lock up properly. He'd wandered, they'd realized their omission after he'd gone, locked and bolted the door after him and then, when the consequences had become apparent, lied to cover their tracks and keep their jobs.

In her notebook she started jotting questions, making plans, testing theories. Did one of the night staff go outside for a smoke, perhaps, and forget to relock the door, locking it later? Mr Foster found it open and slipped out? So why hadn't he slipped back in again? Once more she was trying to follow the maze of a befuddled mind which she didn't understand.

'Jo?' Mike was still on the line.

'Yeah.'

'I'll ring you if we get a sighting.'

'Thanks.' She ended the call.

For a second she allowed herself the luxury of returning to her beloved chief superintendent, Rush's predecessor, Arthur Colclough. 'Good detectives,' he'd advised her, 'never stop asking questions.'

Trouble was focusing on the right questions.

She took another glance out of the window at the fruitless search. 'Did Mr Foster have many visitors?'

'No. He's got no living relatives and, apparently, no living friends.' A mirthless little smile bent her mouth. 'No one visited him. That's one of the penalties of staying alive into your nineties.'

'So how is he . . .?'

'Funded?'

Joanna nodded.

'His house was sold and some of his fees are paid by the council.'

'Where was his house?' It seemed a promising place to start. Maybe he had gone back there to look for . . .

'Leonard Street. Number seventeen. But it was sold eighteen months ago.' The stony, hostile face was back.

'I think we'll take a look there all the same. Can you think of anywhere else he might have gone?'

Sandie Golding shook her head.

'How many staff were on duty last night?'

'Three.' Her eyes were wary now as she continued. 'Two health-care assistants and a qualified nurse. But they'll be sleeping now.'

'We'll speak to them later.'

Joanna paused for a moment, trying to gather her words into the right order. 'The thing I'm struggling with, Miss Golding, is would Mr Foster have been capable of formulating a plan to search for his lost toy? How bad was his dementia? What form did it take? Did he have . . .' she dragged a phrase she'd heard some time in the past, 'short-term memory loss?'

'I don't know. You should speak to the matron about that. She's medically qualified and had more to do with him on a daily basis. She would have more idea of his mental capabilities.'

'Her name?' Pencil poised.

'Matilda Warrender. She'll be on duty later today.'

'Thank you.'

It was a shot in the dark but she decided to pursue it all the same. The missing man's point of exit was still bothering her. It was surely the first step in his disappearance.

'Do any of your night staff smoke?'

Predictably Ms Golding looked bemused at the question. 'I don't know. I really don't know the night staff that well.'

Ms Golding was shutting down. Joanna sensed she would extract nothing more from her. She stood up. 'I need to take a look around, please. The day room, front doors and all the other entrances and exits. Perhaps starting with his bedroom.'

THREE

B ridget was waiting for them outside the door; a shake of her head combined with a slightly doleful expression told Joanna what she needed to know.

Ms Golding led the way, striding ahead quickly, her heels tapping a staccato, business-like rapid rhythm on the wooden floor. Taller than she had initially appeared. More imposing now she had regained some of her equilibrium. She tossed back comments as she turned right, moved back along the corridor and headed towards a curving staircase with carpeted wide, shallow treads. 'He shares his room with Alfred Dean.' A slightly mocking smile warmed her face when she turned around. 'I don't think you'll get much out of him either.'

Joanna shrugged. 'All the same.'

With a little huff of her shoulders, the manager ascended elegantly, head held high, her heels soft now on the carpet. 'Mr Foster's room is upstairs.'

'And he could manage to climb up?' Joanna had a vision: soft slippers, hesitant steps, hands clinging on to the bannister.

'Oh, yes. He *could* get up the stairs. But we do have a lift,' she said, tossing the words back at them as though Joanna and Bridget were prospective clients searching for a place for an elderly relative. Both picking up on the spiel, the two police exchanged amused glances.

Outside a door with a number 11 on; the manager knocked, listened, knocked again and pushed it open.

The room was light and sunny and smelt pleasantly of soap, twin beds taking up most of the floor space. A corner had been used for an en-suite shower room, and as they entered a man shuffled out, behind him the sound of a toilet flushing and a tap still running. He gave them a wide grin which showed his false teeth had slipped. The result was bizarre. Joanna returned his grin.

Once she'd turned the tap off in the bathroom, Sandie addressed him with a friendly arm around his shoulders. 'Alf, love.'

'Aye?'

'These are the police.' Her tone was moderated, as though she was talking to a four-year-old, but very friendly.

'Very nice,' Alf responded, looking Joanna and Bridget up and down with interest. Then he turned faded blue eyes back to Sandie for an explanation. 'They've come about Zac, love. Looks like he's wandered off sometime in the night. They're wondering if you've got any idea what's happened to him.'

The old man plonked himself down on the bed and looked suitably thoughtful before responding. 'I don't rightly know.'

Joanna pulled up a chair so her face was on a level with his. 'Mr Dean,' she said, 'when did you last *see* Mr Foster?'

Unfortunately Alf took his cue from the home manager who'd stepped in. 'Last night, was it, Alf?'

It illuminated a dark corner of his mind. 'Aye,' he said, bright now with inspiration. 'Aye that were it. He were 'ere when I went to bed but when I woke . . .' Again he glanced at the home manager, ''e'd gone.'

Joanna took over. 'Did you hear him go in the night?'

'No. At least . . . No, I don't think so.'

Joanna looked at them both. 'Had his bed been slept in?'

'Yes.' It was Sandie who supplied the answer in a defensive and uncompromising clipped tone, confrontational now as her eyes scanned the room and landed back on Joanna. 'He'd had his sleeping tablets as I told you, around nine, and been seen fast asleep by the night staff at two o'clock in the morning. When they came to wake him around seven he wasn't here.'

Joanna backpedalled. 'So he was seen asleep in bed at two a.m. and was noticed missing at seven a.m.'

'Yes. Of course.' Honesty took over. 'At least . . .' The question flustered her now. 'They probably pop their heads round the door on the two o'clock round and just check, I expect, so as not to disturb the sleeping patients.'

Joanna sensed something in her hesitation. 'So you're saying he went sometime between two and seven a.m.'

Sandie Golding's eyes were definitely evasive as they skittered around the room.

Joanna stood up, walked back to the door. Because of the en suite, from the door, whether the bathroom door was open or closed, whereas Alfred Dean's bed was clearly visible, Zachary Foster's bed was obscured.

Another of Colclough's little mantras.

People who tell one lie are perfectly capable of feeding you an entire pack of them.

Mentally she adjusted the times of potential disappearance. In all probability Mr Zachary Foster had gone missing sometime between nine p.m. and seven a.m., which was a much wider window of opportunity and would have given him the potential for travelling quite a bit further.

She looked to the manager, feeling her face display hostility to the deceit. 'No one heard anything at *any* time of the night? Not Mr Foster creeping down the stairs? Not a door opening, closing, bolts being shot back? Nothing?' Joanna didn't bother making any effort to suppress the scepticism in her voice. Already this was a story full of holes.

And from Sandie's silence she was not about to darn them.

They both knew that even if the night staff had been conscientious enough to check their patients more regularly, unless they'd actually entered the room, they couldn't be sure that Zachary hadn't left his bed any time after nine p.m.

She turned back to Alf Dean who was watching with bright-eyed interest. 'Do you sleep heavily, Mr Dean?'

'Oh aye,' he said, so pleased with himself he was almost patting himself on the back. '*Nothing* would wake me.'

Sandie watched him indulgently. 'He has sleeping tablets,' she said. 'They all do. They knock them right out.' Then she appeared to realize what she had said and pressed her lips together to prevent any more rogue statements escaping.

'Mr Dean, do you have to get up in the night to go to the toilet?'

'Sometimes,' he responded brightly.

'Did you *last* night?'

'I don't rightly remember.' He looked troubled at his lack of certainty.

It was tempting to search the room and then leave. But while Bridget opened drawers and went through the wardrobe, Joanna turned back to the manager. 'How long has Mr Foster been in Ryland's?'

'Eighteen months.'

'But this is the first time he's tried to leave?'

Slowly Sandie nodded. Joanna wanted to ask whether this might be a symptom of worsening dementia rather than a search for his missing toy, but she hesitated to pursue this avenue in front of the bright-eyed and alert Alfie.

But the fact remained that Zachary's first bid for freedom after a year and a half of residence had been successful. Perhaps as much as twelve hours later, he was still at large. The weather was worsening. And that troubled her.

Could this really be over a lost toy?

'How mobile was he?'

A touch of irritation. 'He could get upstairs. He could get around. It wasn't his *mobility* that was the problem.'

Joanna nodded and turned back to Alf who was watching her with an eager, alert expression, almost willing her to ask him another question. Mr Helpful.

So she checked up on another part of the story. 'Had Zac been troubled lately?'

'Oh aye,' he said. 'Ever since he lost his teddy. He was looking for it everywhere.'

Something strange happened with his teeth, so he adjusted them with his fingers – and did a good job. He grinned. 'He was very attached to it. Someone said they'd find it for him.'

Joanna picked up on that. *Someone said they'd find it for him.* 'Who?'

'One of the nurses.'

'Which one?'

And suddenly, without warning, the look of confusion dropped over his face like a fog. Whatever information he might or might not have, it had drifted away, invisible, irretrievable.

The sense of frustration was acute for Joanna, and for Mr Dean, who looked anguished. 'I'm sorry,' he mumbled. 'I'm very sorry.'

'It's all right.'

Joanna kept her frown for the manager. 'Do you have an inventory of Mr Foster's clothes, Miss Golding?'

'I, erm – I – believe so.'

'Would he have been wearing pyjamas?'

'I believe so but I'll have to check with the nurses.' It was proving a useful phrase.

'A dressing gown?' Her eyes flew to the hook on the back of the door where hung two dressing gowns.

'A coat?'

Ms Golding opened the wardrobe door, rummaged around and changed her phrase to, 'I believe so.'

Joanna glanced beneath the bed, piecing together a sequence. Their missing man had put his coat on. He'd planned to go outside to search for Teddy. 'And on his feet?'

The manager's eyes also dropped to the floor beneath the missing man's bed. No slippers.

She looked back at Joanna who picked up the story. 'So it seems that Mr Foster left your home wearing pyjamas, slippers and an overcoat?'

'I'll check and let you know for sure.'

'Thank you.' Joanna was temporarily diverted by PC Anderton rifling through the drawers. 'Found anything, Bridget?'

She held up a plastic fawn behind-the-ear National Health hearing aid, still with a coating of dark earwax.

So their man was going to be hard of hearing, had poor sight, was inadequately dressed.

'Anything more?'

Bridget shook her head and kept up her search around the room.

Joanna kept her eyes on Ms Golding, who was still managing to look affronted, as though all this was way beneath her. Almost as though this whole scenario was the fault of the police rather than due to a lack of vigilance of the staff. Always nice if you can shift the blame for your own omissions on to someone else.

Bridget spoke up. 'I take it he hasn't got a suitcase?'

'No.'

Which set Joanna picturing Paddington Bear. She smiled and patted her abdomen.

Did Zachary Foster pack a bag ready to flit and somehow sneak out unseen through locked doors? Not if his dementia was as severe as she'd been led to believe.

And if it wasn't?

She tried out another scenario. What if the picture of a confused old man in an overcoat, pyjamas and slippers, wandering, apparently unseen, through the streets of Leek, searching for a lost teddy bear, was fantasy rather than fact? She shook her head. It didn't fit. Someone would have seen him. The truth was nothing fitted. She was having trouble fitting *any* picture into a frame.

If he had turned left out of the home, headed out towards the bleak and high ground of the moors, there would have been less chance of him being spotted. But if anyone had seen him out there, an old man wandering around in pyjamas, slippers and an overcoat, they would have picked him up.

Something else occurred to her. Zachary Foster had no relatives, and that meant not only no refuge for him to head to, but equally no one who would kick up a fuss at his disappearance.

'I will need that confirmation of what Mr Foster would have been wearing,' she said. This time she would not mince her words. 'The weather is cold. He's a vulnerable person under *your* care and you're bound to be held responsible.'

Sandie Golding had got the hint all right. Her face paled as she nodded, humbled now. 'I'll ask the matron,' she said finally.

Joanna turned back to Alf. 'Thank you for your help, Mr Dean.' She shook his hand, feeling he looked so eager she should be saying something more to him – that he'd helped – or something else positive. But he hadn't. Not really. It seemed as though Alf felt something was missing too. His expression was still expectant. Joanna was tempted to give him a pat on the head, like an obedient collie, but sufficed with a nod, finishing with, 'And if you think of anything else, Mr Dean, let one of the nurses know and they'll pass on any information.'

'I will. I will.'

She took a last look around the room and tried to visualize the scene: sometime during the night, an old man, sliding his feet into his slippers, crossing the room, opening the wardrobe, taking out his coat and leaving the room to move invisibly and silently down the stairs to the French windows in the day room, somehow magic his way through the doors, out on to the terrace, walk down the drive – and vanish.

And as they left she still felt she was missing some important part of the story.

That feeling persisted as she stood in the doorway and then it morphed into something more specific. Rather than having missed something, it was more that she had glossed over something she should have paid more attention to. She stood still, tried to recapture it, failed. As they left the room, Alf Dean was still watching them from his bed; she was tempted to turn back, start again, take another look, listen harder to the responses to her questions. But she didn't. And she wasn't any nearer piecing the information together. So instead she focused back on the manager. 'Now I need to have a look at both your front and back doors and the French windows, as well as any other exits you might have. And if you can let me have the contact details of your three night staff as soon as possible, and anyone else who feels they might be able to help us find your missing patient . . .'

'Certainly.' This time there was no mistaking the haughtiness in her tone or the square of her shoulders as she marched ahead.

FOUR

The front door was a Yale, easily turned from the inside in the daytime. Sandie Golding went through the arrangements at night. 'Once the evening staff have left,' she said, repeating her earlier version, 'the night staff deadlock the door, put the key in the office which is then locked, and the spare they keep on them until morning.'

'And the back door? I take it that's the one leading from the kitchen?'

'A similar arrangement. The night staff assured me that this was what they did last night. Exactly as they did every night.' Her face and tone were equally severe.

'I'd better take a look.'

The front door appeared secure. The door that led from the kitchen was larger.

'I take it this is where deliveries came?'

'Yes . . . but.'

Joanna inspected them. As she'd said they were currently unlocked, but there were bolts on the inside, the key visible.

'That's removed at night and kept with the night staff.'

Joanna looked around. The kitchen was large, plenty of stainless-steel surfaces. All looked neat, clean and organized. A few of the kitchen staff watched her curiously as she tried the door, opened it and closed it again.

'He couldn't have left through here,' Sandie Golding reiterated. 'We're particularly careful as there was some pilfering a while ago.'

Joanna looked at her. 'Anything serious?'

Sandie Golding shook her head. 'Petty stuff,' she said. 'Food mainly. We disciplined the member of staff. It was an internal affair.'

She didn't enlarge and it was unlikely to have a bearing on Mr Foster's disappearance, so Joanna turned her attention to the two fire exits.

'The Fire Service check them annually,' Ms Golding put in. 'Apart from that they are not used.'

Joanna pushed against them each in turn. Not easy to open. And judging from the debris when she finally got them to budge, they were functional but rarely used. Certainly not last night. She ran her fingers around the edges. Zachary Foster hadn't left by either of these.

So she stood in the spacious day room, now full of residents, some simply sitting, a few reading. The television was on in the corner but no one appeared to be taking much notice. The lady in the corner was still knitting furiously but stopped and gave her a sweet smile as Joanna approached. 'I'm nearly a hundred, you know.'

It was Bridget who responded. 'Really? And you can follow a knitting pattern? I never could.'

'They knit squares for refugee blankets,' Ms Golding said disparagingly.

'Yes,' the lady said, determined to continue the conversation. 'They send them to Iraq, you know.'

'Syria,' was Ms Golding's response.

Joanna stopped by her chair. 'Do you know Mr Foster?'

Pale blue eyes met hers. 'Of course I do. He lives here, with us.'

'Well . . .' Joanna hunkered down beside her. Difficult with her pregnant bump. 'He does live here with you, but he appears to have gone walkabout.'

After a brief stare the lady looked down at her knitting. 'Looking for his teddy, I expect.'

'Yes.' This was bordering on the surreal.

The lady continued. 'He was so upset when Teddy vanished.' She knitted a couple more stitches before giving another smile. 'We used to call him Christopher Robin. Pooh Bear, you know.' She began to hum and Joanna straightened up.

'That's our Shirley,' Sandie Golding said, smiling. 'Not quite the hundred she's so fond of boasting about. Not even ninety, actually. But we indulge her.'

'Thank you, Shirley,' she said, bending back down to speak in her ear. 'Most helpful, dear.'

The look she gave Joanna was an eloquent opinion. *Rantings of an old lady.*

But there was some truth in the woman's version.

They continued towards the French windows, passing a sprightly woman with a darkly tanned face poring over a jigsaw trying to slot in a piece. She turned it around, upside down, and finally lost patience. 'Bah.' In frustration, unable to fit it in, she threw it on the floor where it joined a few more. Ms Golding raised her eyebrows and again gave Joanna a meaningful look, this time a hunt for sympathy, a *Look what I have to put up with.*

Joanna kept her face wooden. The other residents looked up with interest at the stranger in their midst.

The French windows lay ahead, rain rattling against the glass, Joanna noted with concern. Zachary Foster would be getting very wet – unless he'd found shelter. Which again caused her to wonder. How aware would he be of the weather, of danger? Simply befuddled, wandering without direction or plan?

She peered out. The doors overlooked a wide terrace where, presumably, in warmer weather the residents would be able to sit out and enjoy the gardens, a large lawn ringed with mature trees, both firs and deciduous. Through them she could see uniformed police still checking the area but there were no shouts of discovery. She tested the handle. Locked. Think stable doors, she mused. But the key was now *in* the lock and turned easily. She glanced up. As Ms Golding had said, the bolt was at the top of the door, in the centre, a second bolt halfway down near a hook. A chair patterned with footmarks stood to the side. This was how the staff reached that awkward, central bolt. Not terribly safe. A ladder would have been more stable. But also less manoeuvrable. Their man could not have reached it without standing on the chair – unless last night that top bolt had not been shot across. Joanna was tall, five feet eight inches. Today wearing two-inch heels made her about the height of their missing man. And she was strong. Standing on the floor she reached up, hand just about touching the metal. But to shoot back the top central bolt would have been an impossible struggle. Had the door been bolted with the upper bolt fully engaged, even if their man was as strong as she, he wouldn't have been able to shoot it back without climbing on the chair which, in turn, would have been difficult for a doddery, confused nonagenarian, which was how the staff were describing their missing patient. In fact, looking at Ryland's security measures, even if his cognitive function had been reasonably normal, it would have been a challenge to have escaped. She checked with the manager. 'This was found locked and bolted this morning, so *after* Mr Foster had gone missing?'

Sandie Golding nodded and sucked her teeth in disapproval.

'And the key was hanging up in the right place?'

'Yes,' she replied stiffly, reluctantly and resentfully.

All three of them knew this scenario was a physical and mental impossibility.

Bridget Anderton gave a little twist of her mouth and nodded towards the steps, all three thinking along the same lines. Wide inviting steps down to the lawn and a path which disappeared round the side, leading to the front drive and escape. Joanna pushed the door open, letting in the weather, a howling, hostile wind and rain spattering on to the floor.

She stepped out.

The day was cold and getting colder, an easterly wind rattling through the trees, making the outside appear a hostile environment jeering at their futile quest. Joanna pictured faltering steps, slippers slapping on slippery stones, a coat clutched around him. Surely if he had left this way the natural response would have been to turn around and re-enter the dry, stifling warmth and familiar surroundings of the home?

She took a few paces forward, holding her mac tightly around her. The rim of trees was only one or two deep. Through them she could see the edge of the road and the glittering roofs of houses beyond. Either side of the steps stood two sturdy terracotta flowerpots, battered by the weather but obstinately still clinging on to late-flowering, bedraggled roses. A cigarette had been stubbed out in one. Joanna looked at it thoughtfully before slipping on a glove and placing it in an evidence bag. Then she descended the steps and took the path around to the front drive before coming back again. If the old guy didn't turn up soon they might need to try and retrace his steps, maybe see if a reconstruction jolted anyone's memory. But at least she could see no evidence of foul play. No blood, no signs of a struggle and no marks of a slip. Again she returned to her narrative. The night staff had left the doors unlocked and unbolted. Mr Foster had wandered out on some muddled mission to try and find his teddy bear. Someone had come out here, at some time, for a cigarette and locked him out.

As she turned around, heading back towards the faces watching through the window, her primary thought was that – if these details leaked out – Ryland's residential home might have trouble filling their places.

But that was not her concern. Her priority was to find him. The longer this dragged out the worse it would be for everyone – even her. Back at the station she was bound to get her leg pulled over this hunt for an old man and his toy and her failure to find him. She climbed the steps and pushed open the door, catching the manager unawares, who started and jerked backwards as Joanna barked out questions. 'What is his mobility like? I mean more specifically. How fast can he walk? How far can he walk? Can he climb? Could he have managed these steps? Was he unsteady on his feet? Would he be likely to fall? Does he have problems with balance?'

Sandie Golding froze with a picture she was reluctant to share. Of an old man tottering around the day room, moving from chair to chair, holding on tightly for support.

In which case . . .

Her answers dragged out reluctantly. 'His mobility wasn't great.'

'How far would he have been able to walk?' Joanna's tone was insistent.

The manager bit her lip and tried to wriggle out of this one. 'Hard to say,' she said.

'Try.'

Sandie Golding's picture expanded. She pictured the old man, shuffling in slippers too big for him, shoulders and back bent with age, dragging the ancient toy behind him. 'Maybe . . . three – four hundred yards.' *On a good day, a really good day*, Joanna added mentally. *But he is not within four hundred yards of anywhere that hasn't been searched,* she was thinking. And perhaps this indisputable fact was, at last, beginning to get through to the manager.

Sandie Golding's mask suddenly slipped, possibly because her focus was on the fallout from the case. 'Is there really *no* sign of Zac?'

Joanna didn't respond straightaway but studied her face. What was really bothering her? The bad publicity this was bound to generate? Pity for an old man confused and exposed to inclement weather? Trouble from her boss, Mr Haldar? Affection for the old guy?

As Joanna shook her head she would have liked to have uttered a platitude, that she was sure he'd turn up soon, but now she was sketching out a further, darker narrative. A body, still hidden from plain sight, in a skip, fallen into a river or reservoir, half buried on or in a patch of dereliction. And none of these scenarios looked good for any of them.

So as she absorbed the indisputable: an old man, confused, wandering in a futile search for a lost toy, she started to plan. She looked at the chair and wondered whether they should be taking it to the lab to examine it for shoe or slipper prints. So far it was the only tangible item they had. So she nodded in that direction. 'We'll be taking this.'

Sandie Golding didn't demur. Joanna was realizing they needed to intensify their local search, spiralling outwards from Ryland's. They needed more manpower. And they would include his old address, 17 Leonard Street, the house where he had lived with his mother until he'd been admitted here. He might be hurt or dead. It was unlikely he was still on his feet and had wandered over there, but this was a strange case and normal rules of solving crime were not applicable. It was possible there was no logic behind Zachary's disappearance and the obfuscation the result of a few trivial and pointless lies. But if they didn't find him soon, the likelihood was that the cause of death would be exposure and the blame would be laid at the door of the police. It wouldn't just be Ryland's which would be the focus of adverse publicity. She could almost write the headlines herself: *Police's failure to find missing man results in shameful death of ninety-six-year-old.*

So as SIO, however trivial the case might initially appear, it was up to her to formulate a plan. The next step would be to try the police sniffer dogs, comb through CCTV camera footage and alert the public. Leek still had a few old-fashioned bobbies who walked the beat, even through the night. And in the morning plenty of workers scurried around, arriving for work or heading home after a night shift. The High Street bustled from early morning. Shoppers, market traders, farmers, hikers, commuters, schoolchildren. And so far no one had seen him? Or any sign of him? Had he then turned the other way? Not into town? Perhaps turned left towards Tittesworth Reservoir? But that was two miles away. Not the four hundred yards quoted by Ms Golding. And even on a Monday morning, Tittesworth was unlikely to be deserted. Someone was always there – dog walkers and hiking clubs who would stride round the five-mile periphery. Climbing the long steep hill towards Ramshaw Rocks, watched over by the Winking Man, was the least likely option. Joanna had tackled the climb a few times on her bike. Stiff and steep. No place for a tottering, elderly, confused gentleman.

Sandie Golding took them back to her office where she copied out the contact details for the three night staff and promised to have confirmed the list of clothes Zachary would have been wearing. They wandered back outside into a blustery autumn day. So far the snow was holding off, but the wind was almost bitter enough to slice you in half.

FIVE

The search team was headed by PC Gilbert Young, a thirty-something-year-old officer who had moved from Stoke a year or two ago. He was an earnest, honest guy with a shaven head to join his male pattern baldness, an embryonic beard and a crooked grin which made him appear permanently embarrassed, as though he wasn't sure how the grin would be received. He greeted them, shaking his head. 'Nothing,' he said. 'No sign of him.' He scratched his head, looking around. 'He can't have gone far but he isn't here, Inspector. I mean there's not much in the way of grounds. There's nowhere for him to hide.'

Joanna moved in closer. 'Any sign of blood? Trauma? Injury? Broken branches? Footprints?' She tried and failed to make a joke of it. 'Or rather slipper prints?'

PC Young's returning smile was almost sympathetic. 'No.'

She put a hand on his shoulder. 'Keep looking.' He nodded and turned around.

And they left.

When they were back in the car, manoeuvring out on to the road, Bridget spoke. 'That was all a bit unsatisfactory, wasn't it?'

'On all scores,' Joanna agreed.

Bridget was still looking concerned. 'We should have found him in the grounds, trying to find his way back in. But he's not there.'

'Mmm.'

The PC turned towards her. 'So what's your plan, Jo?'

'The usual. Spiral outwards.' She kept her eye on the road and confided in Bridget. 'My concern is that at some point we'll find a body. Somewhere neglected, out of sight. If he's died of exposure we'll be held responsible. Not the home. But an old man like that? A trip, a fall, together with the cold. It wouldn't take much. We'll probably find him or his body somewhere nearby.

So rather than spread to the wider area, we'll concentrate around here, use that as the centre of the search area.'

'And if he doesn't turn up?'

'He will.' Joanna turned to look at her. 'He's somewhere, Bridget. Bu-ut *if* he doesn't show, we'll give it another twenty-four hours then spread the search area. I hope we do find him, alive.' She smiled. 'He sounds quite a character. And we'll send someone round to Leonard Street just in case he's taking a trip down memory lane.'

PC Jason 'Bright' Spark was detailed to check out the address in Leonard Street and was already on his way to number seventeen.

It was a terraced house on a narrow street, in amongst a tangle of such places on the southern aspect of Leek. An ex-mill-worker's cottage, with a front door that opened straight out on to the pavement. It was currently inhabited by a Mrs Janet Baldwin.

Jason pulled up outside the front door. Even from here it was easy to see Mrs Baldwin cared for her home. Neat curtains draped back behind spanking new white UPVC windows, polished glass gleaming in the afternoon sunshine. The doorstep was swept and polished brick red, the door freshly painted in Racing Green gloss with a brass knocker in the shape of a horse's head. Jason knocked, stood back respectfully, knocked again. *No one's ever in*, he was thinking, just before the door was opened and a woman of around sixty smiled up at the tall cop. But as the uniform registered her smile faded and she looked concerned.

Jason held up his hand. 'It's OK,' he said. 'No bad news.' He risked a joke. 'You're not about to be arrested.'

The woman laughed at that. Clapped her hand to her heart, 'Thank goodness for that,' she said in mock relief. 'I must have a guilty conscience, mustn't I?'

His response was stolid. 'Haven't we all?'

She prompted him then. 'Sooo if I'm not in trouble, why are you here?'

'Sorry. Sorry. An old gentleman has . . .' he rejected the word 'absconded', substituting the phrase, '. . . gone missing from an old people's home.' He had his lines ready. 'He's a bit confused – lives in the past, you know. He used to live at this address until a year and a half ago. We just wondered if he might have headed back here, somewhere familiar, you know?'

The woman nodded. 'I heard it. It was on the news on Radio Stoke,' she said. 'Ninety something? And he's missing? The old man who used to live here?'

'Ninety-six,' PC Spark confirmed. 'And yes – apparently.'

Then it dawned on her. 'Oh, Mr Foster. I hadn't made the connection.'

Jason grinned.

'Ninety-six,' she mused. 'I hadn't realized he was as old as that.'

'Yes. A good age.' *But not for running away from safety towards the unknown, the cold, possible danger.*

Spark pursued his quest. 'So have you seen him?'

Janet Baldwin shook her head. 'No.'

'You've not seen anyone answering to the description?'

'Not a sign.' Said a little more emphatically. 'I have not seen an old man hanging around here.' She was looking offended now. 'If I had I would have rung the police.'

PC Spark felt he had to rescue the situation somehow. 'Well,' he said genially. 'As you probably know, old people tend to live in the past so I just thought I'd check it out.'

It seemed to work. The smile was back and he finished jovially. 'If you should see him you ring this number,' and he handed her a card.

'I will.'

She was about to shut the door on him.

'Thank you,' he managed, just before Mrs Baldwin did just that.

Joanna spent most of the day extending the search, assigning more officers to the task, a few sent into the town to home in on CCTV footage. Any moment now, she thought, their man would turn up. Or his body.

And she arranged to interview the staff who had worked Sunday night.

But as the day progressed and the weather worsened, realism kicked in. Any sighting of the missing man was increasingly likely to be of his body.

Sandie Golding rang at three, itemizing Zachary Foster's missing clothing and confirmed that it consisted of:

One pair of striped pyjamas,

One pair of slippers (brown),

One navy overcoat wool mixture Marks & Spencer.

And that was it. He should be easy to spot in that outfit. No one could mistake him for a shopper. He was an obvious escapee from somewhere.

Then she rang Matthew and told him she wouldn't be home until after eight.

He wasn't too happy. 'New case?'

'I'll tell you all about it when I get home.'

'I hope you're not doing too much, Jo.'

'No. I have a lovely soft case which involves an elderly gentleman who's absconded from a residential home. We'll track him down soon and I'll be home. In the meantime, I'm just interviewing the staff who were on duty last night.'

'OK,' he said. 'Well, it sounds safe enough.'

She chuckled, picturing him in their new house, probably looking at colour schemes for the nursery. *Don't paint it blue.*

Since they'd moved in they had spent almost every single evening looking at colour schemes and paint charts, shade cards and swatches of material. Luckily they had found themselves a lovely painter and decorator who was racing through the rooms and was married to a seamstress called Trixie who could knock up a pair of curtains in as much time as it took Vincent Scofield, her husband, to transform a room. Structurally Briarswood was sound, so no major refurbishment had been necessary apart from the four bathrooms. It was a large Victorian semi sprawled over three floors. Four if you counted the cellar. The ceilings were high and the rooms spacious – too spacious in Joanna's opinion. It lacked the cosy intimacy of Waterfall Cottage and didn't yet feel like home. The furniture they'd moved from Waterfall seemed to have shrunk – the rooms looking empty and under-furnished. As Matthew had spoken she could hear an echo, his voice bouncing off the walls.

She tried to reassure him. 'I've spent at least half the day sitting at my computer. I don't think I'm exactly working too hard.'

He slipped into being uxorious, something which had increased since she had been pregnant. As though she was extra vulnerable and needed protection. 'Don't make it too late, Jo. You need your rest, you know.'

She wasn't sure whether to appreciate his concern or to be riled by it. Perhaps a little of both. She swallowed any resentment. 'Duty calls, my darling.'

'Hmm.' He couldn't resist tacking on his current mantra. 'I wish you'd finished work.'

She laughed. 'And do what, Matthew? Nothing? Come on. You know as well as I do. If I was home I'd be scuttling around the antiques shops searching for stuff. Compared to that, being at work is a doddle. And a safe one.'

'I was hoping we could maybe have dinner out?'

'Not tonight, Matt. Another night maybe?'

'OK,' he said grudgingly. 'I'll do myself some pasta then or something.'

'Yeah. Great.'

Mollified now, Matthew chuckled, happy at the turn his life was taking: a family home, a child, even his parents near.

As she put the phone down she felt a wash of deceit, knowing she'd omitted to mention that having used her bike that morning – prior to having been handed this less than major case – she had planned to cycle home. If Matthew had known he would have insisted he come to fetch her. But as far as possible, she denied any restriction resulting from her pregnancy. Cycling being the chief one of these. It was a constant issue with her husband.

Back at the station there was plenty of CCTV footage for the PCs to work through but so far no sighting of an elderly gentleman, at least not their elderly gentleman.

The three night staff trooped in a little before seven: a night sister, Joan Arkwright, and the two health-care assistants. All three looked tired and worried. At a guess they had not had much sleep but had spent the day tossing, turning and considering their future and maybe concocting a story. It was possible they had already collaborated and worked out what they were going to say, checking that their stories matched. They were in uniform ready for their next shift. One in dark blue, at a guess the trained nurse, the other two in white overalls. Presumably they would be heading straight for work from here.

Joanna began by thanking them for coming and explaining that this (in spite of the surroundings) was an informal interview. 'No crime has been committed so no one,' she said, looking at each of them in turn, 'is pointing a finger. This is simply a fact-finding exercise. You understand?'

They nodded.

'So begin by introducing yourselves.'

The thin woman who looked as pale as a vampire spoke up. 'I'm Joan Arkwright,' she said. 'I'm the night sister, in charge of Ryland's through the night.' She licked her lips. 'I've worked there for the past eight years.' Her voice rose. 'This is the first time . . .' Joanna held up her hand to silence her. She didn't need the nurse's résumé or protestation of innocence.

The two health-care assistants looked every bit as nervous as their senior. Susie Trent was a forty-something, plump, motherly sort, whose waist was lost in folds of central fat and whose bosoms looked heavy and very substantial. Amelia Boden, in contrast, was a skinny little thing who looked too young to be on night duty but presumably wasn't.

Joanna's effort at putting them at their ease had done little good. They all three continued to look uncomfortable, shooting anxious glances at one another; to her trained eye, they looked as guilty a set of collaborators as was possible, as though they had abducted Zachary Foster themselves.

She tried again. 'I'm not here to pick holes or point the finger. That's not up to me. I just want to find Mr Foster as soon as possible. And for that I need to ascertain facts. First of all, excluding the fire exits, take me through your locking-up procedure for the night. The night Mr Foster went missing, who was in charge of locking up?'

The vampire night sister spoke up. 'I do that,' she said, suddenly fearless.

'So the front and back doors were both locked?'

'Deadlocked.'

'The keys?'

'I keep a set on me all the time. The spare set is in a locked drawer in the office which is also locked. Mr Foster could not possibly have left through either of those doors.'

She seemed anxious to help, her tired eyes opened wide.

'I've checked the fire doors,' Joanna said. 'I don't think they'd been opened for a while. I don't think he left through there.' The night sister's eyes were flickering. Joanna could read her mind. 'And so,' she said, 'we come to the French windows that lead from the day room to the terrace and a path which goes round to the front drive.'

She looked at all three of them. 'Whose job was it to lock and bolt that door last night?'

Joan Arkwright spoke up. 'It's my responsibility.'

'So . . . last night? Take me through your actions, timings.'

'We come on duty at eight thirty in the evening. There's an overlap of about half an hour so we can have a handover.' She looked at Joanna and enlarged. 'The evening staff let us know if there are any issues regarding the patients.'

I'll come back to that, Joanna thought, and let the night sister continue.

'The evening staff leave at just before nine. I lock up behind them. Anyone wanting to re-enter Ryland's after then would have to ring the front doorbell.' She shook her head. 'No one did last night.'

Joanna turned her gaze to the other two. 'So did any of you exit through the French windows – for any reason?' She placed the transparent evidence bag containing the cigarette butt on the table between them.

The silence hung in the air. No one seemed to breathe.

She rephrased the question. 'Did any of you go outside during the night, maybe . . .' she dropped her gaze to the evidence bag, '. . . for a cigarette?'

Silence accompanied by shifty eyes and a quick retort from Ms Trent. 'We're not supposed to.'

Joanna waited for the silence to flush someone out. And finally.

'I might have done,' Susie Trent admitted.

'What time?'

'Round about two o'clock.'

'Were the French windows both locked and bolted?'

Her eyes flickered for a nanosecond towards the night sister then away. 'Yes,' she said finally.

People lie for all sorts of reasons; the same, motley collection as the motives for murder. Love, hatred, fear, greed, jealousy. And this lie? Formed out of loyalty. Susie Trent was not going to drop her colleague in it. But her colleague had picked up. She glanced at the HCA and looked away again but couldn't resist adding, 'I *know* I locked *and* bolted the day-room doors. I hung the key back on the hook, shot the bolts across and pushed the chair back against the wall.'

Susie Trent flicked another glance towards her and, wisely, moved on quickly to her version. 'I did go out – for a cigarette – after the two o'clock round. I locked and bolted the doors again after me.'

'When you came to the door,' Joanna repeated, 'was it locked and bolted?'

The nurse nodded.

'And the chair? Where was that?'

But her two colleagues were looking at her accusingly, the younger one, Amelia, unconsciously angling her body away from her colleague.

And the HCA defended herself further, her face reddening. 'The chair was against the wall.'

'And when you came back in?'

'I know I locked up properly. I'm really careful about that.' She seemed close to tears. Then she looked up. 'I *know* I locked the door,' she said. 'I followed the correct procedure.'

Joanna turned to the others. 'Did either of you two go outside *before* two a.m.?'

Both shook their heads. Joan Arkwright was looking defiant, her eyes angry.

Joanna was silent for a moment, letting the statements all sink in. She glanced at Bridget, whose face was impassive and unemotional.

Joanna looked at each of the three nurses in turn. 'You see my problem here, don't you?'

All three of them nodded miserably, now avoiding each other's gazes, focusing on her.

Joanna let the silence extend before moving on.

'Who was on duty the evening of Sunday the twenty-first before you arrived?'

The answer came promptly, as if they had been waiting for an opportunity to shift the blame elsewhere. 'Jubilee Watkins, Ned Sheringham and Shawna Wilson.'

'Did you see them all leave?'

Joan Arkwright summoned up some dignity – and fight. 'We don't actually *watch* them go, Inspector.'

Joanna gave Bridget a swift glance. *Touchy on that subject, wasn't she?* Or maybe she still felt she had to defend herself in front of her two colleagues.

Joanna turned her attention back to the hapless Susie Trent, who was beginning to look like a deflated balloon. 'You smoke on the terrace?'

She nodded.

Joanna offered her an escape route. 'Ms Trent. Is it possible you "forgot" to bolt the French windows after you, just thought you had?'

That drew a tight-lipped, firm response. 'No. I remember climbing the chair to shoot the bolt. I remember,' she insisted. 'No. Besides . . .' There was unmistakable hostility growing between the three members of staff. 'The doors were properly locked and bolted and the chair pushed back this morning.' She sat back and folded her arms.

Joanna kept her voice gentle for her next question directed at Susie Trent. 'So how do *you* think Mr Foster managed to leave the home?'

'I don't know.' She spread her hands, appealing to be believed. Reddened, work-roughened, hardworking hands. Honest hands?

She continued questioning Susie Trent. 'You insist that when you let yourself out at around two o'clock to go for a smoke you had to shoot back both bolts, take the key from the hook and unlock it?'

Susie's shoulders drooped. 'Yes.' Her eyes studied the floor.

Joanna pursued. 'Where was the chair?'

'Against the wall.'

Again Joanna offered her a way out. 'And you *insist* you shot both bolts across and locked the door when you came back in *after* having your cigarette?'

Susie Trent gave a jerky nod.

Joanna nodded. 'Susie,' she said, 'when you were outside, smoking, did you see anyone else there?'

She shook her head.

'Where did you stand?'

'Just outside the French doors.' Which bore out the cigarette butt in the flowerpot.

Joanna gave her another chance. 'Susie, I want you to think carefully. We are all capable of convincing ourselves that we committed an action we have made many, many times before. One action on one day blurs into the same action on another day. Or not. Sometimes we transplant our actions into what we are *supposed* to have done, or what we *wished* we had done, freeing ourselves from being forgetful.'

Her response was a tearful shake of the head.

'Was anyone in the day room when you let yourself out?'

She shook her head.

'Or when you came back in?'

Another shake of the head.

'How long were you outside for?'

'Three minutes. Something like that.' She showed a touch of bravado accompanied by a watery smile. 'I didn't time myself.'

'OK.'

Joanna moved on. 'This morning, who opened the door?'

Joan Arkwright held her hand up to shoulder level. 'I did.'

'And the door was locked and bolted. And the chair?'

They looked at each other blankly and this time it was Amelia, the HCA who looked about fourteen, who answered, prompting them. 'Against the wall, wasn't it? Where it always is.'

'Right.'

Inwardly Joanna sighed. The obvious and easiest assumption was that returning after her cigarette, Susie Trent might have locked the door, possibly even removing the key, but she had not shot the top bolt across. Thus leaving an exit point for Mr Foster on a quest.

But if the night sister was telling the truth and Mr Foster had made his escape earlier in the night, someone must have locked and bolted the door *after* he'd exited. Which meant, in turn, that he could have tried to re-enter Ryland's via the same door that he had walked through, but had been locked out. By her side Bridget waited, watchful, eyes scanning the three women in turn.

SIX

Joanna shook herself free and returned to safer ground. 'OK. So take me through last night's events.'

As no one spoke straightaway she prompted them. 'You say you arrive about eight thirty.'

Nods from all three.

'And you have a handover between half eight and nine.'

Joan Arkwright resumed her role as spokesperson. 'Yes – we hear the report on anything unusual to do with the patients.' She lapsed into corporate speak. 'It's part of the Ongoing Care Plan.'

Resisting the temptation to roll her eyes because she hated jargon, particularly as, working in the Force, she was subjected to an overdose of the stuff, Joanna nodded. There were times when jargon could be useful. Joanna tried to make use of this 'Ongoing Care Plan'. 'When you had your handover on Sunday evening, was anything mentioned about Mr Foster?'

'Yes.' Joan Arkwright's eyes brightened. Surefooted as she skipped over this ground. 'Yes. They said he was still upset about his teddy bear.'

'They said,' Susie Trent put in, 'that he was *agitated*.'

'Agitated?'

'Yes.'

'Agitated enough to try and search for it outside the home?'

They looked at each other, less sure of their lines now. 'Did you talk to him about it?'

'When I was giving him his night sedation,' Amelia put in bravely, 'I said that we were all trying our best to find it.'

'And were you?' Bridget's soft voice was nevertheless a well-inserted probe.

'Of course. We were all keeping an eye out for it.' Susie Trent was reverting to a sulky defence. Since the questioning about her night-time cigarette, she had resorted to folding her arms, which gave her a defensive, slightly stroppy look.

'OK. So you, Amelia, tried to reassure Mr Foster that you'd

keep an eye open for his teddy bear.' She wished this investigation wasn't tumbling down this rabbit hole straight into CBBC.

'Yes.'

'And then?'

'We did the rest of the night-time drinks and gave them their medication like we always do.'

Joanna almost smirked at the memory the word 'medication' provoked. *One Flew Over the Cuckoo's Nest*. *'Medication time.'* Which in Nurse Ratched's tone had sounded an ominous threat.

'So you're locked up, drinks and sedation given and then you settle down?'

More guilty looks exchanged between all three. Joanna could picture it. A nice, warm, cosy coffee room. Positively soporific.

'There's bells to answer and we do rounds through the night,' Amelia put in.

'OK, we'll talk about that in a minute.'

Joan Arkwright's irritation came bubbling to the surface.

'Surely you should be out there, searching for him? Not finding out how he left. We *know* how he left.'

'Do we?' Joanna's voice was soft but underneath she was furious. If these women had done their job properly, Zachary Foster would be tucked up alongside Mr Alfred Dean in room eleven and she would be investigating a proper case. Not an old man looking for his teddy bear. She kept that thought to herself and her voice deliberately cold as she repeated. 'Do we? How?'

Sister Arkwright kept her stare up. 'Through a door,' she said finally, still grumpy.

Joanna didn't bother going down the 'Which door?' or 'When – exactly?'

Instead she addressed all three. 'As we speak, there are more than twenty officers searching both town and country for *your* missing patient.' She omitted to point out the obvious fact that twenty officers engaged in looking for Mr Foster was twenty officers taken away from other duties. But even though she hadn't pointed this out, she could hear the accusation souring her voice. The baby was squirming inside her. She was uncomfortable. She wanted to pee. She wanted to be home, with Matthew. He might be overly protective, possessive, proprietorial even, but there were times when that was just what a woman needed. And this was one of those times. She wanted to shower, change into something comfortable, feet up on the sofa. Not here.

But she had a job to do and no answers yet so she continued with her jibes. 'The resources we're expending are considerable.' She was tempted to finish on a note of admonishment but resisted bleating about limited resources or mentioning the fact that the police could be better employed than searching for an old man and his teddy, both of whom should have been safe.

Instead she continued with her line of questioning. 'Did you have any visitors during the night?'

'No.' All three of them chorused this answer.

'So it was just you and your forty-six patients. Minus one by the morning,' she couldn't resist adding.

Joan Arkwright chewed her lip.

Joanna moved on. 'So . . .' She produced a floor plan. 'Take me through the night. Was it a quiet night on Tuesday or were you *rushed off your feet*?' A swift, insightful glance from the night sister told her she'd picked up on the irony.

They all looked at each other, checking, Joan Armstrong providing an answer. 'Reasonably busy.'

'So when did you last actually *see* him?'

This time it was Susie Trent who spoke up for all of them. 'I looked in on him and Alf about two-ish.'

For some reason, perhaps believing the PC would be more trusting (right), her eyes were on Bridget Anderton when Joanna prompted the lie. 'So?'

Susie Trent licked dry lips. 'They were both fast asleep.' She waited nervously while Joanna, smiling, picked the inevitable hole in this. But leaving Susie a way out. These were not villains but innocent liars caught in their own trap. It was up to her to snap it open.

'You stood in the doorway? Or did you enter the room?'

'Just in the doorway.'

Joanna paused, savouring the moment before she produced her trump card. 'You couldn't have seen Mr Foster from the doorway, could you?' she pointed out gently.

Susie hung her head but there was an attitude of anger about the action, a sharp breath drawn in through her teeth, a silent, *What's it to do with you?*

Joanna pressed the point home. 'So you didn't actually *see* him, did you?'

She shook her head.

After a brief pause, Joanna moved on. 'When exactly did you realize Mr Foster had gone?'

They looked at one another, guilty all.

Again, Joan Arkwright answered for them all. 'Not until this morning. Just after seven. We were looking for him everywhere.' Her eyes flicked round the other two inviting their agreement. Obediently they nodded.

'You looked inside the home?'

'Top to bottom,' Susie put in.

'And in the grounds?'

'We didn't have time.'

Alarm in all three pairs of eyes.

'So your call came in to police at . . .' Joanna glanced down at her notes, '. . . just after eight.'

Again Susie Trent made an attempt to be helpful. 'The day staff come in at seven forty-five. They went outside and had a quick look for him. When none of us could find him either inside or out, we called the police.'

It was time to wrap this up. 'Let me point out something to you all. You didn't actually see Mr Foster after you gave him his night sedation at around nine-ish. So he could have left at any time after that.' She turned to look at the hapless HCA. 'If Mr Foster left *before* you, Susie, had your cigarette, you would have found the door both unlocked and unbolted. When you secured the door you would have locked him out.'

She looked appalled. 'Are you saying . . .?'

Joanna continued. 'It seems unlikely that he wandered out *while* you had your cigarette because you would have seen him. If, on the other hand, he wandered out *after* you'd had your cigarette, that is, after two thirty, the door would have been unlocked and unbolted this morning. You see my quandary? We have a frail old man, confused, somehow able to walk through doors which were locked and bolted. And, even more incredibly, he locked and bolted them *after* he'd made his escape. Now then, I wonder whether any of you might want to revise your statements?'

There was no response from any of them. They were frozen.

Joanna addressed her next question to all three of them, moving on as though her previous allegation had been passed over. 'So during the night he must have come down the stairs. I take it you spend much of the night in the coffee room?'

No one denied this. 'Did any of you hear something unusual during the night? Someone wandering around? Voices? Doors opening, closing?'

All three shook their heads and looked puzzled.

'Nothing?' She looked at all three faces in turn and read exactly that – nothing. 'You didn't hear Mr Foster coming down the stairs?'

Again, they shook their heads.

'Did he usually use the lift or was he able to manage the stairs himself?'

Amelia Boden spoke out. 'He could manage – if he hung on to the bannister. He was slow, though.'

And Joanna was wondering how the hell this old man who had to clutch the bannister to descend the shallow steps of Ryland's staircase had climbed a chair to unbolt a stiff lock that even she had problems with, descend the patio steps, of which there were five and which had no steadying handrail, and then presumably make his way down to the front of the house – gravel drive so steps would be audible – and disappeared into thin air.

Sometimes it was the simplest of cases which were the most impossible.

But if Mr Foster was somewhere in the grounds, he would have been found by now. She knew the uniformed team, including Jason Spark. Although prone to excitability, he had a boyish enthusiasm for his work and, more importantly, he was thorough. If Zachary Foster was within a few hundred yards of Ryland's, he would have found him, however well-hidden. Besides, they'd roped in Holmes and Watson, predictably named, but the Force's bloodhounds all the same. They were trained sniffer dogs, and had turned up a number of bodies.

Not this time.

Usually at some point during an investigation, as facts were

unearthed, some sense and order started to appear. In this case
it was the exact opposite. The more facts she learned about this
elderly man's disappearance, the more confusing and impossible
it seemed.

Joanna puzzled over this while the three nurses waited for her
next question.

She stood up and crossed the small interview room then turned
to face them. 'You do understand,' she said, 'that no crime has
been committed. A little carelessness, yes. Possibly some misun-
derstandings or faulty memories . . .' She was leading them
towards a way out. 'But no crime.' Her reassurance had been
meant to put them at their ease, feel freer to perhaps leak some
facts they had, up until now, kept back. Clarify times and the
annoying point of the locked or unlocked, bolted or unbolted
door. But all she got were three pairs of eyes, all with the same
hostile, stony, deceitful stare. And so she produced the next card
she'd been holding up her sleeve, which DC Alan King had
copied from her description.

'This is a rough ground-floor map of Ryland's, plotting the
day room, the kitchen, the ground-floor bedrooms, windows and
doors. I wonder, would you show me on this diagram where you
sit when you're not busy seeing to patients?'

The innocent question flooded them all with the same guilt
and Joanna filled in the gaps. Somewhere warm, comfortable,
somewhere where they could doze the night away; possibly not
central enough to hear *everything* that was going on but where
they could still hear residents' bells. 'Here?' She jabbed her
finger at a room nearer the front door, a room she guessed the
staff used in the day for coffee and lunch breaks and at night,
no doubt containing a few comfortable-looking armchairs, as a
room to relax in. It was placed so anyone descending the stairs
could reach the day room without passing that door. And from
the glances they exchanged which were conspiratorial, she
guessed she'd been right.

From the main front door, apart from the snug, there were
two two-bedded rooms, one to the right and the other to the
left. The sister's office, which they claimed was locked, was
tucked away on the right, beyond the stairs. The kitchen
was at the back.

The day room was on the left, the entrance reached by a short corridor. If her guess was correct, Zachary could conceivably have descended the stairs, crossed the hallway and entered the day room without them being aware if they were comfortably ensconced in the room she was mentally calling The Snug.

She deliberately marked it with a red, felt-tipped cross. It was bold enough to appear an exaggeration. Eying it, Joan Arkwright responded in a professional tone she'd somehow recovered: 'We spend the first part of the night checking up on everyone, giving out a hot drink, night-time medication, checking who wants to go to the toilet. That takes until around eleven, eleven thirty sometimes. And, of course, by six a.m. they're all awake again.'

'So between say midnight and six a.m. where are you?'

The night sister drew in a deep breath, took in the red cross and answered with a touch of asperity. 'When we're not answering the residents' bells or doing our rounds . . .'

Which consist of peering in through the doorway at a pile of drugged-up geriatrics . . .

'We're in there.'

The Snug.

Joanna jumped right in. 'With the door open or closed?'

The night sister looked affronted. 'Open. Of course.'

'And you can hear the bells in there?'

The nod was unmistakably hostile, Joanna's lifting of stones to reveal the creepy-crawlies beneath visibly resented by all three.

C'est la vie.

Joan Arkwright added, 'A light comes on if a bell is pressed.'

But her expression was guarded. No need then for pseudo-politeness. 'Was last night very busy answering bells? You were running up and down stairs all night?'

'The usual. Two or three times every hour. It generally quietens down between half two and five.'

'And when you are answering bells? In which parts of the home are you?'

A deep sigh. 'Upstairs mostly. Mrs Williamson – she seems to need to go to the bathroom every hour or so.'

The others nodded their agreement with gusto. Clearly Mrs Williamson's toilet habits were well known. 'But none of you noticed Mr Foster out of bed, wandering?'

Shakes of the head. 'Does he usually wander in the night?'

Susie Trent answered for them all. 'Not Zac. He's no trouble. A sound sleeper – usually.'

Joanna noticed she'd tacked the word on as an afterthought and picked up on it. 'Usually?'

'Since his little teddy's gone missing, he's been a bit more restless.' She smiled at the memory. 'Like a kid,' she said. 'Goes to sleep cuddling it, his face pressed against it. Like a child has its comforter.'

Which pulled Joanna up short, a thought intruding. *Would the child that was bumping around inside her have a 'comforter'? Curious that she knew so little about him – or her. Not even its sex.*

She shook the thought away. 'OK. So for some of the time during the night, when it's quiet, you sleep?'

None of them even attempted to answer this one but the looks they exchanged said it all.

Oddly enough it was Amelia who responded. 'We might doze for a moment but sleep – no.'

Joanna let the quiet seep in under the door and permeate around the room.

Night Sister Joan Arkwright apparently felt compelled to add her two penn'orth. 'We might have had forty winks.' It was the only admission she was going to proffer.

Joanna frowned because the scenario sounded unlikely. At some point Mr Foster, whatever his physical and mental state, had crept downstairs and let himself out. So she felt compelled to ask again. 'During the night you heard *nothing*?' She knew she should have moderated the incredulity in her voice when she caught Bridget Anderton's surprise.

Two of them shook their heads but Amelia Boden frowned and met Joanna's eyes. 'I thought I might have heard something,' she said. 'But I think it must have been part of a dream I was having.'

'When you say "something"?'

She half closed her eyes. 'Whispering.' And then she tried to explain it away. 'Maybe it was a real voice but it was very, very soft and quiet. I can't be certain.'

'Did you decipher any words?'

She smiled and shook her head.

'Whose voice did it sound like?'

Again the young woman smiled, shook her head and shrugged, effectively detaching herself from her previous statement.

Joanna pressed her. 'Male or female?'

And then Amelia turned full circle. 'If I did hear anything, it must have been Zac, muttering, mustn't it?'

'What sort of time would you say that you heard this . . . whispering?'

'I don't know. About . . .' She thought for a moment. 'Midnight, maybe? Two or three – I can't be certain.'

Her two colleagues were looking at her with tolerant, amused exasperation, so she moderated to, 'I can't really say.'

'And did you wake then?'

'Briefly. It didn't sound anything too worrying. I checked that none of the bell lights were on but it was all quiet. Nothing alarming. I listened for a while and decided it was nothing, so I carried on dozing.'

They were waiting for her to dismiss them so they could head towards their night's work.

Joanna watched them. Joan Arkwright, the trained night sister, was so pale she looked as though she never saw the light of day. Before her shift had even started she looked exhausted. As she left, Joanna regarded her with curiosity and a certain dread. All the surveys indicate that broken nights led to depression and ill health, even early death. So why did Sister Arkwright choose this life? Because there was no option? Because the pay was better? Because it fitted in better with her home life? An avoidance of the hustle and bustle of the day? Autonomy, given that she was, quite definitely, in charge, with no one watching her work?

The phrase, broken nights, jangled in Joanna's ears like a shop bell. Pretty soon, when this lump of a child was finally born, she would be having plenty of those. She'd heard too many mothers talk about being so exhausted they would have mortgaged their soul for eight hours' sleep to fool herself that she would escape.

She tossed the apprehension aside and ended the interrogation with the usual request that if any of them remembered anything, however trivial, they would contact the station.

Then she dismissed them, making the comment after they'd gone.

'A few holes in that.'

PC Bridget Anderton agreed.

Before leaving for the evening she checked around the station. Their man was still missing.

SEVEN

Just one bit of solid information was waiting for her. Sandie Golding had left a message, passed on by the desk sergeant. It appeared that they'd checked their inventory. The staff had checked through his belongings and all his other clothes were in place, including the ones he had worn on the Sunday, the last day he had been seen.

She'd added a postscript. 'It appears he also took the substitute teddy bear.'

Joanna looked at the note then up at a pair of amused dark eyes. 'So that helps me exactly how?'

His response was to broaden his grin. 'Not found him yet?'

She shook her head, still irritated at what she perceived as the triviality of her current case.

But the day was about to get worse.

At eight p.m., trying to block out the fact that this was Zachary Foster's second night out in the cold, Joanna gave up. It was time to go home. The search would continue through the night but, as time moved on, the likelihood of the old man being found alive was decreasing. She changed into her cycling gear and stepped outside. The temperature was hovering just above freezing, joined now by a dismal drizzle, slippery beneath the wheels. Outside it was as dark as a coal mine. Even though her ride home was shorter than when they had lived in Waterfall Cottage, less than two miles, which would take her ten minutes, she wasn't relishing the idea. And even wearing her fluorescent jacket and with a good set of lights, visibility was poor. Her expanding abdomen was not helping her balance. She made a decision. This would be her last cycle home until after the child was born. As she mounted her bike and flicked back the pedal she was already regretting her decision that morning to cycle in to work.

The cold seeped through her cycling leggings and both thermal layers. She could even feel the rain making her breathable waterproof cling to her. She could have rung Matthew and asked him to come and pick her up. He hated her cycling anyway now she was pregnant, and would have been along in minutes if he was home from work. Matthew's job, like hers, could mean unpredictable hours, so there was no guarantee he would be free anyway, or at least that was what she told herself. But . . . She patted her stomach. She would *not* give in to this pregnancy. She would not. The baby would *not* win. *She* would. *It* would not stop her cycling.

She couldn't wait to get home, have a shower, change, make some tea. That was the plan. Beyond tea, she decided, little else. A flop across the sofa, preferably curled up with Matthew and some mind-numbing TV. That was the plan.

And that should have been the end of the evening. But, as Joanna tried to ease the discomfort of her cycling shorts, which were uncomfortably tight now (no one, apparently, makes *maternity* cycling shorts, she'd realized), and move on to the main road, she immediately met a swell of traffic. Though the trip was less than two miles, it was an urban ride with heavy traffic and poor visibility. And to top it all, the rain was turning suspiciously sleet-like. Poor old guy, she thought, as a lorry passed, splashing her with a shower of rain puddle. Her lights, though mud-spattered, were adequate but, like many cyclists, she still disliked riding in the dark. Particularly in built-up areas where motorists could be dazzled by oncoming headlights and the rain and lamp-posts made a confusing vision. A motorist herself, she knew how tricky it was picking up on a cyclist's presence and judging his or her speed. Motorists were often impatient and she mistrusted them all in the vulnerable position of a cyclist. Some passed within an inch, leaving no room for a wobble.

However, there was one big consolation in cycling home: thinking time. Riding a bike is the perfect time for contemplation. And there was plenty to think about even on this short journey home. Someone out of those three nurses was lying. Possibly two of them. And her suspicion fell on Susie Trent and also, possibly, that weary night sister. Once she'd got to the bottom of that, the case, and the old man's whereabouts, would soon be solved. Or . . . she corrected herself: at least she'd know how the old man had got out and it would narrow the time. It would not, however, explain why they had so far failed to find him.

This seemingly simple case, which she had been insulted to be handed and had anticipated solving within half a day, was beginning to look a little less obvious. A little more devious.

Her thoughts swished in time with her legs. She could understand why the night staff had covered for one another. Loyalty. But, partly due to this, the obfuscation was over timing. The cover-up meant that they couldn't even ascertain the basics, such as when and how had Mr Foster actually left the home, let alone why. A lost teddy seemed a flimsy excuse. But to a confused mind?

So, as she turned out towards Ball Haye Road her thoughts moved on too. Where was he now? She felt her face screw up both in puzzlement and against the wind, which was biting into her cheeks. She was having trouble seeing. And so, it appeared, were the motorists, who were practically shaving her legs as they passed too close. Where would this confused, frail, elderly man have headed for? Jason had reported that he hadn't headed for his one-time home. Was he holed up somewhere, alone, confused and afraid? Or was he already dead?

If his mobility was as poor as she'd been led to believe, he couldn't have gone far and without anyone seeing him. Deep in thought, searching for answers even to the most basic of questions was possibly why, late, tired, distracted, in the dark, pregnant and in a hurry, when a car flashed past her on full beam, she failed to avoid an invisible pothole and landed in the gutter, kissing the pavement, bumping the baby and hitting her head on the kerbstone. As she sat up she could feel blood trickling down over her eyebrow.

'Bugger.' She looked down at her torn Lycra leggings and knees scraped like a ten-year-old's. Matthew would be furious. He was overprotective towards his pregnant wife, and this would hand him the perfect excuse for banning cycling for the rest of her pregnancy.

Which she'd planned to do anyway.

Maybe, she thought, over-optimistically, he wouldn't be home yet. She could sneak in, clean herself up and . . .

Fat chance.

She remounted and, cycling more slowly and more warily now, she headed towards home.

Her wish, that Matthew would have been detained at the hospital so she could clean herself up before he saw her, was not granted. His BMW was already in the drive and inside the house the lights were on. He was actually looking out of the window as she rounded the house to put her bike in the shed. She saw his unmistakable long shape and, as he spotted her and waved, she sensed that he stiffened. He'd already seen the bike, perhaps her drooping shoulders and, Matthew-like, had started to fill in the gaps.

Within a minute he was out through the door. 'Joanna, what on earth?'

Five minutes later DI Joanna Piercy was stretched along the sofa looking rueful, gazing over her expanded abdomen at the bottle of red wine sitting temptingly in front of her (banned by her vigilant husband) and ignoring the stinging from her grazed knees. She looked up at Matthew, who was reading her the riot act about cycling while pregnant and what a fall could have done to his (our?) child.

Her explanation of, 'Just a pothole, Matt,' had done nothing to soften his mood. He was really angry. And now she was rebelling. 'Oh, for goodness' sake, Matthew, stop fussing and being overdramatic. It's just grazed knees and a bump on the head. I took a tumble – that's all.'

Perhaps even Matthew realized he'd gone too far. 'Jo.' He sat down beside her, rested his hand on her – their – baby bulge and smiled at her, green eyes warm with affection, before leaning forward and kissing her on the mouth, those same green eyes soft but also unmistakably uncompromising. 'All I ask,' he was saying, 'is that you stop cycling.' The green eyes were pleading with her now, his mouth curved in a beseeching smile. 'Darling, it's not for ever. Just until after he's born.'

She argued resentfully but silently.

Yeah, yeah. It was right to give up alcohol. She agreed with that. She didn't want a drunk as a baby. She didn't actually want a baby but now it was inevitable. The one concession – or should that be bad habit? – she had refused to give up had been her cycling. Matthew had begged her to stop. She hadn't and today she had paid the price and he had been proved right. He had warned her that any fall could harm their child. They both knew tumbles were often a part of cycling. Two wheels are not exactly stable, particularly when you're carrying a large load up front. Ubiquitous potholes causing loss of balance, exacerbated by her weird shape and selfish drivers, darkening nights and worsening weather added to the risk score. And, though Matthew was doing his best to be conciliatory, she knew underneath he was furious with her. Her attempt at defence sounded feeble even to her.

'It's *good* for the baby.' Mentally adding: cycling not falling off! 'Gives it a burst of oxygen and' – sly look at husband – 'it's keeping me fit ready for the delivery.' Something she had unsuccessfully tried to shove right to the back of her mind. And thanks to PC Anderton, her fear of it was moving to the fore.

Matthew pulled away to stare at her. He'd read her mind. 'Look, Jo,' he said. 'You're fit and healthy. You'll be fine giving birth.'

'You can't know that, Matt.'

'No.' As always his voice was steady, his reasoning logical. 'You'll be in a hospital. I'll be with you. All the time. Right through. Darling . . .' He accompanied the sweet words with a brush of his lips on her cheek. 'You'll be fine,' he repeated. 'But . . .' She knew that frown, particularly when combined with a squaring of his chin and fingers running through that honey-blond hair, ruffling it to an almost artistic style which indicated not calm but turmoil. 'If you fall off or get knocked off by a vehicle, it could cause all sorts of problems. God, Joanna,' his anger burst through, 'it's not worth the risk. You're just being stubborn.'

Her sigh, which sounded like a dolphin's exhalation through its blowhole, was her only response.

He hadn't finished. 'Jo. Darling. Stay off your bike until after he's born.'

'It's . . .' she began to repeat her mantra, '. . . good for me and good for the baby.'

But he anticipated it. 'And when you fall off? As you have today? How exactly is that good for the baby, Joanna?'

She shrank back against the cushions. She knew he was angry with her when he called her Joanna in that particular tone of voice.

As usual Matthew had had his responses ready, up his sleeve. And also, as usual, he was right. She shoved that bit to the back of her mind.

'I *haven't* hurt it.'

Matthew moved back towards her, again put his hands on the bump as though he was palpating it to check the veracity of her statement, feeling for the child to move. 'Possibly not,' he agreed, 'this time.' He'd left the pause just long enough for her to worry. 'But that isn't the point, Jo,' he said. 'You *could* have hurt him.'

Her response was the only one *she'd* had up *her* sleeve. 'I wish you'd stop calling it *him*,' she said irritably, tempted to put her hands over her ears to block out this premature sexing of the child, but determined not to lose *every* little skirmish. 'It might be another daughter.'

Another Eloise? She almost shuddered.

He opened his mouth to speak but she pre-empted him. 'And no, I don't want to know what it is.' Thinking, *I'll face that one when I have to.* 'But what with Korpanski treating me as though I was made of porcelain, giving me an insult of a case and you . . .' She appealed to him, made one last attempt to get him on her side. 'Matthew, I find it hard to breathe with all this fuss. Being on my bike, legs pumping, wind through my hair, oxygen in my lungs. It feels great.' She reached for his hand and squeezed it. 'To be honest, apart from my disgusting shape, I've never felt better.'

'Disgusting shape?' And the green flame lit his eyes again but this time brighter, fiercer, as though someone had tossed copper sulphate on to a blaze. Or insulted his 'son'. 'Joanna,' he said, those eyes locking into hers. 'You've never looked more beautiful.' Again, his hands stroked her bump. 'Holding, nurturing our child, you are perfect.' He accompanied the flattery with a kiss before drawing back. 'And anyway, your shape will return.' He picked her hand up and, green eyes now watching her mischievously, brushed it with his lips in an old fashioned and strangely erotic gesture. 'Stop cycling, darling. For the sake of our son, put your bike away. Just for these last couple of months?'

'Oh, please,' she snapped, never a good loser but having to accept that this time she was on the losing side. 'I'm pregnant. It isn't terminal cancer.'

'Yes,' he said, voice steady, reasonable as ever. 'You're pregnant and what I want more than anything in the world is a *healthy* son.'

'Christ.'

He pulled back but she was roused now. Why did he always use the first person? It wasn't just *his* child. It was *theirs*. *She* was playing *her* part. That *I* went too well with the possessive pronoun *mine*. Not *ours*. Not *us*. Not *we*. Always *I*: *His* son – or daughter. Her lips twitched with anger.

She glanced down at the mound. The child was moving around, in agreement with its father probably, and it was making her uncomfortable. Pressing against her spine it was making her feel slightly sick and a bit dizzy. How *could* he be excluding her from something that was so obviously and patently growing parasitically inside her?

Matthew had shifted away but was still looking at her, perhaps picking up on her gritted teeth. But his eyes still burned, his chin was firm and his mouth set. She knew this expression only too well. She would not budge him. And he would not give one inch.

And now he was about to say it.

'I won't forgive you, Jo,' he said in his quiet and most dangerous voice, 'if you harm our son by selfishly refusing to give up *anything* that might endanger him.'

She met his eyes and knew she would not shift him. Matthew was the most stubborn man she had ever met. And this was him at his most extreme. Even as she opened her mouth to defend cycling with her arguments that it wasn't a dangerous sport – that the danger came purely from the motorists and unpredictable road surfaces; that these days she only cycled into work, less than two miles – she knew she was on to a loser. The wound on her forehead and the pair of grazed knees bore their own testimony.

And she had to acknowledge the truth.

Resentful but accepting the inevitable, she nodded and managed a smile. 'OK, Matt, you win. No more cycling,' she said, adding softly, 'until after—'

Matthew still wasn't quite satisfied. 'Don't take *any* risks.'

Fussing over a bumped head and a scraped knee, she thought, inwardly acknowledging damaged pride and an argument lost in his quest for this perfect son, this ultimate ambition, this child, this fulfiller of all his life's desires. *Matthew*, she wanted to say to him, *be real. Life isn't perfect. Girls happen. The son may be a daughter. There are no guarantees. Life itself is unpredictable and has a habit of biting you on the backside. Matthew.* She wanted to appeal to him. But she didn't dare. On this subject Matthew was not only intransigent but very, very touchy.

'And Jo,' he said, determined to capitalize on this gained ground, 'there's something else. Give up frontline policing. Please?'

EIGHT

Two weeks earlier. Friday 5 October, 6 p.m.

In the small front room of a terraced house in the moorlands town of Leek, Staffordshire, on the first grey day of what threatened to be a long and harsh winter, Kath Whalley was pissed and pissed off. In fact, she hadn't really sobered up since she'd left prison a few months ago. She was sitting in the cramped room, dimly lit by one solitary sixty-watt bulb, with her three mates, Fifi, Debs and Chi. Her father was letting her use the terraced house he owned. 'For now,' he'd warned. Then added, 'Best if you go it alone, Kath.' As he'd spoken he'd watched her warily, anticipating a violent response.

She'd stared him out so he'd changed his timescale to, 'Long as you like, love.' She'd entered the house ahead of him before grabbing the keys, turning around and slamming the door in his face. No need for words. Her dad understood her only too well. She'd go when she was ready.

He'd shifted off the doorstep and headed back home as fast as he could.

And so, months later, she was still *in residence*.

The room bore scars of previous tenants as well as of Kath's rages: walls painted cream with patches of damp and marks where objects had been thrown or spilt, and the door pockmarked with holes on which Kath had pinned up a crude picture she'd drawn of a woman, anatomically and explicitly correct, bright blue eyes, thick, curling dark hair and – to remove any doubt of the person's identity – around the neck she'd drawn a placard with the name, Detective Inspector Joanna Piercy. The detective's large blue eyes worked perfectly as dual bull's-eyes. But there were other equally good, larger targets.

'Damn.' She'd only gone and missed the eye, stuck one on the bitch's nose. It quivered for a moment before dropping to the floor. Kath leaned against the back of the sofa and closed her eyes.

She was held together by the sticky tape of hatred and the burning need for revenge. Kath considered herself a tough character. But last time the prison she'd ended up in had not been Drake Hall, the local women's open prison, but some stinky place in bloody Derbyshire. Called a 'reoffender' now, the open prison had been swapped for the closed establishment which meant no little trips out for drugs, booze or liaisons (not that Kath was into blokes, her attitude being that they had their uses but most of the time they were just plain useless). In this prison the inmates were not crime virgins but women with experience. They had taught her a thing or two but, being away from Staffordshire and home, her friends and family hadn't been able to visit. Or else they hadn't *wanted* to make the journey. Initially, before she'd made a couple of friends, she had felt isolated, her anger compounding by the hour while she'd plotted her revenge. With help.

Isolation had been a new experience for Kath. Surrounded by her like-minded family they had normally worked together. But sending Kath to one prison, Hayley to another, Tommy to yet another and Ma and Pa to Winson Green she had, for the first time since her birth, been alone.

She'd sat in her cell, seething.

Until this prison sentence, Kath's assaults had been instinctive, a sudden flash of fury that resulted in fists, feet, head making contact, bones crushed, blood spurting. She didn't plan it. It just happened (which had not impressed the prosecution at her trial for an assault on an elderly lady). And afterwards she neither reflected nor regretted her actions. They just happened and were forgotten within minutes – at least by her. Maybe the victims spent some time in hospital, maybe not. It wasn't her business. But Piercy had got under her skin, made a passionate plea at the trial. Impressed the jury; even her defence (a weak, lily-livered guy with odd eyes and a broken nose) had admitted, admiringly, that the DI had been a worthier opponent.

Kath had noted the words. So how much more impressed would the good townsfolk of Leek be when she finally beat her enemy? Now all she needed was a plan. She threw another dart and this time struck gold – the black pupil in the centre of the left eye.

As she'd been sent down she'd started to think. The stretch had been shit but she had used the time wisely, working things out with help from some of the other inmates who had been full of ideas and suggestions. And when she'd come out her three henchwomen had been waiting.

Hardly taking their eyes off her, she was watched by them now as she chucked her fag on the floor and ground it out in the carpet, leaving yet another scorch mark. She smelt the melting nylon and screwed up her face. Disgusting. One day she'd give up. Just not yet.

She kept her eyes closed while her three mates waited for her to speak. But they would have to wait. Kath was occupied in her half-dream world, her mind testing out various scenarios, each one ending in a different torture. Rip nails, stamp on face, gouge out eyes, punch her till her teeth all fell out. And the final triumph? She would kick her belly until it emptied and she bled the child away. And then she'd watch while her blond husband left her.

Prison had taught her things. The other inmates hadn't known her reputation, so she'd stayed quiet for almost a week.

Until . . . She'd grabbed someone who'd pissed her off once too often, got her in a headlock and crashed her against the sink until she'd flopped to the floor. Not quite unconscious. They'd made such a fuss, alarms and screws rushing in; it had earned her an extra six months on her sentence, but it had also earned her the respect she'd expected. From then on no one dissed her. Not even the screws. There is only one way to earn respect in prison.

Kath opened her eyes, looked at her three mates with a sense of satisfaction and took in a long, deep breath. They were only too aware that the Kath who came out of prison was a different version of the same person who had gone in six and a half years earlier. Tougher, crueller, cleverer, even more of an expert in the art of inciting fear. Never knowing when someone will come up behind you, try to gouge your eyes out, slam you on the head, break your jaw, trip you up on the stairs, gives you a heightened awareness. There are a thousand ways to vent your hatred on someone both in and out of prison. But whatever her status 'inside', none of the inmates had feared her like these three stooges. The stretch had left its mark but she had learned things in there too. Prison had its uses. It is an educational establishment as well as a correctional one. In her case the correctional part missed out in favour of the education she'd received. She chewed her cheek.

NINE

Monday 22 October, 10.35 p.m.

Matthew had added insult to injury by washing her grazed knees, spreading filthy-smelling iodine ointment on them, which stung. (Don't want them getting infected.) And finally tucking her in bed and bringing her some hot chocolate.

She'd looked at the steaming mug in disgust. 'Hot chocolate.'

And felt sure that in Matthew's face there was a hint of mischief as he handed it to her. She took the mug and looked up at him. 'Matt.'

He sat on the bed, his eyes on her, waiting. 'Matt,' she said again, 'promise me one thing.'

He raised his eyebrows in preparation.

'I'll behave this time,' she said. 'I won't be cycling again until after the baby is born. But Matt, no more children. Just this one.'

He gave a little smile, a smaller nod. But not until she'd read disappointment in his face. 'You hate being pregnant that much?'

Unable to lie she disguised her answer by taking a sip from the mug. It was ridiculously sweet. 'It's not just the pregnancy. It's . . .' she heaved a great sigh, '. . . well, bringing up a child . . . all that entails.' Then she dived for cover and took refuge. 'Being pregnant is so restrictive.'

He looked surprised. 'Just because you can't go on your bike?'

'No – more than that.'

He voiced his question with a raising of his eyebrows. 'Work?' She said nothing but watched him warily and he tried again. 'Is it work?'

That was when she nodded but with a wry look. 'If you can call my current case work.'

Now he'd won, Matthew was magnanimous. 'So . . .?' he queried, smile registering faint interest.

'A ninety-six-year-old man with dementia absconding from a residential home apparently in search of a lost teddy bear?'

She had to hand it to her husband. He did his very best not to laugh. Trouble was he didn't succeed. The result was a loud snort. But he was still listening. One thing Joanna really loved about her husband was the opportunity to pick his brains.

'Matt,' she said a little later, after drinking more of the disgusting hot chocolate. 'How long would my old man last out there?' She took another sip, made a face. 'I mean he's old. He's confused. Is he likely to still be alive?' She glanced towards the sleet rattling against the windowpanes. 'In this weather?'

As was his habit, he didn't respond straight away but spent some time considering her question from more than one angle.

'Depends,' he said finally. 'On his BMI. Body fat. Is he slim or well covered?'

'I'm not really sure. I suppose tomorrow I'll get a more detailed description. Maybe a picture.'

'Well, he'd last better if he's got some body fat.' He paused, frowning. 'It's an instinct to find shelter, even though he might not really know where he is if his mental state is confused.' He too watched the rain cascade down the window and his frown deepened. 'All in all, I'd say he's more than likely to be dead.'

'Mmm. Rotten end to a long life.'

And he agreed.

Somehow or other he managed to fit his arm around her and the child and they went to sleep.

His good humour lasted through until the next morning.

Tuesday 23 October, 7.45 a.m.

She was woken by a knock on the door, the rattle of coffee mugs, a cafetière and the scent of buttered toast. She sat up. 'Breakfast in bed, Matthew Levin? Are you going to keep this up until I give birth?'

She would have forgiven him anything for that grin which seemed to wrap up anything bad. 'Absolutely, Jo. Got to look after my family.'

My family. The phrase sounded unfamiliar, even in her thoughts. But he meant her and the child. His family.

'After all, there's two of you now.' A stickler for the absolute truth, he added, 'Well, almost.'

'I'm hardly likely to forget it.'

He flopped down beside her, almost spilling the coffee and catapulting the toast on to the bed.

'Jane was really sick,' he said, 'when she was . . .'

She didn't know which was the worse image – the thought of Jane, his ex-wife, being treated like this, Eloise a growing and developing foetus, or the thing that was fast growing inside her.

She closed her eyes to all the images and accepted the coffee and toast. He'd noticed her frown and ignored it, but not before she'd seen the look in his eyes. 'I need to get up . . .' And then she knew why she was reluctant to leave this cosy place. 'Matt,' she said.

'Mmm?'

'What do people look like when they've died of hypothermia?'

He turned towards her. 'You really want to know?'

'Yes – as probably today I'm going to be faced with it.'

He lay back, folded his arms behind his head and stared up at the ceiling. 'Do you mean what happens to them?'

'Yes. Will he have suffered?'

He shook his head. 'No. They initially start to shiver; their skin goes white and cold. Peripheral shutdown.' He turned his head. 'Confusion sets in, slurred speech, sometimes rapid breathing and they feel tired. Basically they just fall asleep.'

'It sounds peaceful.'

'Basically,' he repeated, 'it is a peaceful death.' And then he couldn't resist. 'If you do find him, Jo, you'd better warn the team. Sometimes they look dead but they aren't. Just in a state of suspended animation. When you warm them up they start breathing again. The mortuary resurrections? Often the result of hypothermia.'

'Thank you. At least I know more about the probable death of our old man.' She put the tray on the side table and threw back the covers. 'Time I got on with finding him then – unless he's already turned up, dead or alive.'

And with that she headed off for her morning shower.

TEN

Tuesday 23 October, 8.30 a.m.

Korpanski caught up with her as she was exiting the car park. He took in her car and grinned. 'Not on the bike then, Jo?'

She glared at him. 'Don't push your luck, Korpanski.'

He raised his eyebrows. And waited, knowing the storm would soon break.

It did. 'I'm actually banned from cycling by my beloved husband,' she said. 'He's all but locked it away.'

Wisely Korpanski still said nothing. But he smirked.

'Actually,' she said as they headed across the car park towards the entrance to the station, 'I fell off on my way home last night.'

'Ah.'

'Grazed knees and the tiniest bump on my head,' she confessed.

And Korpanski couldn't stop the guffaw that opened his mouth and bellowed right across the yard. And after a minute or two she joined him, adding, 'Matthew wasn't impressed.'

Still laughing, they entered the station, but were greeted with a shake of the head from the desk sergeant. She approached him. 'Can you get in touch with Ryland's Residential Home and ask them to email over a photograph of our missing man, please?'

'Consider it done.'

Hearing this, Korpanski had been about to tease her: *Not even found the teddy bear?* It had been on his lips but, after one look at her face, he decided not to risk it, instead following her into their office.

She plonked herself down on the swivel chair in front of her desk and prepared to log on to the computer. 'I wish it was men who had babies,' she grumbled. 'They wouldn't be saying . . .' she scrabbled the air, '*it's just for a few months.* They'd . . .'

Korpanski burst out laughing. 'You look so funny, Jo.'

She jabbed at a few keys, something like a glare beaming out of the stormy eyes.

While Korpanski waited for the storm to pass.

Unpredictable as ever, it didn't take long. She looked at him ruefully. 'Scooting through a puddle and the next thing I knew I was lying face down on the pavement.'

'Shit, Jo,' he said. Then he caught her eyes and clamped his mouth together. A little squall was still present.

'Don't you start,' she warned. 'Just don't bloody well start, Korpanski. The baby is fine. Matthew, however, is not. He practically had a nervous breakdown when I got in with my front wheel buckled. He hasn't stopped making a fuss about it ever since. Honestly. He nearly wheeled me all the way to the hospital to insist on a total body scan.'

Korpanski said nothing but continued to watch her, very guarded now. And something unexpected, something he'd never thought he would feel so strongly. Not for his DI. He felt protective.

'That's not all,' she said, avoiding his eyes.

He came up behind her and put a friendly hand on her shoulder.

'Let me guess,' he said, breathing in a scent of shampoo, lemons and soap. 'He wants you to give up front-line policing.'

She nodded.

'It's policy anyway, Jo.'

She nodded again. 'I know, but . . .'

And then she fixed her mind on the job in hand. 'I guess I'd better get on with the search for my old man.'

'Yeah.'

She began by checking with the uniformed team who had been detailed to search Ryland's and its surrounds. And the answer was still a negative.

'He's not turned up?' Joanna was incredulous. 'Not alive or dead?'

'No, Jo.'

'Any sign of him? Slippers? Footmarks?'

PC Paul Ruthin shook his head. 'Nothing.'

She still felt this investigation was not exactly challenging. But answers were eluding her. An old man wanders away from a residential home. Police can't find him.

Hardly headline news. But all the more irritating for its very triviality.

But whatever the case, it was her case. A professional is a professional. Pregnant or not, she was an officer of Her Majesty's Police Force. It was up to her to work through it until it reached its conclusion. And the next step was to escalate the search, call a briefing and address the roomful of three detectives and four uniformed guys, reflecting that a few years ago there would have been double this number.

And in her opinion Mr Foster's fate would be known.

Looking at her team she sensed they felt the same as her, that this was a minor case which would be wound up by teatime.

Much of a briefing consists of going over the same facts again and again, searching for some explanation while a physical search is being carried out behind the scenes.

'So,' she began, 'on the surface I agree with you. A minor case but puzzling too and with some anomalies.' She pinned the photograph emailed from Ryland's and took a good look at the missing man's face. Zachary Foster looked every single minute of his ninety-six years. His expression was earnest, blue eyes hooded by sagging skin. His face was thin. His eyes, a pale, icy blue, looked confused and appealed for understanding. The faintest hint of a smile played around his lips; the smile wasn't a confident one, but ingratiating. He looked vulnerable, lines of worry creasing his cheeks. His hair was, as described by Sandie Golding, sparse and white. You could see the shape of his head.

She turned away from him, feeling she was failing to respond to his mute appeal. His obvious vulnerability made her feel even worse for failing to find him.

She turned back to her team of officers, using the whiteboard to feed them the facts.

'Zachary Foster. Age: ninety-six. Wearing striped pyjamas, brown slippers and an overcoat. Resident of Ryland's Residential Home for the last eighteen months. Prior to that he lived at number seventeen Leonard Street, Leek. PC Jason Spark has visited that address but the current owner, a Mrs Janet Baldwin, hasn't seen anyone answering to this description in the vicinity. Mr Foster was born in that house and lived there with his mother who died many years ago. He never married and had no children. There are no close relatives.'

Joanna turned her attention to the street map of Leek and the wider surrounds. Reservoirs, moorlands, peaks and climbs, but her eyes always returned to the town with its busy, cramped streets. She frowned. Leek was nothing if not congested. And congested meant many pairs of eyes. So where was he, this one old man who had so far evaded discovery?

She picked up. 'According to Ryland's staff, Mr Foster's mobility was limited, but in spite of that an intensive search of the immediate area has failed to find him. And so . . .' she heaved in a sigh, '. . . we must escalate the search.' She paused before adding, 'The likelihood is that we find a body. The weather has been cold.'

She paused. A briefing is an ideal opportunity to a) review a case and b) brainstorm. But as Joanna scanned the room she couldn't see any bright sparks of ideas. The faces looked as uninspired as she was by the review.

So after a brief pause she continued, 'Mr Foster suffers from dementia and had a stroke two years ago which affected his mobility and his speech. He drags his foot and slurs his words. Which makes it all the more extraordinary that we haven't found him – yet.'

Now she saw that a few members of her team were frowning.

'There are some troubling accounts of his disappearance. Let's look closely at the staff of Ryland's who were *supposed* to be looking after him. One qualified nurse and two health-care assistants.' She turned back to the board and wrote:

Night Sister Joan Arkwright and two health-care assistants, Susie Trent and Amelia Boden.

'They initially claimed that he was last seen around two a.m. by the night staff. I'll come back to that. They said that Mr Foster appeared asleep.

'He was officially noted missing at around seven a.m. by the night staff. I said I'd come back to the claimed observation at two a.m. This turned out to be not quite so. Ms Trent actually did not see our missing man at two a.m. She stood in the doorway.' She returned to a room plan she'd drawn earlier. 'Mr Dean, the resident who shared a room with our missing man, has a bed that is clearly visible from the doorway, but Mr Foster's is concealed by an en suite bathroom. So in fact the last sighting of Mr Foster was at around nine p.m. when he was given his night sedation.'

She searched the room for inspiration and found none, so continued. 'Mr Foster has never absconded before nor shown any desire to escape the residential home.'

She scanned the blank faces. 'So you might want to ask yourselves if anything had triggered this disappearance?'

Again there were more expressions of puzzlement than of clarity or inspiration.

She helped them out. 'It transpires that he had appeared upset lately as a teddy bear his mother had given him – and to which he was very attached – had been lost.'

She gritted her teeth, ignoring the looks, partly puzzled, partly amused which passed between them, before turning back to the board to draw up a list of checks.

'So, quite apart from the fact that we don't know when he left, there is the point that none of the three night staff witnessed his flight, plus we still don't know how Mr Foster made his escape.

There are five potential exit points. The front and back doors are deadlocked and the keys removed. I've studied the two fire exits and am satisfied that he didn't leave through either of these. Which leaves the French doors exiting the day room. All the doors are apparently locked and bolted when the staff working the evening shift leave the premises at around nine p.m.'

Again she listed them on the board.

Jubilee Watkins

Ned Sheringham

Shawna Wilson

'After the two o'clock round, Susie Trent went outside for a smoke and insists the French windows in the day room were locked and bolted when she exited, and that she secured them when she came back in. PC Bridget Anderton and myself are returning to Ryland's later today and will be checking up on this. My theory is that Ms Trent found the doors unlocked and unbolted and, believing the night sister, Joan Arkwright, forgot to secure the doors, is covering for her out of loyalty. It seems the most logical explanation.' She tried to bring some levity into the room. 'Unless, that is, our man managed to exit through a locked and bolted door and secure it similarly behind him.'

It raised a couple of very weak smiles.

'There is no CCTV in Ryland's, but there are plenty scattered around the town. So far there have been no sightings.' She ploughed on. 'A thorough search of the premises and surrounds has so far shown no sightings either.'

She stood still for a moment, paralysed by this one odd fact which, added to the others, seemed impossible. *No one* had seen him?

She could see her puzzlement reflected in her team as she wound up. 'I don't need to tell you that the weather has hovered just above freezing for the last two nights and our man was wearing pyjamas, slippers and an overcoat.'

More scribbling and she recalled Matthew's words of warning. 'Elderly people who have hypothermia sometimes are not dead but in a state of suspended animation, so if you do find him make sure a doctor examines him.'

Korpanski was standing at the back of the room, watching, with some sympathy. She smiled at him, which he returned – with interest – in the form of a wide, encouraging grin. But she was aware that she was stumbling over something more than just the strange facts of the case. She didn't and couldn't possibly understand what this word dementia meant. She'd heard it often. But what did it actually mean? Had he simply wandered off to look for this 'teddy bear'? Right under everyone's nose? Creeping down the stairs without anyone hearing or seeing? Maybe Matthew would be able to explain. Sometimes it was very useful to have a medic for a husband.

She wound up the briefing. 'Obviously we want to find him alive but at the same time the likelihood is, considering the weather and the fact that he was elderly and confused, that what we will find will be Mr Foster's body.'

Grave faces nodded back at her.

'The next stage will be to go public, put his photograph around on social media as well as speaking to people in the town. We can sift through CCTV to try and ascertain which direction he left in. Rope in the ever vigilant and frequently misleading Joe Public . . .' sniggers all round, '. . . and sift through all the detritus, false sightings, misleading information that involving *vox populi* or rather *mens populi* will inevitably drag in.'

She glanced at Mike, still standing at the back of the room. Even from that distance she could read humour in the dark eyes. He was mocking her, putting his hand over his belly and grinning. One day in the future he would drag this humiliating briefing up and they would laugh about the day she had been sent out to search for a demented old man who was himself on a confused quest for a long-lost toy. 'So . . . any questions?'

PC Gilbert Young, a balding, shaven-headed constable who had recently moved from Stoke, put his hand up. 'What do we know about this home?'

She corrected him. 'Ryland's *actually* calls itself a residential home. It's been open for twelve years and in general it has good reviews. All four and five stars, a big band of happy relatives, praise for the humanity of the care assistants and their bosses. The manager is Sandie Golding and the matron Matilda Warrender. The owner is a Mr Sadiq Haldar but I don't think he has much to do with the actual running of Ryland's. I've yet to interview the matron. DC King has searched the home through the PNC. Nothing. We've never been summoned there before and there have, apparently, been no problems. Just an annual clear fire inspection.'

She looked around the room. 'PC Anderton and myself will be returning to Ryland's and interviewing more of the staff. In the meantime, go out and find him. Please?'

Korpanski watched her, deep in thought. Some women look beautiful when they're pregnant. Skin, hair, and that joyful expression on their faces that they are preparing to meet the child they already half know but have only seen in strange, ultrasound images. Fran had been like that. Beautiful.

He wouldn't exactly call Detective Inspector Joanna Piercy beautiful in her pregnant state. There was a sense of irritation, of frustration in her manner, but something *had* changed in her. It just took a little longer to see it. She had softened. The inspector he had first met all those years ago had been spiky, defensive, determined to prove herself superior. A lot of that attitude had gradually been shed like the scales of a snake or a lizard when it has outgrown its skin. Maybe that was what had happened. DI Joanna Piercy had become Mrs Matthew Levin. And as such had outgrown her skin. As he stood and watched her he also acknowledged his own part in the conflict; resentful at having a female inspector to work under, he had been angry and obstructive. Not any more.

As the officers filed out he walked towards her to stand by her side and, like her, studied the map. 'Any ideas, Mike?'

Her finger trailed to the northeast moorland, the A53, and the road which eventually reached the spa town of Buxton.

'That,' she said, 'is my fear. If he's somewhere out there we might never find him.'

'You can take the helicopter out.'

'For now,' she said, 'we'll focus on the town. But then . . .'

She trailed her finger to the left of the A53. Just beyond Blackshaw Moor was Tittesworth Reservoir and to the west of that, Rudyard Lake. Her finger moved down the map, following the road that led towards the Potteries. She moved her finger again to trace the A520 which threaded through Cheddleton, crossing the Caldon Canal and finally reaching Stone. And then her finger touched the A523 which led south-east towards Ashbourne.

'He wouldn't have got that far, Jo,' he said.

'No. For my money he is still here.' She touched the town map and the maze of streets.

'But the thing that puzzles me, Mike, is . . .' She turned around, her face near his. 'People here are nosey,' she said. 'They know their neighbours and aren't shy of coming forward and intervening. If they saw a frail old man dressed in slippers and pyjamas, even covered up with an overcoat, not one of them wouldn't ring the police.'

Korpanski stayed silent and she carried on, her eyes trained on her sergeant's face for some hint of inspiration. 'The alternative is that he didn't walk at all.'

'I don't understand what you're implying, Jo.' His features were as blunt as his response.

'What if someone has picked him up, Mike?'

'Why? Why would they do that? And why wouldn't they bring him in or at least return him to the residential home?'

'He might not be able to give them his address.'

'In which case they would have brought him here, wouldn't they?'

And there she was stumped and merely shrugged. 'Search me,' she said. 'I have absolutely no idea.'

She dropped into her seat. Ryland's Residential Home had been practically taken apart. He wasn't there. She had seven officers searching through the town, focusing on the little spots one finds in even the most densely populated conurbations, the places where rubbish is thrown, the dusty attics and damp cellars of derelict buildings. Neglected backyards. Even the graveyard. They had combed the area and would continue to do so. But they were all coming to the same conclusion. He was not within two miles of the home unless . . . Her finger returned to the southern aspect of Tittesworth Reservoir. Mike put a restraining hand on her shoulder. 'You know as well as I do, Jo. Bodies float unless they are weighted down.' Which set her mind tracking along another course. Would the ninety-six-year-old have had the cunning to escape from the home, find his way to the reservoir and commit suicide by filling his pockets with rocks?

'Maybe we should call in the frogmen.'

ELEVEN

Tuesday 23 October, 11.30 a.m.

'Bridget.'

PC Bridget Anderton had been hovering around. 'Jo?'

Joanna flashed her a smile. 'Come on,' she said, 'let's go back.'

In the car Joanna outlined her plan. Bridget was perfect for this, gentle, kind, softly spoken. The staff of Ryland's would instinctively trust her and taking a back seat would allow Joanna a better opportunity for observing responses and reflect on their characters. There was a back story here. Someone was lying but she couldn't work out why – unless it was purely guilt?

Bridget's eyes opened wide. 'You can't think . . .?

Joanna smiled. PC Anderton was a woman who rarely saw harm in anyone. Unusual among the police, who generally saw harm in everyone. Bridget had a husband on long-term sick – no one seemed quite sure of the diagnosis; depression had been mentioned, as had a bankrupt business – but Bridget was loyal and hadn't expounded, keeping her personal life tightly to herself. Which had earned extra respect because, whatever her difficult home circumstances, she was loyal and she wasn't a complainer. If or when she spoke about Steve it was overwhelmingly with a mixture of affection and pity. She managed the home, her children, her husband, her job, and took very little time off. Bridget, Joanna had decided, was exactly the right person to take into an old people's residential home and winkle out salient facts from staff and residents while she played the part of observer. If they needed to interview any of the residents she would deal with them calmly, allay any fears, whereas Joanna knew her impatience and irritation would have crept through. And she *was* irritated. Quite apart from the residential home staff covering up for one another, this was an investigation that should never have been necessary. Sheer bloody carelessness and incompetence was her take.

Bridget had another talent. She was intuitive, sensing omissions in stories and hesitation in the relating of the sequence of events. If this was anything other than a patient simply wandering off into the night searching for a lost toy, they might need all of their powers of observation.

Sandie Golding gave them a very frosty welcome as she opened the front door.

'So you still haven't found him?'

Joanna bristled at the tacit accusation of police incompetence. Tempted to point out – yet again – that this was not police incompetence, but rather a failure on the part of the staff of Ryland's to protect their residents. And she could have added a postscript – that the police investigation was being hampered by the staff's failure to stick to the bloody truth.

'There are a couple of points we need to clear up,' she said, tight-lipped.

Sandie Golding threw her hands up in the air. 'What points? What can you possibly . . .' Her voice trailed away in the wake of Joanna's hard stare.

'My PC has a couple of checks to make and, while she's doing that, I would like to speak to your night staff again.'

'They're on their days off now.'

'Then summon them in. Or I can speak to them at the station.' Joanna gave Bridget a swift exchange. 'On reflection, perhaps that would be the best plan. Ask them to attend Leek police station – at their own convenience – within the next twenty-four hours, please. If they don't attend we'll have to visit them at their home addresses.' Joanna smiled to add casual menace to the threat.

Ms Golding started to object again, 'They may be . . .' Again her voice petered away and she nodded.

As had been agreed, Bridget made straight for the day room, where she was the object of all the residents' attention except for the woman who was still battling bad-temperedly with the jigsaw. She looked up only briefly before venting her frustration on the irregularly shaped pieces of cardboard. The others' interest mounted as Bridget moved the chair and climbed on top of it – not without some difficulty. Chairs are not like stepladders. They are not so easy to climb. At the top she wobbled and grabbed the curtain before shifting the bolt a couple of times. Watched by Joanna as well as the elderly residents and Ms Golding, Bridget climbed off the chair. 'Not easy,' she commented as she landed.

'It's not meant to be,' Ms Golding responded drily. 'It's meant to keep the residents *in* and *safe*.'

Both the police turned to look at her. To have made the obvious comment was quite unnecessary and far too predictable.

Ms Golding was determined to continue with her rudeness and frank hostility. 'Anything else?'

Bridget smiled. 'Yes. Can we take another quick look around Mr Foster's room? And we'd like to inspect the stairs again.'

'I really don't think you'll learn anything from taking another look at the stairs. Or his room.'

Bridget simply continued smiling while Joanna observed.

Sandie Golding was right about the stairs. She watched them critically as Bridget and Joanna stepped up them slowly, making a pretence of examining each step as well as the polished pine handrails.

They moved on to Zachary's room, this time empty. Mr Dean must be downstairs, unless he too had absconded. The room seemed smaller without either occupant and smelt vaguely, but quite pleasantly, of a lemony disinfectant. The window was slightly open, both beds neatly made up. Joanna smothered a smile. Neat, squared-off hospital corners, both beds with pale blue duvets folded back, topped by two pillows.

She opened the wardrobe door. Coats, shirts, even ties. A vague scent of tobacco.

She closed the door again.

'Does Mr Dean smoke?'

'None of our residents do.'

Joanna nodded.

She peered under the bed while the manager and Bridget watched. Opened the drawer in the small bedside table. Inside was a plastic wallet containing a sepia photograph of a woman in a black dress – high neck, long sleeves and a patient stare. On the back was written a year: 1922. It was hard to say how old the woman was – she could have been in her twenties or her fifties. Her stare was unemotional, her expression unsmiling.

'I think that's his mother.' Ms Golding had come up behind her and was peering over her shoulder.

Joanna dipped into the drawer again and came up with another picture of the same woman, possibly younger this time, with her arm around a slightly older woman who was similar enough to guess that the two were sisters.

This time Sandie Golding shrugged. 'No idea,' she said.

Nothing was written on the back. Joanna replaced them in the drawer and closed it. Wherever Zachary was, she thought, she would not find the answer here.

They descended the stairs.

TWELVE

Sunday 7 October, midday
40 Mill Street, Leek

Less than a mile away from the police station, in Mill Street, the atmosphere in the small room was already suffocating, an airless fug of cigarette smoke mixed with stale chip papers. Extracting some security in being together, Debs, Chi and Fifi, her three cronies, mates since before her prison stretch, had slept here the night before, using the cushions from the sofa and some old blankets, while Kath had claimed one of the two bedrooms. Now Debs, Chi and Fifi sat squashed together on one small, sagging sofa, its material heavily marked by carelessness, pockmarked with cigarette burns and splashed with wine, coffee, cider and other substances. Kath sat, alone and regal in the armchair, plotting. She thought best, whatever the hour, when her brain was sharpened by alcohol and sustained with food. Fifi had popped out to the chippy again and Chi had replenished their supply of cider, so the timing was perfect. She felt sharp as a bloody needle.

Revenge. It filled her brain and focused her wits.

She slammed the bottle down on a coffee table so flimsy it staggered on thin legs. She stuck a cold chip in her mouth and picked up another dart, poising it ready to throw. 'I'm going to get the bitch,' she sang. 'I've waited a while for this chance and I am going to soooo enjoy it.' She chucked the dart and this time got her right in the middle of her pregnant belly. She grinned, happy at her aim this time around. She took another swig but then noticed Chi was looking worried and a bit thoughtful. Kath's eyes narrowed. She could smell doubt a mile off. To her doubt meant disloyalty. People were either *for* her 100 per cent or *not*, which equated to 0 per cent. Which meant a traitor. Which meant . . .

She leaned back, eyeing her false friend from beneath her eyelashes, sensitive to the one person in the room who wasn't going to play 'follow the leader'. Maybe it was just that Chi wasn't as drunk as the rest of them. But her instincts were telling her something more. She sat bolt upright, picked up another dart and felt the point of it with the ball of her thumb. 'You got something to say, Chi?'

Sensing danger, Chi shook her head. 'No . . . but.'

Kath leaned forward. 'But what, you fucking chicken?'

Chi tried again, making an attempt to moderate her language as she pointed out the obvious. 'She's a cop. Whatever you do to her, Kath, you'll get it back tenfold. When you get caught you'll have an even longer stretch. You'll be back in clink before you know it.'

For an instant Kath didn't move. She was too angry. Years ago she had lost an incisor. She'd lost it in a fight – but not the whole tooth, and it hadn't really been a fair fight as she'd been holding a baseball bat at the time while her opponent, a one-time friend named Craig, unprepared for conflict, had been unarmed. But he'd still struck a lucky shot with his fists, removing most of the incisor. She had a small jagged piece of it left. When she smiled it gave her a mad, demonic, threatening look. When she was very angry she rubbed it with her finger which was a warning sign to all who knew her. It fuelled her fury by reminding her of things: the nastiness and unfairness of life in general, and in particular it reminded her of the untrustworthiness of false friends like Craig. As she rubbed her finger over it now she could almost taste the wavering loyalty of someone she'd been in school with. Had bunked off lessons with, had smoked behind the bike sheds with – even shared a

boyfriend with, once, in a forgettable threesome. But now? She
could smell that friend's wavering conviction.

False friend. Traitor, the jagged tooth screamed. She needed
to know what was going on in the sly thing's mind. She played
the middle game.

'*If* I get caught, Chi,' she said, glaring.

Chi dropped her eyes.

No one quite knew how 'Chi' had got her name. Her real
name was Rachel. But like the other two, her real name had little
to do with her commonly used moniker. Maybe Chi had stuck
because of the upwards slanting eyes. Or the silky hair that she
straightened to a railroad track. But whatever its origins, the
name had stuck, even though both her parents were as Staffordshire
as oatcakes.

Chi nodded now, her pointy little chin bobbing up and down
in agreement. 'Yeah,' she said, repeating the phrase but with
added emphasis, '*if* you get caught,' counting on the fact that
Kath Whalley was immune to irony, as she was to many other
subtler nuances of the English language. 'I suppose there's always
the chance that they won't connect you with any assault on a
serving police officer.'

She might have said more but stopped abruptly when she
read the level of doubt and suspicion in Kath's face, which
signalled danger and hostility, which in turn triggered a red
alert. Too late, she realized she had just sailed too near the
wind.

Sitting in the centre of the sofa, hemmed in by the other two,
she could not escape the heat and doubt in Kath's gaze.

But Chi had a secret, a plan and an escape route. In that order.
And as Kath continued to stare at her, Chi wondered whether
Kath could read some of it.

She was worried.

And she was right to be. Kath's stare stripped her of her secret.

Nearly three weeks ago, Chi had made a new friend.

Tuesday 18 September, 2 p.m.

Out of Kath's cronies, Chi was the only one with a job. Legit.
Debs and Fifi scraped together some PIP if and when they could

convince their questioner that they had a genuine mental health problem that prevented them from working. They supplemented this paltry income with a few 'foreigners' done for cash, and they supplemented that in turn with a much more profitable and reliable income gained from petty crime, burglary, opportunistic pickpocketing and a bit of drug peddling. Nothing too heavy or complicated. They didn't want to tangle with the big guys so they stayed under the radar. Just satisfying themselves with bits and pieces here and there. They survived by following this simple code: beg, borrow or steal.

Until Kath had come out of jail, when they'd been taken over by her and absorbed into her plans. Trouble was, Kath Whalley was just that bit more ambitious.

Chi had been desperate to escape, and since Kath had emerged from prison her desperation had compounded. Now she would do anything to escape before disaster struck and, together with Kath and the others, she was consigned to HMP.

Truth was Kath frightened her. They'd been at primary school together, and even then Chi had realized that Kath was mad, bad and dangerous to know. But since she had come out of prison she had lost all inhibition. All she cared about now was getting her own back on the detective who had successfully beaten her and put her behind bars. And she didn't seem to care about the inevitable consequences. As long as she took DI Piercy down, Kath wasn't bothered whether she went down too. And that included dragging her three faithful cronies down with her. Which was not in Chi's life plan.

All too often, Chi had witnessed Kath at work, watched her victims cower away from her slaps and thumps and punches. One November night, just before she'd been put away, Kath had invited her to join her in a baseball-bat foray. She'd had a score to settle against a girl who had, she believed, betrayed her. Chi had remained unconvinced. The frenzy of sights: blood, terror, sounds, bones cracking, screams, and the smell. Gore, piss and shit. It had frightened and revolted her so much that she knew she was not like Kath. Never would be like Kath. And since Kath had been released, she'd spent all her time trying to dream up a way of escaping Leek and her one-time friend for ever.

One event in particular had firmed her resolve.

It had been a week or so after Kath had come out. Although it was April, there had been a light dusting of snow and a wicked easterly wind that found its way through your clothes right into your bones. They'd been wandering the town, feeling bored, sour and grumpy, looking through the shops, wondering which bits to nick, when a boy on a bike had collided with her on the pavement and Kath had given him 'what for'. 'Come on, Chi,' she'd urged. 'You can give him a punch too. He went over your foot. I saw him.'

But Chi had had enough. Though she too objected to cyclists on the pavement, this response was just going too far. He was just a kid. She'd seen the terror on his face, the blood pouring out of his nose, the eye already starting to close and she'd shaken her head. 'Let him go, Kath.'

Kath's head had spun round. Chi had caught the blast of fury followed by mockery for her squeamishness. 'Come on, Chi,' Kath had ordered, 'Don't be a wimp. Put the fucking boot in.'

But Chi shook her head and repeated, 'Let him go, Kath.' And surprise, surprise, or maybe because she *was* so surprised, she had. Removed her fist from the boy's collar and turned towards her friend, once she'd warned the terrified youth what she'd do if he told anyone. (*Take your fucking eyes out. Both of them.*) The boy had left his bike on the pavement and run.

Then Kath had turned her attention on to Chi and Chi had felt the sour taste of fear. It didn't do to show Kath anything less than absolute loyalty. She knew what had happened to Craig.

So two weeks later, when Kath had invited her to 'join in' on a punch-up outside a pub, she had, but half-heartedly with weak punches. Kath had finished the job for her, breaking the woman's jaw and pulling out a handful of hair, which she'd brandished like a trophy, her eyes all the time on Chi who'd known Kath was on her guard. She was being watched and tested. And the strain was terrifying. At any moment Kath could turn on *her*, pull *her* hair out, smash up *her* face, burn *her* with acid or bleach, drain cleaner or lighter fuel. If she knew what was in Chi's heart, Kath would wreak her vengeance and she had plenty of actions in her repertoire. It was just a matter

of time before her instincts took over and she realized that Chi
was planning her escape route.

Chi's first step had been to take a real job and earn legitimate
money. Initially bar work, but then she had moved to an upmarket
coffee shop/restaurant named Rosemary's and the manageress,
guess her name (whom Chi suspected of being a lesbian), had
taken a shine to her and quickly promoted her to waitressing
and, though the hours were long and the tips a bit unpredictable,
she quite liked waiting at tables. At least you met normal people.
Families who didn't squabble, shout, get drunk and throw things
around. Couples who weren't yelling at one another every time
they were together. OK, some of the kids were quite disgusting
and their parents rude, but on the whole she liked the work.
Trouble was she wanted/needed to move a long way from Leek
and her psycho friend and find somewhere decent to live. Her
dream was somewhere near the sea, warmer and safer than this
little corner of Staffordshire. But for that dream to be converted
to reality she needed money. Working as a waitress, even when
the tips were good, it was going to take her one thousand years
living on absolutely nothing before she'd have saved enough to
get away. What she needed was a lucky break. A win on the
government lottery. Or else a lucky draw on the lottery of life.
So her antennae were wafting around, trying to pick up that
elusive chance. Chi was an optimist and she felt certain that
something would come her way.

And then it had.

THIRTEEN

Tuesday 23 October, 4 p.m.

Joanna had anticipated this. Call in the frogmen and the press
come scarpering behind them, sniffing out a potential story,
the chance for pictures and headlines.

As they'd returned to the station her mood had been gloomy.
One of the frustrations of this case was that none of the usual

avenues was appropriate. No mobile phone to track (didn't have one), no car number plate to feed into the ANPR (didn't have one of those either). No relatives to interview (deceased), no friends (all dead). The town CCTV had not shown him, and dragging in the general public had brought in nothing fruitful, although a couple of elderly gentlemen had been accosted, insulted at being mistaken for an inmate of a residential home.

To all intents and purposes, Zachary Foster really had vanished into thin air.

The uniformed guys and gals had done their best, poking into streams and skips with equal thoroughness and vigour, but there was no sign of him, his teddy bear, slippers, overcoat or pyjamas. And so far, the feedback from the frogmen at both Tittesworth and Rudyard was that nothing more than an old bike, a shopping trolley and a car number plate had been found. She sensed the team's frustration and irritation matching hers.

The helicopter had done a sweep of the surrounding moorland using heat-sensitive equipment but that had turned up nothing but two dead sheep.

7 p.m.

Sister Joan Arkwright was the first of the night staff to arrive at the station. Out of uniform, wearing ordinary clothes, well-fitting black trousers and a cream-coloured fleece, she had a little more colour in her cheeks and looked ten years younger. She even managed a smile for Joanna. 'I thought I'd better get down here and not waste time,' she said, 'though I've told you everything I know.' She stared at the wall of the interview room. 'I can't believe he hasn't been found.' She pressed her lips together, still frowning in puzzlement. 'It doesn't make any sense, does it?' Her grey eyes held no guilt, only puzzlement. It was as though she was allying herself with the police.

'No, it doesn't,' Joanna responded frankly, keeping her eyes trained on the nurse.

'I'll be honest with you. The only way that Mr Foster could have left Ryland's is through the day-room door. Which, in turn, implies that it was left unlocked and unbolted.'

Joan Arkwright's stare didn't waver. 'I am absolutely certain I locked and bolted the day-room doors just after the evening staff left.'

Joanna let her eyes linger on hers before asking in a voice as soft as velvet, 'So how do *you* think he left?'

'I don't know. I don't know.' Her voice tailed off until she lifted her eyes again. 'Unless someone let him out.'

'Why would they do that?'

'I don't know.'

'And where would he have gone? Why haven't we been able to find him?'

The nurse hesitated before speaking slowly. 'Perhaps he was picked up by a car.'

'By whom?'

The nurse shrugged. 'I don't know, Inspector.'

'So why mention a car?'

Joan Arkwright was frowning. 'Oh, I don't know.'

Joanna waited.

'Sometimes I don't know whether I've dreamt something or imagined it.'

Joanna waited for her to continue.

'Lack of sleep, you know?' She was frowning at the wall. 'It does funny things to your mind.'

'Like what?'

'I wonder whether I heard a car sometime in the night.' She was biting her lip as though the pain of it might force her mind to separate reality from imaginings.

Joanna's response was blunt. 'Did you?'

'I don't know.'

Joanna shelved the possibility for now. She would return to it later. For now, she continued with her line of questioning. 'I'm still surprised,' she said, 'that at some point in the night, time as yet unclear, in spite of having limited mobility, Mr Foster apparently gets out of bed – having had his sleeping tablets – opens the wardrobe door, slips on a coat and walks downstairs. Unseen and unheard by any of you. It's unlikely no one would have heard him unless you were all fast asleep yourselves.' She waited for a response but there was no denial. Just a blank look.

She continued, 'He then crosses the hallway to the day room, drags a chair to the French windows, shoots back a bolt, reaches for a key, unlocks the door, steps outside, closes the door behind him . . .' Here she held up her hand. 'And don't even try telling me he locked and bolted the door behind him, putting the chair back against the wall, because you and I both know that's impossible. My PC struggled with this manoeuvre. I'm pretty sure Mr Foster dragging his leg would have found it impossible.'

The night sister was staring at her. 'Maybe he didn't leave by that route?'

'The other doors were also locked and bolted, the keys with you, and the fire doors were practically jammed up with dirt and debris.'

Joanna left the solution to the nurse who was sitting dumb and puzzled. As was she.

'OK,' Joanna said wearily. She was really tired. She wanted to be home and in a hot bath. In this case she was going round and round.

She had a vague, distant, rare memory of her father. *'Round and round the garden, like a teddy bear. One step, two steps, tickle under there.'*

She was regressing, turning into a child herself. That was what pregnancy did to you. She put her hand on The Bump and for once it was still.

She focused on Sister Arkwright. 'Have you anything more to add?'

'No.'

'OK. Do you know when the other two are calling in?'

She shook her head. 'I haven't spoken to them. I guess they're still asleep.'

Joanna sensed she would not extract any more. 'OK,' she said. 'You're free to go.'

And this, she thought as she watched the nurse file out, is Mr Foster's third night out in the open – or not. It was increasingly likely that his body was somewhere, his death due to exposure.

A swift phone call confirmed that the two HCAs would attend the station first thing in the morning, and Joanna heaved herself into her car, glad now she wasn't on her bike, and headed for home. It was almost ten when she finally arrived. Matthew was slumped on the sofa peering at his tablet screen. He sighed and switched off as she entered. But his grin was warm as he stood up, put his hands around her face and kissed her hard on the mouth before moving back and studying her face. 'You look all in.'

She didn't respond at first but drank in his presence. She loved the feel of him, the tangy, male smell of him, the taste of his mouth, the touch of his hands. Those competent hands she'd watched work with such skill, uncover secrets concealed in the dead. Would he soon be uncovering the death story of Zachary Foster? She ruffled his honey-coloured hair because she loved that too, and watched as it sprang back into its own style. 'I *am* all in, Matt,' she confessed. 'My brain is going round and round,' *like a teddy bear*, she added mentally, 'and coming up with nothing but a blank canvas. None of this case makes any sense at all. And the sillier it is, the more frustrating that I can't find this one, old, confused bloke who, let's face it, is probably already dead. If he's not, if we don't find him very soon he will be, and his death will be yet another one chalked up to police failure.' She knew she was handing him a cue to persuade her to ease up for the remaining weeks before the baby was born, but for once she didn't care. She felt safe here, comfortable, happy in his arms, and she didn't want to move.

'Hey,' he said, searching her face. 'Let me make you a cup of tea and you can tell me all about it.'

It was her dream, to return home to a friend, a loving friend. A husband who cared, and for once she dropped all her defences, took the tea he offered her, sank down on to the sofa and, when he settled beside her, laid her head on his shoulder. 'Thank you for this.'

His answer was another grin wider than the first. His eyes were bright, his manner friendly, open, inviting her to confide in him. So she did, confessing this little mystery which was defeating her and she didn't know why. She asked him the questions that rumbled round and round in her head. 'Why haven't we found him, Matt? I haven't even solved the first part – how he got out. Someone who's never made an escape attempt before. Where is he? What is dementia like? Is it cunning? Could he have plotted a complicated escape plan? Who helped him?'

Matthew shook his head. 'No,' he said. 'Frankly, he's just more likely to have found an open door and stumbled through.'

'What about searching for his lost toy, one he'd had since a child?'

'Yeah,' he said, thinking about it carefully. 'That would be almost an instinct, to find it.'

One of the things she loved about her husband was, when posed a conundrum, he gave it grave and proper consideration. 'I take it your guys have done a proper search of the surround?'

'They're good.'

'But if all you tell me about Foster's limited mobility is true, he has to be within half a mile of the home unless someone's picked him up.'

She told him then about Joan Arkwright's 'dream'.

'We all know we incorporate actual senses or sounds into our dreams, so maybe she did hear a car, Jo.'

'It would make sense as to why we can't find him. But it also makes no sense. Why would anyone abduct an old man who has no relatives, no money, no contacts, and lives in the past?' She thought for a moment before adding, 'And if they did pick him up, why haven't they brought him back when they realized he had dementia? And if he was picked up and they didn't bring him back, why not? And where would they keep him? What would be the point? No one's going to pay a ransom for his return.'

Again Matthew was silent, thoughtful, as he ran through various possibilities. Then he looked up. 'Who took the missing teddy bear?'

She stared at him. 'You think there's a connection?'

'I'm just asking. It's another . . . Aren't you always telling me that no fact, however seemingly small and insignificant, should be ignored? Don't you always search for a logical explanation for everything?'

She shrugged. 'The explanation given by the nursing staff was that it might have been put in the wash, thrown away, somehow discarded.'

'When all the people at the home, from residents to staff, had seen him dragging it around. Didn't you say like Christopher Robin? It's a very clear image. Your man and his teddy bear were inseparable.' He paused. 'And another teddy was substituted?'

She laughed. 'So, follow the bear like the White Rabbit – down the rabbit hole?'

'How long's he been in the home?'

'Eighteen months.'

'And did you say he's never even tried to abscond before?'

'What *are* you suggesting?'

'Cause and effect, my darling.'

'Sure you're not applying too much logic, thinking too hard?'

'Isn't that what you've asked me to do?'

'I suppose so.'

'It's your case, Jo.'

She was silent.

'You've checked his old address?'

'PC Spark went round.' She smiled and brushed his hand with her own. 'Jason Bright Spark. No sign of our missing man there, and the woman who lives there now hasn't seen him either.'

Again Matthew was silent, staring into the fireplace. A log burner was on their list of Things We Want to Do to the House. Maybe by next winter they would be sitting round the comforting warmth of their own log burner while upstairs . . . She could almost hear it. Upstairs a child would be wailing. Screaming for attention.

She moved her attention back to Matthew's profile, almost aquiline, long straight nose, eyes perceptively sharp enough to miss nothing. She dropped her study to the full mouth, the stubborn chin, finally noting, with a smile, his hair: thick, wiry, like its owner with a will and a style all of his own, honey-blond, always tousled; hair that should have belonged to a poet or a musician – not a pathologist.

She smiled. But Matthew wasn't. He was still frowning, tussling with her questions. And when he looked at her, Joanna could already guess what his next sentence would be. He would persuade her to take her maternity leave early.

'I understand you want this case cut, dried and dusted.' She held her breath, anticipating. But now he was grinning. 'I'd be the same, Jo,' he said, mischievously diverting. Then he kissed her. 'I'd be exactly the same.' And she realized she'd never been more wrong. She finished her tea.

'You know what, Matt?'

His response was a raise of his eyebrows. 'I'm not really hungry. I think I'll have a bath and an early night.'

'Me too.'

So the rest of that evening was spent soaking in bath oil, scrubbing each other's backs, Matthew soaping her belly as gently as though he was massaging a newborn. As soon he would. The evening ended up with them dropping between clean sheets.

A perfect end to an imperfect day.

FOURTEEN

Wednesday 24 October, 8.30 a.m.

The two HCAs arrived together, mirroring each other's expressions of anxiety. Unusually Joanna had decided to speak to them at the same time, certain that they would back their colleague's statement unless it threw doubt on their own version of events.

'I just want to confirm the exact sequence of events on Sunday night,' Joanna said.

Both nodded, avoiding looking at one another.

'The nurses working the evening shift – you let them out?'

They looked at each other, apparently surprised at the question. Susie Trent took the lead.

'Well, no – not exactly. We don't *see* them out. They just go and we kind of lock up.'

'Right. So who actually did the locking up?'

Amelia spoke up. 'Sister Arkwright.'

'Did you see her do it?'

Both shook their heads.

'Did either of you check that all the doors were locked and bolted?'

Another negative. But Joanna sensed something. Susie Trent was avoiding her colleague's eyes. Joanna focused her attention on her. 'Did you only go out the once for a cigarette?'

Susie Trent nodded, her face pale and sweating now, her

discomfort infecting her colleague who was looking at her with alarm. Joanna waited a moment before speaking gently to her. 'I have a theory, Susie,' she said, 'that when you went out for a cigarette after doing your two o'clock round, checking the patients . . .' She omitted to mention that in some cases the check had been cursory. '. . . I think you found the day-room door unlocked and unbolted.'

Susie's sigh of relief was like a punctured tyre. She nodded. And immediately tried to justify her lie, speaking quickly. 'I didn't want to get Sister Arkwright into trouble. I just thought she was really tired. She'd done a run of eight nights. She was exhausted. Her kids have been off school for half-term. I wouldn't have blamed her if she'd forgotten to lock just one door. We couldn't have known Zac would wander off looking for his teddy.'

Joanna watched her. At least one conundrum had been solved. 'And the chair?'

'It was against the wall. Where it should be.'

'So when you came back in?'

'I locked and bolted it behind me.' There was something almost self-righteous about her statement.

'Right. OK.'

Remembering Matthew's words the night before, Joanna pursued another avenue. 'When Mr Foster lost his teddy it was replaced with another one.'

Both nodded, puzzled.

'Was it just like his?'

Both shook their heads. It was Amelia who answered for both of them. 'No. His was an ancient old thing. Black. Not very nice. But it was really old. The other one was brown but a lot newer. You'd have thought he would have preferred that.'

'Where did the replacement come from?'

The two women looked at each other then back at her, faces blank.

'We don't know. It just sort of appeared,' Amelia said.

They waited, politely.

'OK. Thanks.' Joanna managed a smile. 'You're free to go – unless, that is, you have anything more to add?'

The pair of them escaped.

*   *   *

Joanna was sitting back at her desk when one of those moments came, a small bell jangling in her brain.

She was gathering facts, trying to put them in some sort of order. Perhaps read a logic not constructed by a ninety-six-year-old man whose brain was being nibbled away, but someone else. So she looked for the sequence.

He'd never absconded before but, the staff had reported, he had appeared accepting and relatively content at Ryland's. He'd settled in nicely, was the phrase they'd used.

The perception was that he had gone to look for his lost teddy bear and got lost himself.

Someone, possibly him, had wrapped a coat around him in preparation for going outside.

No one reported having seen Zac comb through the rooms for the missing toy. So why would he look for something *outside* the home?

Surely his natural instinct would have been to search the place itself? Ask the staff to help. And that was where the irritant scratched away inside her brain. The trouble was she couldn't get a handle on this missing man. And the longer he remained missing, the more desperate she was to find him. She didn't want this case, probably one of her last cases before she gave birth, to be a failure.

But she was stumbling in the dark.

Perhaps the answer lay not with Zac but somewhere else, possibly with some*one* else, not even inside Ryland's. In which case it was time she delved further and interviewed the staff who had worked the evening before he went missing and tried to winkle out a back story – if there even was one.

But this time, partly as punishment for his mockery of her demeaned position as SIO to this ridiculous case, but also because she wanted his perspective, in spite of his protests, she took Detective Sergeant Mike Korpanski and swallowed her mirth at his furious expression. 'You are joking, Jo?'

'Nope.' She smothered her giggles at his disgruntled expression. Getting your own back can be such fun, she thought mischievously, as she noted him grumpily inserting his arms into the sleeves of his jacket. *Ha*, she thought. *Gotcha back. Now who's laughing, Korpanski?* But wisely she kept all that to herself.

One could only push the DS so far and she sensed he was already in a mood. On the way over she shared the HCA's confession. 'When Susie Trent went out for a smoke, she says that the French window in the day room was both unlocked and unbolted.'

'So someone forgot to lock it.'

'Or Mr Foster let himself out through that door, though that seems very unlikely.'

'And that was the last anyone saw of him?'

'Yeah.'

He kept silent as she drove them both over to Ryland's, but while she was driving she'd sensed his attitude was softening and, as she pulled into a parking space, she noted his eyes flickering around. He was taking it all in and she knew later in the day he would be sharing his impressions.

As it was, he kept up his silence while she rang the bell and was admitted.

This time she was connected with a Ms Matilda Warrender who was, she informed her, matron of Ryland's. 'I'm the trained nurse in charge here,' she said crisply. 'If you want to know something about Mr Foster's medical condition, it's probably better you speak to me.' She had gentle, pleasant eyes and a soft speaking voice. Assets for someone in this position. But her eyes, brown flecked with amber, were also wary. Joanna suspected that, like the manager, she was worrying what impact this event would have on the home – and, ultimately, her job.

And for all her gentle and soft manner, she looked as though she would run a tight ship.

'You still haven't found him?'

Somehow she'd managed to tuck in an accusation rather than a defence.

But Joanna was fully aware that if it was the home's fault that their patient had gone missing, it was the police's failure to find him that was generating headlines and, always happy to run a negative police story, perpetuating media interest.

Joanna came straight out with her concerns. 'A few things are puzzling me.'

'Oh?' The matron's manner was quickly defensive.

But Joanna was not to be cowed. 'Yeah,' she said. 'This toy that's—'

'It was a horrible black teddy bear,' Matilda Warrender cut in, her nose wrinkling in disgust as though she could, even now, smell it. 'It was an ancient old thing, but Zac had had it since he was a child and he was very much attached to it.'

'And the substitute teddy bear didn't satisfy him?'

'No.'

'It was nice that somebody went to the trouble of finding another bear to put in its place.'

Matilda Warrender's only response was to press her lips together. 'Do you know who it was?'

'No.'

Joanna avoided Korpanski's eyes, which were threatening to droop with boredom. 'So he was searching for his own toy all over the home?'

'No.' Ms Warrender's eyes clouded and she frowned. 'Not really.'

'And yet you believe that he awoke in the middle of the night, put his coat on, let himself out of the day-room doors, which can't have been easy for a frail, elderly man suffering from dementia, and wandered off to search for it.' By her side Joanna noted Korpanski stiffen. Not asleep now then.

Ms Warrender frowned. 'This is not *my* version, Inspector. It's yours.'

'So what's *your* version?'

The question threw the matron. 'He just wandered off.'

Joanna sighed and met Mike's eyes. This wasn't helping.

'Let me give you the facts, Miss Warrender.' *Another one with no wedding ring.* Joanna spoke coldly. 'Your patient—'

'We call them residents.'

You can call them what you bloody well like, Joanna thought. *How about your responsibility?*

Aloud she conceded the point. 'OK, your *resident* was put to bed here by your staff after they'd, presumably, given him his night sedation.' She wanted to rub this in.

Ms Warrender had picked up on the hostility. 'When you put it like that . . .'

Joanna continued in the same cold voice. 'At some point in the night . . .' Here she met Ms Warrender's eye. 'Your staff appeared vague as to whether they actually saw him after he'd been put to bed at around nine o'clock.'

'They said they'd seen him during—' Her voice was clipped.

'They might have *said* they saw him,' Joanna said wearily, 'but in actual fact they simply stood in the doorway. As you well know, Mr Foster's bed is invisible from that angle.'

Ms Warrender bit her lip and, mercifully, made no comment. Joanna continued without a ripple.

'At some point in the night, after nine thirty but before six thirty in the morning, Mr Foster, presumably still in his pyjamas, put his slippers on and an overcoat over the top, unseen by the staff who were *supposed* to be looking after him, made his way down the stairs and then' – even Mike was wincing at the poison in her voice – 'let himself out through the French windows and vanished. When Susie Trent went out for a cigarette sometime after two a.m., she found the left-hand door leading from the day room unbolted and unlocked.'

The only response from Matilda Warrender was a raising of her eyebrows.

'Susie Trent lied about this originally, believing your night sister, Joan Arkwright, forgot to lock the day-room doors. She lied out of loyalty. But at least it solves the problem of how an elderly, confused man managed to walk through locked and bolted doors and fasten them behind him on a quest for a missing toy.'

The matron drew in a sharp breath and had the grace to blush, but she held her gaze steadily as Joanna continued.

'As we haven't been able to find him, I need to interview all the other staff particularly . . .' she glanced at her list, 'the three members of staff who were on duty on Sunday evening. That is, Jubilee Watkins, Ned Sheringham and Shawna Wilson. Are they here today?'

Matilda Warrender nodded. 'You can use my office.' Her tone was chastened now but ice cold.

'Perhaps you and I could begin with a preliminary chat?'

That earned a vinegary look, accompanied by an if-I-must sigh and a droop of the shoulders. At a guess, Madam Warrender was reflecting less on the sufferings – or not – of her patient and more on the reputation of Ryland's Residential Home. *Care for the elderly our main concern.*

Joanna gave Mike a swift glance and a wisp of a smile but he hadn't quite forgiven her. She got a stony stare back. But it was soon followed by a twitch at the corner of his mouth, which she recognized and returned – with interest.

Once they were sitting down in the main office, Joanna opened with a direct question.

'I'm a little puzzled,' she said, 'about this toy.'

The matron dismissed it with an upward flick of her chin. 'It's just a symptom of his dementia. He cuddles it more or less all the time.'

Joanna acted dumb. 'So how did it come to be mislaid?'

Ms Warrender stared at her, anger bubbling to the surface. 'I don't know.'

'Does it have any significance, apart from being a childhood memory?'

'No. It was just a well-worn teddy bear,' she said with more than a touch of irritation.

'So what do you think happened to it? How did it come to be lost?'

She could sense the matron's irritation and almost hear Mike's tut of disapproval, but she wasn't going to let go of this thread. 'If he held it so close, how did it come to be missing?'

'I really don't know. Maybe one of the other residents "borrowed" it.'

'But it hasn't been found,' Joanna persisted.

Which provoked an even more sarcastic reply. 'We did look for it but failed to find it. And now we're focusing our attention on our resident. Not his toy.'

Joanna gave Korpanski a swift glance. He knew there was something behind this close questioning and was looking a bit more interested. She continued, 'It hasn't turned up?'

'No. But it was such a tatty thing. It could well have been thrown out with the rubbish.'

Joanna narrowed her eyes. 'Did Zac, Mr Foster, spend a lot of time searching for his lost toy?'

'No. He just . . .' Matilda Warrender suddenly picked up on Joanna's thread and stopped herself. She continued slowly, 'Just sat in the corner, keening.'

'Tell me a bit about his mental state.'

'What do you mean?' She was unmistakably on the defensive.

'Reasoning. Could he read a book?'

Ms Warrender shook her head.

'He could feed himself?'

'After a fashion. Sometimes the nurses would help him. He could be a bit slow.'

'Did he wash himself?'

Another shake of the head.

Joanna tried to pick her next words. 'Did he talk? Speak? Make sense?'

'He could talk but . . . I wouldn't really say he made a lot of sense. More he was childlike.'

'Would that fit in with the evidence that at some time during the night he got up, donned his coat and crept out in search of this toy and without anyone seeing him? Would he know somewhere he could go?'

That pulled the matron up short. She was silent as her expression flitted from puzzlement to confusion and then towards defence. 'What are you getting at, Inspector?'

'I'm not sure. I'm simply exploring possibilities.'

'You can't think someone is *behind* his disappearance?'

Joanna didn't respond so Ms Warrender pressed home. 'One of my staff?'

Joanna leaned back in the chair.

Put like that, she thought and pressed home her advantage. 'Perhaps it's time I met a few more of them.'

She and Mike spent the next hour inspecting everywhere yet again: the missing man's bedroom, the day room, entrances and exits. There was nothing there that interested them.

It was the same with the staff. In general they were a pleasant lot, bemused, obviously fond of Zachary Foster, and all of them appeared genuinely upset at his disappearance. One of them, a health-care worker named Caroline Dewar, appeared more upset than the rest. 'He really did remind me of Christopher Robin,' she said, dabbing at her eye with a tissue, 'dragging Pooh Bear behind him. He was always so polite, so sweet-natured. He'd jump to his feet to open the door for you if you were struggling with a tray of cups or something. He was a gentleman,' she said reflectively. 'Lived all his life in Leek with his mum.'

So is likely to still be here, Joanna thought. But we can't find him.

The two evening staff seemed to be able to detach themselves from any blame. 'We put him to bed.'

'You normally did that?'

'If we've time,' Shawna Wilson said, a young woman with a flame of bright red hair. 'It's nice if you come on duty when you're doing nights to find the evening drinks given and they're in bed.' She gave a warm glance at both Joanna and Mike, inviting praise for her consideration.

Mike spoke up. 'Isn't that a bit early to be put to bed?'

'Oh, they don't mind.'

Which Joanna interpreted as, *They don't have much choice.*

Shawna followed that up with a more truthful response. 'They don't do much in the evenings anyway.'

Ned Sheringham was a plump guy, with a slow, ponderous way of speaking and a strong Leek accent.

'He were quiet that night,' he said. 'A bit upset. He were 'appy to go to bed early-like. Cried a bit when he couldn't cuddle Teddy but he had the other one. Just said it weren't right.'

'Who found him the other one?'

'Don't know.' His response was bovine and uncurious.

She was unlikely to get much from him.

The last person she interviewed was a large Jamaican girl, Jubilee Watkins. Jubilee was in her early twenties, swung her ample hips through the door and gave Mike a distinctly come-hither flash of very white teeth. She sat down without being invited and reluctantly tore her gaze away from Korpanski and back to Joanna, whom she treated to a simple nod. Behind the black eyes was a sharp curiosity and an almost animal-like alertness. Joanna liked Jubilee from the start and Mike wasn't impervious to her charms, flashing her a friendly grin – as though she needed encouragement, Joanna thought. Jubilee had a cavernous mouth, which emitted a loud laugh, big white teeth and the lovely curly eyelashes which went with an IC3. But as they questioned her, something else emerged, some-thing shameful, something evasive, which interested her. Exchanging glances with Korpanski, she could tell he was alerted too.

Particularly as Jubilee was anxious to volunteer information.

'I wasn't even on duty the night he went missing. I finish hours before he disappeared.'

Joanna felt Mike's quiver of interest and knew he too had picked up on the swift note of defensiveness.

Believing she might get more out of the girl if she let her sergeant proceed, she indicated with a flap of her hand that Mike should ask the questions. 'You understand why we're here?'

That provoked a wary smile.

'You worked the evening before Mr Foster went AWOL.'

'I finished at . . .'

'We know what time you finished, love. What time did you actually leave Ryland's?'

'Just after nine.'

'You knew Mr Foster well?'

'Of course I did.' She was still on the defensive.

'What did you think of him?'

The girl swivelled her head to meet Korpanski's eyes full on. 'He was – he is,' she corrected, 'a very polite man.'

'You like him?' Joanna let Korpanski carry on with the questioning. Jubilee Watkins would be more likely to drop her guard for the DS. Besides, it was a chance for her to observe.

'When did you last see him?' The same questions they'd asked every member of staff who was working today.

'I don't know. Maybe a quarter before nine.'

'Did he seem particularly disturbed that evening?' Joanna sensed that Jubilee was uncertain where this was leading. And that was making her anxious. She sat forward, watching, observing very carefully.

'He was troubled. That's true.'

Korpanski played the innocent. 'About anything special?'

And that appeared to strike Jubilee dumb. She opened her mouth but nothing came out. Joanna watched her even more closely. The girl's eyes were practically rolling in their sockets, which puzzled Joanna. Everybody knew the answer to this one. So why was this throwing her off course?

Finally Jubilee managed, 'He was upset because a little toy was missing.'

Korpanski continued to act dumb. 'A little toy?'

But Jubilee was not quite that dumb. Her black eyes were suspicious. 'It's just an old teddy bear he lost.'

'And what do *you* think happened to it?'

'I think . . .' She was making this up as she went along. 'I think he must have mislaid it and somehow it got thrown out with the rubbish.'

'You think that's what happened?'

'Oh, most certainly.' Said with confidence.

FIFTEEN

Korpanski was thoughtful as they drove back to the station. 'That girl,' he said. 'I'd keep an eye on her. I think she knows something about the old man.'

'Now do you see why I'm finding the case so bloody difficult?'

'Yeah,' he said. 'I do. You go round and round in circles. One step forward, two to the side and one step back.' He was quiet for a moment before speaking again. 'It's one of those cases that you think you'll wind up really quickly and then you just don't.' He glanced across at her. 'They're the worst.'

'Tell me about it.'

It was as they were winding up for the night that she finally exploded. 'I hate this bloody case,' she said. 'I'm finding it really frustrating and I hate having this thing in my belly.'

Korpanski couldn't hold it back any longer. He too exploded, but with laughter. He moved towards her. 'I'll remind you of this one day, when your arms are full and you're boasting about how big and strong your little baby's growing.'

'You think?'

'I know, Jo.'

They stood for a while, chatting in the car park. 'Somehow,' she said, 'I can't quite get the picture. Unsteady on his feet, having to cling to the handrail when he descended the stairs, and he gets past three members of staff who don't notice a thing. There's a mystery inside that place and it's eluding me. Tomorrow

I suppose I'll have to have a word with Joan Arkwright again and confront her with the fact that Susie Trent found the door unlocked at two a.m.'

'Still going round and round,' he said.

She looked up at the sky. Starry. Cold and clear. 'You know what?' she said, 'I think I'll walk home. Leave the car here. It's a nice evening for a bit of exercise and, as I can't be on my bike, at least I can stretch my legs.'

'My night at the gym.' Mike headed towards his car. She watched him go and with absolutely no reason or logic at all felt swamped with a sense of foreboding. She clapped her palm to her head. What was this? Was this what being pregnant was like – seeing bogeys behind every hedgerow? Why on earth was she transported to a lecture they'd attended together back in 2015? A lecture on security. Keeping safe. And one of the things that had been stressed had been habit. Korpanski went to the gym on the same days every week, at the same time, and he left at almost the same time to the minute. Took the same route home. Opened his front door at the same time. Predictable.

For goodness' sake, she lectured herself, knowing that if she ran after Mike, banged on the window and warned about avoiding regular habits, he'd simply laugh at her. *So get a grip, Joanna. Stop seeing ghosts behind every tree. Stop tilting at windmills and get on with the job which you are currently making such a pig's ear of.*

She turned for home.

Thursday 25 October, 8.30 a.m.

Fourth night missing.

Joanna was studying the whiteboard wondering where he was. Whether he was dead or alive. The general public had, for once, been singularly uninformative. There had been not one single sighting of an elderly man dressed in slippers, striped pyjamas and an overcoat. She knew the details so well now: overcoat: navy blue Marks & Spencer's. Pyjamas: brown and cream striped brushed cotton. Slippers: brown. Even in a police report there wasn't a lot you could say about a pair of slippers.

She had a little picture of him shuffling along, sliding one foot in front of the other, dragging his leg, his face puzzled and frightened as he wandered and searched, shivering at the cold. But he was hardly going to blend in with the crowd, was he? Not in that outfit.

'Mike?'

He was sitting staring into the computer screen. But the trouble with computers is that though you might be intending to do your job, find similarities in the latest batch of burglaries and link them up to one MO and one perpetrator, it is all too easy to divert, search university listings, which was what DS Korpanski was actually up to. His son, Ricky, had done well in his GCSEs in the summer and Mike had a secret ambition. He dreamed that Ricky might end up in Oxbridge. Now that would be a turn-up for the books. Ricky had a secret weapon which both father and son intended to deploy. Built like his father, tall and very fit, he was an expert rugby player. Quick, fast, accurate. And Mike firmly believed that rugby players had a special welcome at both universities. So he believed he might just live his dream. His son at Oxbridge.

'Mike,' she said again, separating him from the dream in one short syllable.

He swivelled round, a fug of guilt wrapping itself around him. 'Jo?'

'I keep looking at this, Mike,' she said, 'and wondering why it feels so unlikely, almost staged.'

His mind was still on the grades Ricky would need at A-level, toying with the added plus of his rugby prowess. 'I know it looks unlikely but that's what happened, Jo. You can't argue with facts.'

'You can't argue with facts,' she repeated, 'except our perception might be distorting things so what we perceive as "facts" might not be quite as we see them.'

His mind still stuck somewhere between Oxford and Cambridge, DS Korpanski simply shrugged.

SIXTEEN

Sunday 7 October, 11 p.m.

K ath knew something was different about Chi. She wasn't looking at her when she spoke but was keeping her gaze low, fixed, it seemed, on studying the stains on the carpet. She was fidgeting with her hands too, in a world of her own. And when she looked at her she noticed her 'friend' was practically squirming under her stare.

'You all right, Chi?'

'Yeah, yeah.' Her response was all an act. Kath was good at sniffing out traitors, but for now she stayed silent and watched her, her anger permeating right through her until she felt she might explode with incandescence.

Chi was trying to hide something.

Chi sat in the corner, trying to pretend she was invisible, that if she kept perfectly still and silent, Kath might stop studying her with that evil look. But her thoughts had returned to a night less than a month ago when she had been on a late shift and the last customer had come in round about ten. A plump, cheerful black girl who'd looked exhausted. 'God,' she'd said to her, 'get me some chips. I'm starving and knackered.' She'd pulled a cigarette out of her bag and Chi had stretched out a hand. 'I'm sorry. You can't smoke in here.'

'I know that. I wasn't going to light it. I just needed to know it was there.'

Half an hour later, when the girl had smothered her chips with more tomato sauce than you see on a body in a Hollywood horror movie, they'd gone outside together to share a fag and the girl had introduced herself. 'I'm Jubilee.'

Chi had held out her hand. 'And my real name is Rachel, but no one calls me that. Everyone calls me Chi.'

Jubilee hadn't made any of the usual comments about her oriental looks, and out of that considerate beginning a friendship

had been born. When Chi had finished her shift, they'd gone up
to the Butter Market, found an empty seat and shared a bottle
of wine they'd paid half and half for. Jubilee Watkins was the
result of a Jamaican mother and a Welsh father. To describe her
as black wasn't quite true. But to describe her as Welsh wouldn't
cut it either. She had wiry hair and dark eyes and skin, but deli-
cate, pretty features and high cheekbones. She was striking at
six feet tall and with a powerful physique which bordered on
huge. Somehow or other, her family had ended up living in
Stoke-on-Trent and, liking the nearby moorlands town of Leek,
she had found herself a bedsit and a job as a health-care assistant
at a local residential home. The talk meandered between drags
and swigs, through boyfriends and work, debt and families, trying
to lose the inches of fat that seemed to have landed from nowhere
around their middles, everything that was wrong with their lives,
and they soon realized they had a shared problem – lack of
money. A theme they developed over their next few outings.
Meeting Jubilee initially had seemed like paddling along with
someone in the same boat, which didn't help Chi's position,
although she was good fun with a wicked sense of humour. But
one night that had changed.

'I'd just love to visit my hometown,' Jubilee said.

Chi giggled. 'Well, it isn't very far to Wales.'

Jubilee gave her a mock punch. 'I don't mean Wales,' she
scolded. 'I mean Spanish Town, Jamaica. Looks a lovely place
on the h'internet.'

Chi giggled. 'Internet, silly.'

Jubilee gave her a hard look. 'I know that,' she said. 'I'm not
stupid.'

Chi had one word, one response to Jubilee's dream. 'How?'

Jubilee regarded her with those big black eyes fringed with curly
lashes. Then she drew in a deep breath and moved in closer to
speak directly into her ear. 'I don't know whether to tell you this.'

Sitting motionless in the corner, Chi remembered the urgency
in her new friend's voice.

Such a little crime, so easy too. Like taking candy from a baby.
Perhaps she should have remembered that all actions have
consequences. By altering the status quo, you interfere. And who
knows where the ripples from such actions might end?

That night Chi had listened. Sceptical at first. But something in her had absorbed the story. She wanted out. She needed to escape but she couldn't let Kath know.

Kath . . . would . . . kill . . . her.

But now, sitting in this dingy room, looking through windows, searching a night sky for even one solitary star, being scrutinized by that suspicious, pale, lardy prison face, she could see that Kath was already wondering. Chi knew that stare. Close on the heels of that facial expression, particularly when accompanied by the finger rubbing of her damaged tooth, came violence. Even against friends who were soon to become ex-friends. Possibly even dead ex-friends. Chi had witnessed it first-hand.

It wasn't just Craig.

Years ago, before Kath's jail sentence, they had had a mate called Patsy. Patsy had had the most irritating, high-pitched, squeaky voice imaginable. It almost hurt your eardrums when she spoke. And when she shouted – or screamed – your eardrums burst like glass shattered by a soprano. It was strange that she'd even been one of their mates because they'd all found her irritating. But she had been one of the gang, right up until she'd pinched one of Kath's fags without asking. Just . . . pinched . . . a . . . fag.

Chi still squeezed her eyes shut and clapped her hands over her ears just at the memory. Kath had seen her smoking a Benson & Hedges, counted the fags in her packet and made the connection. She hadn't needed to ask or check her facts. It had begun. Her assault had started with a glare which had soon morphed into a hand on Patsy's neck and she squeezed and squeezed until Patsy couldn't breathe and her eyes started to bulge. And then Kath had let go. Patsy had staggered out of the bar they'd been in and they'd never seen her again. Anywhere. God only knew what had happened to her.

Significantly there had been no formal complaint – not even from the people in the bar, who had watched, horrified. Nobody spoke. The place fell quiet.

Kath had that effect on you.

And now she was turning that very same stare on to Chi. Chi knew what it meant, and she was frightened.

How she'd guessed something was up, Chi could not imagine,

unless Kath had a sixth sense – but in a way it didn't matter. Far from the prison sentence reforming Kath, she had been further deformed. These days suspicion was enough. And now she was sitting there, glaring at her with that look, finger on sharp tooth-stump, eyes reflective. Without realizing what she was doing, she rubbed her neck at the same time as Kath stopped rubbing her tooth to speak. 'You seem a bit quiet today, Chi. What's the matter, love? Having cold feet as usual? Or is it something else?'

How did she know that?

'No. Nothing.' Chi could hear the waver in her voice.

Kath's eyes were skewering her now. 'You don't seem very keen on my ideas, Chi. You don't want Piercy to get her comeuppance?'

All eyes turned on her, Fifi and Debs slewing around so they could get a good look. Chi glanced worriedly at them, trying to gauge their loyalty to her or Kath by surreptitiously moving her gaze from side to side. Nothing too obvious. She couldn't afford for Kath to realize maybe she didn't have quite as many loyal followers as she'd thought.

But she couldn't read any doubt in either Debs or Fifi. Were they that thick that they didn't realize this was dangerous ground? Surely neither of them wanted any of it? They couldn't be that stupid that they thought *they* wouldn't be implicated in an assault on a serving police officer? But when she looked first at Fifi who was fingering her nose ring, mouth dropped open giving her a vacant look, and then at Debs who had the most unflattering haircut ever – shaved up the sides and little tufts on the top, both of them watching Kath with a sort of mesmerized hero worship, she wondered. They were all wearing the team uniform of ripped jeans and tight T-shirts, Fifi with more success than Debs, who displayed a roll of fat between nipple and knee. In spite of the heaviest make-up ever, all thick black lines and clumpy eyelashes, Debs was still as plain as the proverbial pikestaff, but she did have an impressive pair of 36D cups. Fifi, on the other hand, was so heavily decorated with piercings and tattoos, a lizard down one arm, Chinese writing on the other, pierced tongue, lips, eyebrows and God knew where else, it was hard to decide whether she was grotesque or attractive. But, even with all that decoration, her chest was as flat as a boy's. She was always talking about having a breast enlargement but at a guess she'd never get around to it.

Or be able to afford it.

Fifi blinked as a sticky false eyelash became detached and scratched her eye. She scowled and chuntered, making a noisy fuss over nothing. But Chi was glad of the distraction. Even Kath stopped staring at her for a brief, blessed moment to laugh at Fifi who was tugging at the lash distorting her eye like the rubber effects on a character in a horror movie. But Chi was soon back to being the focus of all their attention. She felt their suspicious stares like tendrils of wet hair down her face. And the worst part? Chi was convinced that Kath's suspicions were seeping through her skin into her cells, making her guilt glow from inside. And then Debs locked curious eyes with her and Chi wondered. Out of the two of Kath's devotees, Debs was the one with insight. Chi read her interest and curiosity even as Kath drove her point home, a sulky tone belying her native paranoia. 'You don't *want* me to get my revenge, Chi? I wonder why not.'

Maybe she did have a sixth sense.

Revenge, Chi thought, tasting fear, salty, on her tongue. It was what Kath lived for; it was what had kept her together through her years in prison, her blood constantly simmering, her brain constantly plotting.

Kath hadn't finished her jibes. 'You scared?' She was jeering now, using her instinct of betrayal as a weapon. All the more frightening, Chi thought, because she was hiding it, like a knife in the folds of a cloak. You didn't know when or how or even whether she would use it. But, Chi thought wearily, she did know when it ripped through the fabric it would not only be DI Piercy who would suffer but her too. If she didn't escape.

She had a go at moving out of the shadow of Kath's suspicions. 'Course not.' She affected nonchalance and tried to disguise her fear by taking a noisy slurp from the cider flagon, swilling it round her mouth like mouthwash before passing the bottle on and only then swallowing. 'I'm right behind you, Kath,' she said, noting that Kath had got bloody fit inside. She was bulkier and more muscular. She looked strong and powerful.

Look at those biceps and those hamstrings. And Kath always had been able to pull a punch.

Chi couldn't stop herself adding lamely, 'But I don't want to end up inside.'

'You don't want to end up inside?' Kath tossed the comment out into the room where it sounded even lamer. Fifi and Debs joined in the mockery with inane leers and splashes of laughter while Kath continued her taunts.

'Oh, someone find her dummy for her.'

Which provoked another laugh from her fanbase.

Prison would be full of knobheads like these, Chi thought. And the strongest and most frightening would always be the ones with the cheerleaders. That was how the world worked. Inside and out.

Her only chance of escape was the plan. And that depended on Jubilee.

Sometimes people are strewn across your path like leaves on Palm Sunday. (Where did they get those leaves from?)

Jubilee had been one of those palm leaves.

SEVENTEEN

Monday 8 October, 11.35 a.m.

They'd passed another stuffy, smelly night on the sofa cushions, Kath queening it upstairs while Chi, Fifi and Debs had put the sofa cushions on the floor, squashed together and tried to sleep.

They woke when Kath burst in asking where the cup of tea was before lurching out of the room. 'I need the loo.' She was avoiding looking at Chi.

Which left her wondering. Was she simply biding her time? Playing her as a cat does a bird. Or had she forgotten last night's suspicions?

It didn't take long for her to find out.

Minutes later, Kath staggered back into the room and dropped into her chair. Debs had disappeared into the kitchen to make a 'brew' while Fifi was barely sitting up, her heavy black eye make-up smeared across her face. Chi stayed watchful, hardly noticing the fug of cigarette smoke, the sickly sweet scent of spliffs and tobacco mingling nauseatingly with cheap perfume and air freshener. (Which didn't do any of the things it said on the can.) She allowed herself a brief respite. What she *smelt* when she closed her eyes was rum and coconut oil; what she *heard* was the swish of waves meandering up a sandy beach, washing over shells and white sand. What she *felt* on her face was heat. What she was *wearing* was not ripped jeans and two fleeces but a pair of shorts and a T-shirt with spaghetti straps. On her feet were flip-flops bought from a colourful boy at a beachside stall, not a pair of boots (wrong size) which she'd picked up from a charity shop.

She closed her eyes and felt nothing but the heat of the sun on her face.

She was to go with Jubilee to Spanish Town, Jamaica. And she knew how.

Kath was watching, sensing something she didn't understand – yet. But she'd picked up on Chi's mood. 'You happy about something?'

Chi's tempting image dissolved and fear crept in. The soothing sound of waves crashing over white sand was replaced by the heavy clang of bolts being shot, the jangle of keys being turned, doors being slammed, screams and taunts, fingernails scratching her face. A whole place populated with Kath-alikes, each one as nasty, cruel and psychopathic as her one-time friend. And the smell that filled her nostrils was the stink of mouldy damp and toilets that needed bleaching. The smell of uniforms and fear.

BANG BANG BANG

She started. That was a real noise.

One of the neighbours was objecting to their music. That was the trouble with terraced houses – two lots of neighbours. Someone shouted, 'Turn the fuckin' noise down. The baby's trying to sleep.'

'Turn it up,' Kath ordered. Fifi stopped fiddling with her newest piercing and stood up, wobbling a bit on her skinny heels, six inches high and thinner than a finger. She tried to remonstrate. 'They'll make a complaint, Kath.'

'And I care?' And then at the top of her voice she shouted, 'Fuck off,' before turning back to Fifi. 'Now – turn the music up.'

6 p.m.

Kath had persuaded a reluctant Debs to drive her to a new housing estate on the Ashbourne Road. She wanted to view The Obstacle. That was another thing she had learnt in prison. Know your enemy. The girl who'd given her that particular piece of advice had killed a neighbour who'd been (deliberately, she said) annoying her. The hostility had come to blows and so the girl, Emmie Clayton, had torched the woman's house.

'Easy,' Emmie said. 'You just make sure the back door's secured and then you chuck a Molotov (plastic bottle full of petrol and a rag in the neck of the bottle) and whoosh. Gotcha.'

She'd wagged her finger at the gobsmacked audience. 'But first I had to plan. That means observation, knowing what nights she'd be in, track her movements, make certain she was going to have too much plonk to get out of bed. Know your enemy.'

So Kath had listened and learned. Planning + Observation = Success. In other words: Know your enemy. Get close to them. Watch them.

And that was exactly what she was doing.

Emmie Clayton's neighbour had died in the fire along with her two-year-old daughter.

Debs parked the car opposite number 18 Badger's Rise. AKA *Chez famille* Korpanski. It's easy to find out where a police officer lives. Half the time a squad car's parked outside. Or you can take the long way round and follow him home from work – or the gym.

From the car they had been treated to the sight of mother and daughter scuttling into their car, a little Clio, heading off some-where and, twenty minutes later, DS Mike Korpanski and his son, Ricky, in shorts and trainers, peering at their Fitbit watches and heading out for a run together. Kath chewed on her burger. 'That's nice,' she said. 'Father and son going out for a jog together. How sweet.'

Debs said nothing but Fifi, sitting in the back, spoke up. 'You're never going to take him on, Kath? He's fuckin' enormous. And he looks as if he works out. Even the kid does.'

Kath didn't even bother to swivel round. 'I got my ways.'

'Why?'

Kath turned her head. 'Because I can never get to her if he's around. He's in the way. He's a fuckin' obstacle.'

Debs clamped her mouth shut. There was no reasoning with Kath when she was in this mood. Or in any other mood, actually. In fact, there was no reasoning with Kath – period.

Kath was thinking.

She'd wandered up past the police station three or four times in the last couple of weeks. Most of the time she'd seen nothing going on and no sightings. But twice she had had a chance to observe.

Piercy, hateful pregnant cow. Her friend's advice echoed in her ears. *Don't just see things from your point of view. Take it all in. Watch and learn.*

God, prison was better than going to villains' academy.

Her target was walking down the steps of the station, her DS by her side. He must have said something funny. She was throwing her head back and laughing, her hands protectively holding her stomach. Or rather, the bump. And Kath, who was learning to be observant and patient, noted something else. The detective sergeant put a hand on her shoulder and smiled at her. The smile lasted just that little bit longer than it should. The hint was that they were more than just colleagues and Kath, with her new-found education, was learning to read between the lines. DS Korpanski would never let anything harmful happen to his DI. She wouldn't get to within six feet of Piercy without Korpanski taking her on. And, looking at the powerful physique and heavy tread, she knew without a weapon she had no chance.

So she had to think this one through.

She'd turned away. Challenges are nothing but an obstacle which needs to be surmounted. It was up to her to surmount this one. And Kath had an idea. It had taken months, but she was beginning to piece together the whole plan. She drew in a breath. It would work. She was almost there. She was just missing one small detail. And she had the feeling that Chi might just hold the answer.

EIGHTEEN

Sunday 28 October, 1.30 p.m.

'Dear boy.'

Joanna saw Matthew in a different light when they were with his parents. And though she would have preferred to do almost anything else on a Sunday, somehow every couple of weeks or so they found themselves in this small bungalow, only a stone's throw from Briarswood, the large, Victorian semi they had recently moved into and which, to Joanna at least, didn't yet feel like home. But here they were, guests of Peter and Charlotte, Matthew's parents. Warm to him, frosty to her, positively effusive towards their granddaughter who seemed to be included on the invites. Even Eloise's boyfriend, the bespectacled Kenneth, got a warmer and more civil greeting than she did.

'Joanna,' said in a haughty, cold voice. 'Hello. How are you?' And without waiting for her response, Charlotte added, 'Come in.'

She'd have treated a Jehovah's Witness more cordially.

Charlotte was a thin woman who looked thinner when her eyes rested on her daughter-in-law. But her cheeks actually flushed with pleasure when they rested on the other members of the family. Today she was wearing a cherry-red sweater and loosely fitting grey trousers. Matthew got a kiss on both cheeks – his parents could be hugely affectionate towards their only son, his sister being a 'sad disappointment'.

The days generally followed a rigid format. Peter shook hands with Matthew and they were led into the day room. From the kitchen came a mouth-watering scent of the Sunday roast – beef one week, lamb the next, and on bank holidays and special occasions roast chicken with homemade stuffing, which Charlotte always made herself and also always announced that fact. At least the food was good.

Eloise and Kenneth got a glass of sherry, Matthew a beer,

while Peter started on the red wine and Charlotte a cup of Earl Grey, but she had the choice of *Earl Grey, dear, or a soft drink?*

Joanna opted for the soft drink. She might as well have opted for bread and water for the relish she felt for elderflower cordial, though Charlotte's roast did smell appetizingly good and she was starving.

Did she and Matthew have to spend their precious free time together here?

And yet . . . She looked across at her husband, ruffled honey-coloured hair, long legs stretched out in front of him, wide grin as he, his father, Eloise and Kenneth, medics all, discussed a recent breakthrough in the treatment and diagnosis of multiple sclerosis. The medical advance appeared to be exciting them all. She was seized with an impulse to cross the room, sit on her husband's lap, kiss those full lips and rumple his hair. He caught her eye and for a millisecond his eyes were warm on hers and she almost imagined he read her thoughts because a mischievous little smile bent his lips further and lit up his eyes. He took a sip of his beer and wiped his lips, still looking at her.

So what would Charlotte, thin faced, thin lips, bent in disapproval, wiping her hands on her apron as she entered the room and announcing lunch was served, have made of that little exchange, Joanna wondered, smiling herself. What if any of them could read her mind as they all made their contribution to the conversation, which had dropped into scientific language and was, to her, as impenetrable as a hedge of thorns?

Synapse? Acetylcholine? Beta-2 receptors? Helper T cells?

Charlotte looked around her, happy as a mother hen regarding her brood. 'Moving down here to Leek,' she said, a hand stretching out to touch her son's cheek, 'was the best thing we ever did.'

'Here, here.' Eloise raised her glass, as did her father and grandfather. Only Kenneth met Joanna's eyes and gave the slightest of smiles which indicated, by raised eyebrows, a question.

And then Matthew blew it. 'And here's to my healthy son.' This time it was Eloise who didn't join in and Kenneth, his eyes behind thick glasses, still perceiving all, met hers again while Matthew continued, obliviously happy. 'I've even chosen a name.'

Sometimes, she thought, particularly when ecstatic, he could be so obtuse, so blind to all but his own delights. Couldn't he feel the permafrost directed at her by three members of his family?

Probably not.

Resentful, Joanna lifted her gaze and stared right into those green goblin eyes. Even Peter and Charlotte looked startled. 'So what is it?'

And Matthew, still not seeing what was right under it, tapped his nose. 'Ah,' he said. 'That would be telling. And besides . . .' And now, at last, he did look at Joanna. 'Besides,' he resumed with a grin. 'That would be inviting bad luck.' Joanna swallowed back a retort. She didn't like exposing any weakness in their relationship in front of Matthew's parents or Eloise.

Adding to her discomfort, Charlotte, her mother-in-law, managed to put her foot straight in it.

'And you're still working, Joanna?' How did she manage to inject so much poisoned syrup into the question?

'I'm doing mainly desk duties.'

Matthew was giving her a stormy look as he absorbed her sulky tone. 'Joanna,' he said, not without a touch of malice, 'is searching for that old man who has apparently gone AWOL along with his teddy bear from a residential home.'

'Oh, that case?'

Thank you, Charlotte.

Eloise couldn't resist making her contribution. 'Haven't you found him yet?' Her tone was scornful but before Joanna could dredge up a suitable response, her stepdaughter continued, 'Honestly, Joanna, how difficult can it be? He's ancient. He can't have gone far.'

Then you fucking well find him.

For once Charlotte made an attempt to soften the insult. 'It is rather strange that you haven't found him.'

I'm not exactly working alone, Joanna thought tumultuously.

Somehow she maintained her dignity and her frostiness. 'Yes,' she said, in a calm and polite tone of which she was very proud, 'we all realize this. A lot of time and manpower has been spent searching the immediate area. You're right. It is odd. He can't have gone far.'

Peter, in the crassest manner, tried to make a joke of it.

'I wonder which you'll find first,' he chortled, 'the old man or his teddy.'

Unsurprisingly no one laughed, although Kenneth's mouth gave a suspicious twitch.

And now, even Joanna could see the funny side of things. She glanced across the table at Matthew. The corner of his mouth was also twitching and she realized he was suppressing a smile and her heart warmed towards him. She gave him a ghost of a smile back and for a moment they were two people who loved each other, depended on one another and would soon be bonded and joined by another. The Little Stranger.

And then the spell was broken. 'Gramps . . .' Amazingly, was it Eloise who was about to restore the status quo?

Her grandfather turned to look at her, his face soft with indulgence.

Eloise scooped in a deep breath and gave Joanna a sly glance. 'Will you and Granny come to my graduation next year?'

So the apparently 'innocent' question was anything but. (Was anything Eloise said ever innocent?)

Eloise opened her mouth and eyes wide. Peter and Charlotte exchanged an uncomfortable look while Matthew frowned and appeared to freeze.

And Eloise continued, triumphant now. 'I *know* they say only parents.' One of those little simpers was aimed at Matthew. 'You'll be there, won't you, Daddy?'

For once Matthew could see exactly where this was heading. 'Of course.' He kept his voice steady but his look shifted towards Joanna, at the same time raising questioning eyebrows. Since she'd been pregnant he'd seemed to want her mood to remain calm and optimistic, as though that would ensure a healthy environment for his child to be born into. He sensed this was about to threaten his carefully manufactured status quo. And erupt.

Eloise couldn't stop the triumph from spreading across her face like soft butter on hot toast. 'And Mummy.'

Nothing on earth would have persuaded Joanna to attend Eloise's graduation, but she still felt the girl's malice. In the future there would be a few occasions, all connected with their daughter, when mother and father would need to be together.

Perceptive too, Kenneth was frowning as Eloise delivered

her final shot. 'And you, Joanna, of course, will be busy with
the baby.' A covert glance at Matthew. 'Unless, of course,' she
almost sang out her next sentence, 'you're already back at your
beloved work.'

Surprisingly, Matthew actually recognized the depth of her
malice. He put his knife and fork down with a clatter. 'That's
enough, Eloise,' he said sharply. 'You don't need to keep goading
Joanna.'

And now it was Joanna's mouth that had dropped open. She
almost felt like applauding this first, until she realized he wasn't
so much protecting her as protecting the mental state of *the
mother of his unborn 'son'*. And possibly the unborn 'son' too.
Her mood spiralled downwards.

She almost clasped her hands together across the bump, hoping
it was a son. To have a daughter anything like Miss Eloise would
be the worst conceivable fate. She couldn't imagine anything more
horrendous. It would be like parenting Damian from *The Omen*.

Kenneth also put his knife and fork down and raised his hands.
At first Joanna wondered whether he was about to applaud
Matthew's defence of her, until she saw his long, bony fingers
spread out in a Halt sign and realized it was directed at Eloise.
She wanted to warn him. Careful. If you want your relationship
with Miss Eloise to continue undamaged, you don't challenge
her on the subject of her stepmother.

And then Peter put another two penn'orth in. 'You'll have to
make certain you pass before you start issuing invitations, Eloise.'

Charlotte's contribution was: 'Apple crumble, anyone?'

NINETEEN

Thursday 11 October, 5.30 p.m.

Chi and Jubilee had met for an early evening drink which
was planned to stretch into late evening. Two ciders in,
Jubilee started to tell her new friend her secret. Chi knew
that Jubilee planned someday to return to a Jamaica she'd never

actually seen, but she'd discarded it as a pipe dream. What she hadn't ever understood was how on earth her friend, practically on minimum wage, was going to raise the fare.

And then Jubilee let her into her secret.

Chi had listened and then she had listened hard while Jubilee tried to persuade her.

Chi stared at her and Jubilee put a hand on her arm. 'Just think,' she said, 'it's dark and it's cold in this country and for the next five months it is going to get darker and colder. But out there . . .' She half closed her eyes and held her hand up, palm towards the sky, fingers spread, peeping through them as though to block out the sun. 'Out there,' she said, 'it's sunny all the time. We can get a job in a beach bar.' She laughed, mouth wide open, showing teeth dazzling white against her skin the colour of milk chocolate. 'Drink rum all the time. And the boys.' She whistled. 'They are just gorgeous. Quite beautiful. Stripped to the waist.' She nudged her friend. 'Rippling with muscles.'

They both giggled – Chi almost coyly.

'And you'd really split the money fifty-fifty?'

Jubilee nodded. 'I promise,' she said.

They stubbed out their cigarettes, clasped hands solemnly and headed back to the bar. This called for a celebratory drink.

But Chi couldn't quite believe her luck and checked again. 'You're sure?'

Jubilee nodded.

And then Chi realized why this generous offer.

Working in the restaurant she met people. Lots of people. All sorts of people. Sometimes she and Jubilee giggled over the snooty ones or the ones who argued about the bill. The ones who had a tipple too many or spilt their wine. The smart clothes some of them wore, the stories some of them told, the old ones who wore too much make-up, their skirts too short exposing knobbly knees, fashions twenty years out of date, the badly behaved children and couples who stormed out after a very public and noisy row, the times they'd had to call the police as violence had broken out, the time someone had thrown a brick at the window. The glass had not shattered but a large crack had appeared and Rosemary told her that her insurance had doubled. The stories Chi related to Jubilee often made them laugh as they

swigged their cider straight from the flagon. It made for enter-
taining conversation and was a welcome change from the subject
of Kath Whalley.

There was one story, Chi realized now, which had given
Jubilee the idea.

Her name was Diana . . .

Chi could remember the conversation almost verbatim a
month or so ago.

'Sixty if she was a day.'

Jubilee had laughed, put her hand over her mouth as Chi
had described the customer. 'Wearing a really tight leather skirt
and a low-cut silver top. And so much jewellery she almost
needed Securicor.'

They had both laughed at this, but Jubilee had stopped first.
'This woman,' she said. 'You got to chat to her? Who is she? She
sounds rich.'

Chi had made bits up then. 'She is rich. She's an antiques
dealer.'

And for some reason Jubilee's mouth had clamped shut.

It was only now that Chi was realizing the significance of that
encounter and the consequence of relating it to her new-found
friend.

So now as Jubilee told her little story, Chi was not only listening
– she was understanding too. She would have her part to play.
And that would earn her fifty per cent.

She drew in a long, deep breath. 'There's only one way to
find out.'

Jubilee nodded, black eyes sparkling. 'Up to you, Chi.' She
paused, watching her friend, trying to gauge her reaction. 'You
don't have to come in on it if you don't want to. I can do it all
without you. But if you want to hitch a ride with me straight
off to Spanish Town, Jamaica, far away, you are very welcome. We
can easily get work in a bar over there – right on the beach – maybe
even open one of our own with the money. What do you say?'

Chi foresaw all sorts of problems ahead. A veritable obstacle
course of problems. But the prize was huge – escape from Kath,
who wouldn't have a clue where she was. And even if she sent
her a postcard, Kath was never going to find her way to Spanish
Town, Jamaica. More likely back to HMP Foston Hall.

She tried to find the weak spot in Jubilee's plan. 'You've never even been to Jamaica. You might not like it.' She corrected this to, '*We* might not like it.'

Jubilee had put her hand on her arm. 'My father tells me all the time what it is like over there. He tells me it is Paradise. You think he would lie?'

Chi frowned. 'Why did he leave then?'

That earned a very hostile look from her new friend. Chi regarded her back, trying to discern Jubilee's true character. Was she another Kath? Was she about to jump from the frying pan straight into the fire?

But then Jubilee gave one of her mouth-wide-open belly-laughs and Chi was reassured. They clasped hands but she wasn't so sure about their destination. The stories she'd heard from Jamaica had been more about organized crime (out of the frying pan?). Yardies. Guns.

As though reading her doubt, Jubilee spoke. 'Not Spanish Town,' she said once she'd stopped laughing. 'It's not violent there. That's Kingston.'

But now the doubt had surfaced, Chi tried to retreat. 'I need to think about it.'

And there was always the possibility that Jubilee's plan wouldn't work, that her facts were wrong.

But she looked out of the window at the dark and deserted streets of Leek, saw a vision (nightmare) of Kath's face, her pig-nose squashed flat against the glass, watching her with that suspicious look that could so easily and with only the slightest provocation translate into a beating. They might be 'friends', but it was Kath's version of friendship, which consisted of her going along with her plans – whatever they were. If Kath got a sniff that she was planning to run (Fly), she would be lucky to escape with her life. Chi sat rigid, suddenly miserable, as she foresaw another immediate future, one that included no sun. More like plastic surgery, if not an undertaker. There were only three ways life with Kath was going to end up. Maimed, dead, or in prison.

And she feared all three alternatives. Prison would surround her with people like Kath. Suddenly the thirst for a different life made her reckless, the lust for Jubilee's version of an island in the sun almost making her dizzy. It was a risk but only a small one. If she was going to disappear she needed money. Not just the wages and tips from Rosemary's. This chance was being offered her on a plate. If she didn't grab it with both hands, it would slip away and that would be that.

So, mind made up, she looked at her new friend who was sitting very still, hands folded together as though in mute prayer. Waiting for her decision.

'OK,' she said. 'I'm in.' Which meant she needed to do some groundwork.

TWENTY

Monday 29 October, 8 a.m.
Leek Police Station

After yesterday's lunch and the unhelpful take on the case, from Eloise in particular, Joanna was only too aware of the lack of progress in finding Zachary Foster. So she regarded the officers attending the morning briefing and tried to find something to spur them on.

She had a quick word with Mike, sharing with him the direction of her curiosity.

'Go for it, Jo,' he said. 'It's not as if you've got any other leads for them to follow. At least this sounds feasible. Not some geriatric magicking himself through locked doors and disappearing.'

So, speaking to the room of watchful faces, she confided in them.

'I have two possible leads,' she said. 'Amelia Boden, one of the health-care assistants, thought she might have heard whispering in the night.'

PC Gilbert Young looked up. 'Any idea of time?'

'Unfortunately she couldn't pin it down.' She hesitated. 'Amelia Boden incorporated it into a dream. Possibly the time was as early as midnight but it could have been as late as two or three a.m.'

She had their rapt attention. 'But if Mr Foster left Ryland's before Susie Trent went outside for her cigarette at around two a.m., it would fit in with both nurses' claims – Sister Joan Arkwright's insistence that she *did* lock and bolt the door and Susie Trent's disclosure that when she left by the day-room door it was already unlocked and unbolted.'

The room was very quiet now as each officer tried to make sense of the version DI Piercy was giving them.

Joanna drew in a deep breath. 'There is another point that has puzzled us in this case. How did a frail old man with limited mobility manage to travel so far from the residential home where he'd lived happily for a year and a half that we have not been able to find him?'

She waited before speaking. 'The night sister, Joan Arkwright, thought she might have heard a car. Again, she couldn't be certain, neither could she give us any idea of time. But it would explain the anomaly in this case, i.e. that we have been unable to find Mr Foster in spite of his limited mobility and confused mental state.'

She noted a few were nodding their agreement.

'So . . .' She scanned the officers. 'We now have two lines of enquiry, but neither is definite. We don't have times and we certainly have absolutely no idea of why he went. But the fact remains that we haven't found Mr Foster yet.' She turned back to the board, met the rheumy old eyes and made a silent apology to the elderly gent. Then she turned back into the room. 'Come on, guys,' she said, 'let's find out what's happened to this old chap. He must be confused and frightened. That is if he's still alive. If he is, let's bring him home.'

At the back of the room, Korpanski was doing a silent clap. He grinned at her and did a thumbs-up. As she reached him, he said, 'Well done, Jo.'

But her response was muted. 'We still haven't found him, Mike. And you must see as well as I do that neither of these statements is exactly proof of anything.'

'It's the best we can do, Jo. You can't do more.'

And she had to be content with that.

TWENTY-ONE

Friday 12 October 2 p.m.
Mill Street

One of the cellmates Kath had shared with was a woman in her forties called Marjorie, though if you called her that she'd probably break your nose – or worse. She liked to be called Lakshmi after the Indian goddess of good fortune, although Marjorie suited her much better. She had very pale skin, freckles and frizzy ginger hair, though again nobody would have described it as that unless they fancied facial surgery. Kath never knew what 'Lakshmi' was in for and she never asked. Some people boasted about the crimes which had resulted in them being banged up. Many – no, most – protested their innocence or at least claimed they had only had a peripheral part in the crime, or else they'd been provoked beyond human tolerance. But Marjorie, or rather Lakshmi, never said a word. Not even how long she was in for or when she was eligible for parole, which intrigued Kath. Kath would have liked to have known what she had done. After all, she'd shared her confidence. And to know she was a killer or a sex-mad lesbian would at least have put her on her guard. But on the subject of her crime Lakshmi kept schtum – unlike on practically all other subjects, particularly philosophy. Her own brand of this branch of science was spouted out on all available occasions. During their sentence the prison had been in lockdown for almost a month after an inmate accidentally set fire to his mattress. The result was that Kath and Lakshmi spent rather a lot of time together.

Because Kath didn't know what crime Lakshmi had committed, she was a little wary of her and put up with behaviour she wouldn't have tolerated from anyone else on the planet. Lakshmi had a habit of sitting for hours cross-legged, humming or chanting or, more interestingly, spouting out words of wisdom. And for some reason, probably connected with her cellmate's silence

about her crimes, or maybe just because she'd been a captive
audience, instead of scoffing, Kath had listened to her stories,
even though instinct told her that Lakshmi's stories were more
attributable to her own particular brand of philosophy than that
of the real Indian goddess. One of the stories she had been fond
of telling was the tale of a man who'd brought a poisonous snake
home after he'd found it run over on the road half dead. Feeling
sorry for the reptile's plight, the man had picked it up, taken it
home, put it somewhere warm, given it a saucer of milk and a
dead rat to eat. (Lakshmi wasn't absolutely certain about some
of the detail so, she said, she'd had to fill it in.) To the man's
delight the poisonous snake had recovered. And when it was
strong it crawled out of the warm comfortable place and bit the
man. Just before he died, the man, justifiably pissed off, said to
the snake, 'I rescued you. I took you home. I fed you and kept
you warm. I gave you milk to drink and a rat to eat. And now
you are recovered you've bitten me. And I will jolly well die.'

Again more Lakshmi's words than the original story.

The snake replied, 'Whatever you did for me you should not
have forgotten. I . . . am . . . a . . . snake.'

At which point the man died. She and Lakshmi had practically
wet themselves they'd laughed so much over this story. And,
periodically, when they were about to do something particularly
bad, they would make eyes at each other and whisper.

'You should not have forgotten. I am a snake.'

Out loud, to herself, as she tried to work out the logistics of
her plan, Kath said it now.

'You should not have forgotten. I am a snake.'

And, this Saturday lunchtime, 'I am a snake' had a sixth sense
that something was going on behind her back. She leaned back
in her chair and stared at her friend. 'Not working today, Chi?'

'Later,' Chi said, not looking at her. 'I'm doing the evening
shift.'

Kath nodded, her skin prickling with the instinct that there
was something different about Chi these days. Her face looked
different. Practically cheerful. Which was worrying. She was
even walking differently these days. There was a positive spring
in her step. She was bloody bouncing along. What right did she
have to be so frigging happy?

Chi should not have forgotten – she was a snake.

She tried again to get to the bottom of this.

'You in love?'

Chi stiffened, on her guard. 'No.'

Kath moved forward, perching her ample rear on the very edge of the chair, resting her elbows on her knees and fixing her mate, possibly soon to be her ex-mate, with a stare. 'Well, something's up,' she said in her snake-voice. 'Something's different about you, my friend.' She half closed her eyes and waited until inspiration found her. In the silence she heard Chi give a noisy gulp, which told her something but not enough. 'You're plotting something, aren't you?'

'No.' Chi felt sick with apprehension. Kath could so easily ruin this. Kath could ruin anything. She hardly had to try. And when Kath was thwarted . . . She didn't even want to think about the bloody nose, the shattered knee, the way Kath Whalley could wield a baseball bat. She was going to have to draw on all her acting skills and divert her. *Head her off at the pass*, as her dad used to say.

Kath appealed to her trusty team of cheerleaders. 'What do you think?'

Fifi took a couple of noisy cow-chews at her gum as she angled her gaze towards Chi. 'See what you mean, Kath.'

Debs said nothing but her eyes slid down her like a cobra's. And she was bending her head forward so her hair partly concealed her face. Chi felt the calculating falseness radiating from her, the secrecy, and knew Debs was hedging her bets. Already working out how she could use this to her advantage, wondering which side of the fence she should fall. Debs always was the smarter one. She would back the winner. Chi met her gaze fearlessly. It wasn't Debs she worried about. The question was, who would be the winner? And what would happen to the loser?

Having so far failed to flush her out, after a prolonged stare, Kath moved on to something else and Chi breathed again. At least Kath quickly got bored and moved on to some other scheme.

But Kath was not going to let go.

Half an hour later she stumbled to her feet. 'I'm going out,' she said.

*   *   *

How and why do places acquire a bad reputation?

Geography? Folklore? History? All are capable of giving a place a bad name. Legend begets legends, attracts poets and story tellers and in the end no one can really separate fact from fiction. Stories stick like flies to fly paper. Lud's Church, a silent, damp crevice in the rocks of the Peak District, is just such a place.

Somewhere the sun doesn't ever shine and ice has been recovered as late as July, a hidden area deep in the moorlands. A narrow entrance leads to a flight of steep, slippery steps which descend along a path lined with dripping, overhanging, moss-covered stones, seeming to close the intruder in a grave. The walls are decorated with ferns and overseen, oddly enough for this place more than sixty miles from the nearest sea, by a ship's figurehead, the female form reminding one of a bloody event, the martyrdom of the beautiful daughter of a Lollard preacher who died for her father's faith. This is, apparently, fact.

Walking along the floor of Lud's Church you cannot be unaware that you are trapped; the escape route is even narrower than the entrance which itself is concealed. You do not stumble across Lud's Church by accident, which is why the Lollards used it for their illegal services, hoping to avoid being burnt at the stake as heretics, the result of an edict passed by Henry IV. Even today if you visit Lud's Church do you still pick up the faint scent of burning flesh on the wind? Interpret stains on the dripping stones as the blood that sprang from the martyrdom of Alice, the Lollard preacher's daughter? Killed by a bullet from an arquebus?

Friday 12 October, 2.50 p.m.

Kath recced the spot and almost rubbed her hands.

Perfect.

At school, when she'd bothered to go, stories had been read so she was aware of its history. The one she'd liked best was the story of Sir Gawain, knight of King Arthur's, who made a vow to the Green Knight (who, unlike Piercy, could replace his head when removed with a sword) that he could return the blow in a year. Kath stomped down the steps, slipping on the moss and hurting her back. Oh, this place was so perfect. All she had to do was get Piercy here alone. Without that Polish thug, the body-building detective sergeant. Kath could handle a pregnant Piercy but not him as well. So first he must be incapacitated. That was taking a bit of working out. She was still missing one ingredient, but she had a feeling that the problem would soon be solved.

She turned to go, away from the stories and legends, away from the Vikings, the Lollards, the summer snow and the headless knight.

And now Lud's Church would acquire another gory story to join the rest. But this one would be 100 per cent true.

The Legend of Detective Inspector Joanna Piercy.

In the future, grannies would terrify their kids with threats. 'You know what happened to that policewoman lady. If you don't behave, I'll take you to Lud's Church and leave you there.' And the children would melt into good behaviour.

She just had to work out how to remove DS Korpanski.

She'd spent the last week staking out Joanna's sidekick. Well over six feet tall and with bulging muscles, she needed to have a careful think about how to remove him from Piercy's side because she was never going to be able to take him on. Watching him and his family had given her some ideas. There was Korpanski himself, a wife who was half his size, petite and pretty. She seemed to work irregular hours, whereas the two teenage spawn, a lanky boy and a girl who was a clone for her mother, attended school, neat in their Westwood College red and black. DS Korpanski spent Wednesday evening at his gym, though sometimes he went for a run with the lanky boy. They seemed close, laughing together as they jogged side by side. She watched them all with interest but not hatred. She was conserving that for Piercy. However, it was unarguable that DS Korpanski was an obstacle. A large one.

Time she called in a favour.

A few days after Kath had found her perfect spot, she wandered up to The Cattle Market – a pub perhaps named so farmers needn't lie to their wives. When asked why they were so late home they could respond truthfully. 'I were just at Cattle Market, love.' And the wife would sniff and accept their version.

Kath pretty much knew if she headed there on a Wednesday,

Leek's market day, when deals were struck, wallets could be pinched and information traded, she'd bump into a couple of her dad's mates. And Angus and Chad would do just about anything for money. It was time to see just how far she could push them.

As anticipated, the pair were huddled over pints in the corner, looking wonderfully seedy and wary as they raised their heads and recognized her, lifting their hands in greeting.

'Kath?'

To their discomfort she crossed the crowded bar and sat down opposite Chad Newick, a skinny, ill-looking man with grey hair too sparse even for a comb-over and Angus, a tubby, red-faced man with a permanent scowl.

'What's up, Kath?' It was he who addressed her, a note of anxiety in his voice making it sound plaintive.

She sat down, thumped her elbows on the table, face in her hands and glared. 'Fancy earning some money?'

They exchanged glances, worried. While earning money was a permanent problem for the pair of them, they had their limits, and both knew Kath was the sort of person to stretch those limits. But needs must. They needed money which was in permanently short supply. Not bright enough to work the benefits system and with a zero chance of securing gainful employment, their options for earning were limited. The labour market wasn't exactly wide open to them. No skills, and if they got as far as an interview, their technique put off almost all employers, particularly when accompanied by either Angus's scowl or Chad's toothy leer. Angus's last job had been hedge-laying for a local farmer – cash in hand. And that hadn't ended well – the cash had been less than he'd been expecting and had ended with the farmer having a bloody nose and vowing Angus would never work again in the farming community, a prophesy which had more or less come true. The hedge didn't do too well either after a liberal dose of Pathclear.

So they might be worried but they were also broke. They didn't have to ask Kath whether this would be cash in hand or whether it was strictly legal. She would already know they didn't work any other way. Chad didn't even have a bank account. And nothing Kath ever did was legal.

But, anxious glances exchanged, Kath's job might prove . . . complicated. Ah, well. Complicated meant more money, surely? Chad gave her a sideways glance and responded. 'What for?'

Kath gave them the best smile she could manage. It sat on her face like grease on the surface of the water in a washing-up bowl. 'Just a little job,' she said. Then, addressing Angus, she asked casually, 'Still driving?'

He nodded, wary.

'Good,' she said, the smile still sitting on the surface of her face, not reaching her eyes or reassuring either of them. 'Little driving job.' Then even more alarming. 'Let me buy you a drink.'

They were going to need it.

Eight minutes later Chad exploded. 'You are fucking kidding.'

But when she told them how much money this little jobby was going to earn them, they looked at each other and smiled then nodded.

Angus bit his thumbnail. 'Don't suppose, Kath, you'd consider just a little bit more?'

She chilled him with a look and a shake of her head. 'I don't think so, Angus.'

He took refuge in a long swig of beer and she stood up. 'I'll be in touch.'

TWENTY-TWO

Monday 15 October, 10 a.m.

Diana Sutcliffe sounded curt when Chi eventually managed to speak to her, opening with the tentative, 'I don't know if you remember me.'

'No.' Her response was flat and unfriendly.

'I work at Rosemary's.'

'Oh, the waitress.' It wasn't a great start but Chi ploughed on. 'I think you might be interested . . .'

And then Diana Sutcliffe listened.

Chi had her story ready and trotted it out, word perfect: a

great-great-aunt, *terribly* affected by the tragedy, who had bought it for her great-grandmother. But even to her it sounded thin, suspicious, amateurish and totally unconvincing. It wouldn't fool this canny, sour, greedy businesswoman for a minute. Even if they were right and Ms Sutcliffe ran with the story, she had no doubt that when she produced the item the dealer would run rings round her. In the background she could hear the sound of an auction taking place.

'*Give me fifty . . . sixty I have . . . Seventy? No? Sixty. Sixty-five . . .*'

She started on her spiel. 'It was my gran's. It belonged to her mum's mum.' Too late, she realized she should have been blurrier on the detail.

'Her name?' Her voice was razor sharp.

Chi had to improvise. 'She shouldn't want me to give it.'

There was a long pause. In the background the auction was still going on. She heard the gavel knock down twice but Diana was still silent while Chi fretted. They'd been worried the dealer would try and cheat them, but at least they'd counted on her giving them ready cash. The silence stretched. Maybe she was checking the internet on her phone?

Chi's mouth was dry with anxiety. They'd pinned everything on this.

'I need to see it before I can verify it.'

Chi tried to sound nonchalant. 'Yeah. Of course.'

The dealer's voice was crisp. 'And without provenance and proper documentation the price will be affected.'

Chi could hear a distinct lack of enthusiasm in her voice.

'Right.' A prickling of interest began to replace the initial boredom. 'I'm in London at the moment but I can meet you in Leek on Friday. I'll see it then. If it's genuine we can talk about the money.'

Chi was panicking. 'You couldn't make it tomorrow, could you?'

'My . . .' A mocking tone. 'We are anxious, aren't we?'

Well, you would be bloody anxious if you were me – with all the baggage this is dragging in.

The sarky old cow couldn't resist adding, 'Even I can't fly on my broomstick and be with you tomorrow.' And then Chi revised her opinion of her as Diana Sutcliffe added, 'particularly with all the cash you might want. It'll have to be Friday.'

They agreed to meet at the coffee bar on the market square. And now all they had to do was cross their fingers and wait.

Which left them both fidgety.

TWENTY-THREE

Tuesday 30 October, 9 a.m.

Perhaps it had been over-optimistic to hope that the two spurious leads might lead to any progress. They'd even commandeered the chair from Ryland's and dusted it for footprints, which appeared to reveal that a multitude of different shoes, makes and sizes had stepped on it but nothing that looked remotely like an old man's slipper print.

The newspaper headlines just about summed it up.

Police Admit They Are Baffled!

Who'd leaked that particular line, she couldn't know. Maybe, having nothing else helpful to say, the hacks had made it up. But it was uncomfortably close to the truth. She didn't want the fate of this vulnerable old man to remain a mystery, but it was definitely heading that way. She knew she shouldn't, but she'd read through the article on her tablet and felt even more fed up.

DI Piercy, assigned to the case, seven months pregnant (unflattering photograph) *was quoted as saying 'the police are baffled' and so on . . .*

It might be the truth but it wasn't what she had said. She'd actually said that investigations were continuing behind the scenes. How they'd translated that to the 'baffled' line was beyond her. OK, she hadn't been able to add the fable that the 'police were following leads'. It wouldn't take much of a brain to know that there were no leads. Not really. A couple of dreamt-up clues that might or might not exist, the possible sound of a car, the whispering.

She'd had the uniformed guys look at the drive just in case there were tyre tracks on the gravel, but the drive was used by all the visitors to Ryland's. They had two lines of enquiry but nothing concrete, nothing to go on. Nothing real.

She sat, glaring at her screen.

Any poor show by the police could be used as a political football and prove that the lack of funding had resulted in this pathetic failure.

And it felt pathetic. Outwitted by a ninety-six-year-old with dementia. She had to agree with the papers. It didn't exactly make her look like Albert Einstein. The question that was beginning to haunt her was: was someone else involved in his disappearance? If so, who and why?

Tuesday 30 October, 2 p.m.

That afternoon, feeling that she couldn't justify two officers, she went alone to Ryland's and re-interviewed all three members of the night shift who'd been asked to attend again. Sister Joan Arkwright initially insisted she'd spent much of the night in her office writing reports, checking drugs. But when Joanna questioned her more closely about hearing the car, she looked upset. 'I was exhausted,' she said. 'When I'd locked up and we'd settled everyone off, I thought it best if I had forty winks in the coffee room.'

'OK,' Joanna said. 'What sort of time?'

'Eleven-ish. I just dropped off.'

'And the others?'

'Everywhere was quiet, settled. We left the door open. We would have heard if Mr Foster had come downstairs and left. He would have been asking us about his teddy bear. All day, they told us, and all the night before he'd been upset so . . .' Her voice tailed off.

Joanna waited but sensed nothing was about to be forthcoming. 'So?' she asked delicately.

'We gave him an extra sleeping tablet. He was upset and we're allowed to use our discretion.'

Joanna thought about this. 'So he would have been very drowsy.'

'Yes.'

'Perhaps had trouble managing the stairs . . . alone?'

The night sister nodded.

Joanna tucked this little fact into her brain.

Next she spoke to the two HCAs, again together. She wanted to bounce their stories against one another and find the truth. They had been much more involved with the residents, hands on, taking them to the toilet through the night, checking the rooms periodically. Though their shortcomings in this department had been exposed, Joanna was convinced they *did* do the rounds at intervals. What the intervals were was open to doubt. But she couldn't shake their stories. Susie Trent was clinging to her version that she had found the French windows unlocked and unbolted but had locked and bolted them on her re-entry from her fag break. 'I hung the key back on the hook and put the chair in its usual place with its back against the wall.'

'Can I just check? When you found the door unlocked, did you look outside to make sure no one had wandered out?'

'I didn't exactly look,' she said. 'I stood on the terrace. I would have noticed if there was anyone around.'

'Was there a car in the front drive?'

'I wouldn't be able to see from there. It's round the corner.'

'OK.'

'Our cars are always parked round the back,' she explained. 'It's only visitors who park at the front.' She smiled. 'It makes the place look nicer.'

'Did you see any lights around the front?'

Susie Trent looked puzzled at the question. 'We-ell, through the trees you can see the lamplights from the road.'

'OK.' She addressed her next question to them both. 'When you were doing your rounds through the night, did you notice any other residents wandering around?'

'No.' Both shook their heads.

'Was anyone particularly restless that night?'

This produced a second negative.

Joanna looked from one to the other. 'Have you thought of anything else since we last spoke?'

Both women shook their heads.

'OK, you can go.'

She wandered back into the day room and looked at the chairs standing around the perimeter of the room.

Plain wood stacking chairs with a solid seat, similar to the one currently in the crime-scene forensic department. This time, after studying it for a few minutes and seeing nothing new, Joanna tried to mount it. Her pregnancy might be making her awkward and unbalanced but apart from that she was relatively fit. It was no easy feat to climb on this chair and reach the bolt. She was now even more certain that it hadn't been Zac Foster who had opened this door. Not by himself. Which meant that if the night sister was telling the truth and she *had* locked it, then someone else *from the inside* must have shot back the bolt.

Perhaps the same someone who had had a car waiting, headlights probably switched off.

It was a game changer.

She returned to her office with a huge sigh. Mike Korpanski surreptitiously watched her and sensed something in his colleague's attitude was shifting. She shared her thoughts with him and watched his face darken. 'Can I just run stuff past you?'

He sighed but couldn't resist the appeal in her eyes.

'What if our elderly man was abducted?'

'By whom? One of the night staff?'

'Well, they were the only ones around.'

'It makes sense,' he agreed, 'and at the same time it makes absolutely no sense.'

'Yep.'

Then he saw *that look* in her eyes.

'You all right there, Jo?'

'No, Mike,' she said. 'Frankly I'm not. I'm sick of being portrayed as a woman who's lost her marbles because she's pregnant. I'm sick of being the Aunt Sally for the underfunding of the entire police force and I'm also sick of being haunted by this story of a confused old man who's apparently fallen down a rabbit hole in a quest for his lost teddy bear, probably helped by one of the nurses in a fairly pleasant residential home.'

He started to speak but she interrupted him. 'Have you read any of the headlines? And the cartoons are even worse. I'm drawn, in a uniform I don't even wear, chasing Christopher and his . . .'

Korpanski held up a warning hand. 'Careful, Jo, you'll be owing money to the swear box.'

That drew a smile which in turn calmed her down. 'If I'm right, he must either be dead or someone is sheltering him.'

He opened his mouth to speak but again didn't get the chance.

'And, by the way, to add to the list, I'm also sick of my step-daughter needling me about my failures as a detective inspector. Will that do for you?'

Devoid of an answer, struggling not to smirk and knowing she would see through any attempt at appeasement with a wild guess, Korpanski simply shrugged, tempted to return to his computer screen and finalize the figures for violent crime in Leek for the year . . .

'Mike,' she appealed, 'how can I make sense of this? If, as seems probable, a member of staff helped him to escape, someone else must have been driving a car.'

Korpanski gave a cautious nod.

'He has no obvious contacts, no friends or relatives to shelter him. The manager said he doesn't have any visitors. We've covered the moors and the town is well populated, so someone must be sheltering him or holding him against his will.'

'Have you no clues, Jo?'

She shook her head.

'What shoe prints did they get from the chair?'

'Plenty,' she said. 'Too many, if anything. It seems anyone and everyone used it to reach that top bolt. No discernible slipper prints,' she added.

She was silent for a moment, going over known facts. 'And I can't completely rule out the possibility that the door was not locked in the first place. After all, Joan Arkwright has admitted she was dog-tired after a run of nights. She might have forgotten to lock it, thinking that she had, in which case I can't exclude the fact that Zac wandered outside and was locked out when Ms Trent returned from her fag break. But it still doesn't explain why we can't find him.'

Korpanski simply nodded.

'The night staff told me no one was wandering around the

home when they did their rounds, so somehow he sneaked down-stairs and out of the home right under the noses of three members of staff.'

'Who were probably or possibly fast asleep.'

'I don't think so. Not all three. Not at the same time. Not deeply asleep. Maybe just dozing. And he had had an extra sleeping tablet.'

'They didn't do a proper check on the residents, though.'

'No.'

And the explanation for the door being unlocked?'

'Susie Trent said she just thought Joan Arkwright had forgotten to lock up properly.'

'But now you think it's possible someone let him out?'

She nodded.

'That opens up some strange possibilities.'

But she ploughed on. 'What possibilities? He's hardly a candidate for a Getty-style kidnapping, is he? No one's going to pay a bean for his release.'

'Agreed.' The muscles in his neck twitched. He was now *desperate* to return to his computer screen.

But she hadn't finished. 'There's been no reported sighting, so either we're still failing to find a body or someone is harbouring him.'

Korpanski shook his head. 'Come on, Jo,' he said, subconsciously echoing Matthew's words. 'This is an old man who's gone walkabout. He'll be found dead, possibly from exposure, somewhere hidden, out of town.'

But her eyes still held that tenacious flame. 'No, Mike. That is not what has happened. Even with more than a nine-hour head start alone, he wasn't going to get very far walking, I guess, at a snail's stumbling pace.'

He was grinning with his next remark. 'I don't think snails stumble, Jo.'

Her lips twitched too. 'You know what I mean. We've all seen elderly folk taking an age to cross a road, stumbling, slow steps. Someone *must* have helped him. And my money's on a member of staff.'

Sensing she still hadn't finished, Korpanski waited before offering, 'He might still be somewhere obscure.'

'You think our uniformed guys aren't savvy enough to search wheelie bins and derelict, empty buildings, or cars carelessly left unlocked?'

He shrugged. 'There's always some place, Jo.'

But she was shaking her head. 'Not within four hundred yards there isn't.'

He grinned. 'Maybe he had a sudden spurt of energy from somewhere.'

She held up her hands and shook her head. 'There's another dimension to this. I don't know what it is but . . .' She glanced across at her sergeant and knew he wouldn't appreciate her thoughts. That there was an undercurrent here which she sensed but could not articulate.

Korpanski was growing fidgety; an avalanche of crime figures needed collating and he couldn't see where this conversation was going. 'So, you want to run anything else past me?'

'Yeah,' she said decisively, 'I do. This isn't about a ninety-six-year-old man who is so confused that he's attached to a teddy bear his mother probably gave him when he was about five and has absconded to search for it.'

Korpanski shrugged. 'So what is it about?'

She shook her head. 'I don't know.'

When he greeted this with silence she added waspishly, 'You're not being a lot of use to me at the moment.'

'Sorry, Jo. I've got other things on my mind.'

'Like what?'

He lifted his eyebrows. 'Crime figures mean anything to you?'

'Yes, but live crime is what we're all about.'

'Sorry,' he said again.

To which she retorted, 'If you're so sorry, why are you smirking?'

Korpanski did his best to wipe the smirk from his face and look serious.

'Jo,' he said, an idea forming. 'If he's attached to his old teddy bear which you think he might have had for around ninety-odd years, what about trying somewhere familiar? Maybe his old school?'

Now she was smiling. 'OK,' she said. 'Unlikely but not a bad idea. Although I doubt the schools he went to in the twenties and thirties will be in the same buildings. But it was half-term last week so no one around. It's a long shot, but I'll send some uniforms round to all the schools, check them out. Mike.'

Korpanski waited.

'Thanks.'

He grinned at her and for a moment they both simply savoured the friendship.

Korpanski screwed up his face, recalling something in his past. 'I have to say, Jo, this doesn't sound like the dementia I always imagined. Not like my grandma, who reverted to speaking Polish and thinking the Nazis were coming.'

She smiled and shook her head. 'No.' Then she started to giggle. 'I was just thinking, it's almost as though two brains planned his escape. Mr Foster and his teddy.'

They both laughed out loud at this, Korpanski doing a teddy bear impersonation, paws held up to his face. But as she gathered her papers up on the desk and stood up, she felt an overwhelming sense of dejection.

'Come here, Jo,' he said. 'Let me give you a hug.'

'Difficult with . . .' and she indicated The Bump. He did it anyway and she took comfort from the powerful musculature of Korpanski's shoulders, built from hours at the gym.

And it did make her feel better.

TWENTY-FOUR

Tuesday 30 October, 3.20 p.m.

Korpanski wasn't about to shed any further light on her thorny problem but at least he'd handed her a spark of an idea. She picked up the phone to summon a couple of uniforms and gave them their instructions – to find out which schools were around in the 1920s and 1930s in Leek and search any premises or areas where they had been, as well as current school buildings.

What if she'd been looking at this the wrong way round? Focusing on the wrong place.

Not an old man missing but an old toy missing. Cause and effect, Matthew had said.

She picked up the phone and connected finally with Matilda Warrender, the matron of Ryland's. Without preamble she dived in.

'Tell me more about Mr Foster's teddy bear.'

After the briefest of pauses, which Joanna translated correctly to *This is a joke?* the matron responded, audibly supressing surprise and a chuckle which escaped. 'He'd had it since he was a little boy . . .' Joanna did a quick calculation. Zac was born in 1922.

'So he was given it around 1926 or so?'

'I suppose so.' She couldn't have been less interested.

But Joanna pressed on. 'I think you said it was black?'

The matron laughed. 'Yes, a really tatty old thing.'

'Can you tell me anything more about it?'

'Such as?'

'I don't know. Anything.'

'No.'

'And the bear that replaced it? What was that like?'

'Oh, much newer.' A pause. 'And it was brown nylon fur. Not black.'

'Where did it come from?'

'I haven't the faintest idea.'

'No one's admitted finding it for him?'

'No.'

'Would you mind asking all your staff who gave him the substitute toy?'

'If you want.' Maybe realizing she was bordering on sounding rude, the matron added, 'It didn't do much good anyway. He wouldn't have anything to do with it. He just threw it on the floor, although I think he did pick it up later.'

'Thank you.'

Joanna put the phone down.

Wednesday 17 October, 9.30 p.m.

It hadn't been as easy as she'd thought. Even though he'd had his sleeping tablets, Zac was restless, almost as though he knew something was going to happen tonight. Added to that his arm was tight around the bear and she could hardly release it. Even when it was safely in her hands he gave a little moan and reached out. Lucky she'd brought the substitute.

She bundled his bear into a bag and couldn't wait to leave.

Thursday 18 October, 7.45 a.m.
Ryland's Residential Home, Room 11

Even before he awoke he knew something was very wrong. Something didn't smell right and it didn't feel right either. Without opening his eyes he touched it tentatively, stroked the fur, tried to find the button on its ear, put the paw into his mouth and then he knew. It was the wrong one. He opened his eyes and sat up in bed. Looked at it and gave out a howl.

One of the nurses came in response. 'What is it, Zac?'

He held out the teddy bear and howled again.

She took a brief look before trying to soothe him. 'It's just your teddy.'

He shook his head. 'Not mine. Not mine.' And he threw it across the room while Alf watched curiously.

The nurse stroked his head. 'Course it is, love.' She picked it up and held it out to him. He took it and again flung it across the room, glaring at her. 'Not mine. Not mine, not mine. Someone stole it.' And again he set up the agonized howl.

Jubilee heard it from the other end of the corridor. So he *had* noticed. The guilt seeped into her from her feet up.

Zachary Foster lay back in his bed, even more confused than usual as he tried to work it out. Someone had taken it. He looked around and saw Alf staring at him. He threw back the covers, sat up and walked towards him. 'Have you took it?'

'Took what?'

'My bear. Teddy.'

Alf shook his head, doleful. 'Sorry. No.'

Zachary gave him a hard stare then gave up and returned to his bed, still puzzling.

'Time to get up now.' Shawna approached him cautiously. Word was that Zac was being difficult this morning.

Zac folded his arms and lay back against the pillows, shaking his head. 'I'm not getting up today.'

'Come on, Zac,' she pleaded.

He lashed out then, catching her arm so she winced. 'Not until you find it.'

This, she thought, was tiresome. There wasn't time for patients to be difficult – or violent.

Zac lay in bed trying to work it out.

Who took it?

He ticked people off on his fingers. He couldn't remember all their names, even though they all wore name badges. Stella? Was there a Stella? He thought there was. Well, there might be. The girl with almost white-blonde hair. No her name wasn't Stella. That was somebody else he'd once known. The nurse's name was . . . He screwed up his face. Something else beginning with 'S'.

There was another girl with red hair (dyed, he thought; it was too bright to be natural), whose name he couldn't remember, and another who was from the Far East. Not her, he thought. Suzy Wong, he called her. Not her. He liked her. She smiled a lot and patted his arm; though people from the Far East were supposed to be inscrutable, she was not. She giggled a lot. Funnily enough she had a Welsh name. Something that sounded like Near.

There was an Indian girl who giggled a lot too. He couldn't remember her name either. Not her. She was too pretty. And friendly. But the one he liked best was the big Jamaican with a loud, hysterical laugh that bubbled up from her belly. Jubilee. There never was anyone better named. Maybe Jubilee would help him find it.

It could never be her who'd taken Teddy. She was far too nice. She wouldn't steal from him. He'd told her the story and she'd listened, her eyes kind and understanding.

So who was it? Someone sly and greedy. Someone who wanted his little treasure. Well, he would find out who it was and report them to the police. They wouldn't get away with it. He looked at the wrong teddy he'd just hurled to the floor and felt a bit sorry for it now. That was no way to treat a teddy just because it wasn't his. Maybe it was somebody else's treasured thing. Someone who was even now searching for it. And he'd treated it badly. Hurt it. He picked it up and put it on the end of his bed from where it gave him a sad, lopsided, apologetic little grin.

When the afternoon shift arrived, Jubilee and the other nurses who'd worked through the morning had to give a report. And this threw Jubilee into a quandary. Zac had been kicking off about his beloved bear. Should she mention it? She needn't have worried. Shawna was making a fuss about the bruise that was beginning to form on her arm.

'He seems to have settled down a bit now,' she said, 'but maybe tonight he'll need some extra medication.'

It was duly noted down.

Jubilee stood through the other nurses' reports, still feeling the moment she'd slipped his hand from around his beloved childhood toy and replaced it with the charity-shop bear. Even then she'd had a pang of conscience. But he'd hardly stirred. The cocktail of sleeping drugs meant *all* their patients slept like babies and gave the staff a quiet night.

Her eyelids drooped as she abstracted herself.

If she was to get to Spanish Town, they needed to convert that bear into money as quickly as possible and get away.

They needed cash. Quickly.

'Jubilee?'

She gave her report without mentioning Zac's loss and thankfully went off duty.

Thursday 18 October, 5 p.m.

Chi had always known she wouldn't be able to stand up to one of Kath's interrogations. She collared Chi when she'd packed Fifi and Debs down the chippy. And when Chi tried to slide by to go with them, Kath had her by a shoulder-grip that practically had her on her knees. 'Not you. You stay here. I want to talk to you.'

Like I have a choice?

'Don't think you can play a double game with me.'

Chi shook her head. 'Double game? Not with you, Kath.'

Kath gave a slow shake of her head, eyes steadily focused as though she was puzzling something out. 'Something isn't right with you, my friend. You're up to something.'

She spoke slowly and deliberately and Chi recognized the threat behind it. Her legs felt like jelly. She was wobbly with terror. She felt sick too. Planning the escapade with Jubilee had seemed such fun. Such a simple, easy way of making a packet. The old man, Jubilee had assured her, probably wouldn't even notice the switch. So it was a win-win situation, a victimless crime. But if Kath became involved it would be a whole new ball game. Chi wasn't brave. She was frightened. Last week she'd seen Kath punch a woman for sneaking into a parking space ahead of her at Sainsbury's. Only the fact that the woman had moved her head so the punch had landed on her ear had saved her from a broken nose or a split lip and Kath from another stretch inside.

'You're trying to keep little secrets from me.' Chi knew that tone of voice too. Not loud – shouting, screaming – but quiet and menacing.

Chi shook her head, tried, one last time, to protest, to wriggle out of it. Their plans would soon come tumbling down if Kath got involved. She made a weak attempt at protest. 'No, I'm not, Kath. I promise. I am not keeping any secrets from you.'

Kath leered and held out her hand. 'Give us your phone then.'

Chi stared at her and knew this was the start of something very bad.

Kath scrolled through the messages without saying a word while Chi tried her hardest not to breathe. *If I don't breathe,* she tried to kid herself, *she'll forget I'm here.* She focused on keeping her knees perfectly still and waited while Kath continued to read. Then she looked up. Sometimes Kath shocked her not just with her nastiness but with her insight. After reading through a few more messages she read one out. *OK. Speak to that lady and see about getting the money. Soon.* Chi cursed herself for being so careless, leaving the message on her phone for Kath to read. She knew what she was like – suspicious.

Her face didn't move a muscle.

Kath's eyes were like marbles, cold glass marbles. Her smile looked evil. Little more than a curve of her mouth.

With the result that when Kath smiled, it was only marginally less threatening than when she ranted or lashed out or put on that *quiet* voice. Because anyone who knew her was aware what would come next. And those who didn't would still never forget that smile or the action that inevitably followed.

Kath drew in a deep breath, scowling as she read out the message again.

OK. Speak to that lady and see about getting the money. Soon.
'What's all this about?'

Inch by inch, word by word, the story leaked out, like urine from a terrified person with poor bladder control.

But for the first time in her life, Chi sensed that Kath was both surprised and impressed.

'You're sure?' Kath dragged deeply on her fag. She rubbed the jagged point of her tooth and then she looked up. 'What's your plan then?'

This was when Chi opened her mouth but her throat seemed tied up with barbed wire. 'Umm.' She regarded Kath with trepidation, unsure just what she could or should say, and finally coming up with, 'To get the money.' She was praying that Kath didn't follow this up with, *And then what?* She didn't want to tell her about Spanish Town. She just wanted to disappear.

But Kath's response mirrored her own previous question, one word. 'How?'

'How what?'

'How do you intend to get the money?'

Chi thought for a moment and knew she had to tell her about Diana Sutcliffe.

Kath's response was predictable. 'And you trust her?'

Chi shrugged. 'I don't have a lot of choice, Kath.'

'The old man – will he make a fuss?'

'If he does, Jubilee says that no one will take any notice. He's got dementia.'

'And once you've got the money?'

This was the bit Chi had been dreading, the weak link in her story. Knowing Kath would sense the true version, Chi confessed. 'Spend it, I suppose.'

Kath was thoughtful a while longer, her eyes narrow and suspicious, while the other two, back from the chippy, simply stared, eyes rounded. 'How?'

Somehow she *had* to head her off. She affected nonchalance, studied her fingernails. 'I don't know, Kath. Jubilee might be wrong. It might be a bit of absolute shit.'

Kath countered this with, 'But you trust her.'

Chi shrugged, dragging out all her acting skills. 'Sort of.'

Kath fell quiet while Chi froze. Something cold trickled down her spine. As slowly as an ice cube melting.

Then Kath smiled. Her friend should have remembered. *She was a snake.*

She could see just how she could use this.

'I've got a suggestion,' she hissed.

Three minutes later, Chi was drowning in a barrel of treacle. The place where reggae music played all night and the sun shone all day, where she wouldn't have to bundle up six months of the year, where she could drink rum and coke and sleep on the sand, vanished as abruptly as a dream when you wake to the alarm clock and realize you're late for work.

She felt sick.

In contrast Kath was just starting to feel excited. She had known that her plan was missing one vital part. But now she could see her way through and Chi and her Jamaican friend were going to help her.

Thursday 18 October, 8 p.m.

The conversation with Kath had unnerved Chi. As soon as she could, she took the opportunity to surreptitiously get in touch with Jubilee. She wandered upstairs to the bedroom and pulled out her mobile phone.

'I got good and bad news,' she said.

And now Jubilee was tense too. 'Give me the good first.'

'I'm meeting Diana Sutcliffe tomorrow.'

'That is good news. And the bad?'

'Kath's got wind of our plan.'

'How much of it?'

For a moment Chi didn't respond. Then honesty prevailed. 'Most of it.'

'So what does she want out of it?'

'I don't know for sure.'

Jubilee's response was predictable. 'Is this Kath girl going to be trouble?'

'She could be.' She had entertained her new friend with some of Kath's milder exploits but had stopped short of describing Kath's true nature and how that manifested itself. But Jubilee was smart enough to have picked up the implication. 'What do you think she will do?'

'I don't know.'

TWENTY-FIVE

Tuesday 30 October, 9 p.m.

Even Matthew had stopped asking her how the case was going, and that rubbed it in even more. Though he wasn't usually interested, he made some show of asking about her cases as he shared the more interesting parts of his work with her.

The baby was growing fast, kicking with energy, and as it thrived she felt that it was sucking her own energy. She seemed to want to sleep for most of the time. She still had weeks to go but even Matthew appeared impressed at her size. One night he'd asked her if she was sure of her dates.

'You think it'll come early?'

He palpated what he called the fundal height and nodded. 'I wouldn't be surprised, Jo.'

She felt a sudden panic. 'It's not twins is it?'

'No.' He smiled. 'Just a bonny bouncing, beautiful boy.'

And this time she was too tired to argue.

The night was warm, the room cosy with the log burner blazing away. Joanna lay on the sofa, her mind working. Matthew was reading a magazine, or rather the *Journal of Forensic and Legal Medicine.* She watched him deep in concentration. At times his lips moved or he frowned. Once or twice he shook his head, as though disagreeing with the content. Then he looked up and saw her watching him. Somehow he sensed she wanted to say something and, carefully marking his place, he placed the magazine down. 'Jo?'

'Matt.' She began tentatively. He was all attention now. All smiles. He knew she wanted his opinion on something. 'Can I run something past you?'

He nodded, still smiling.

'I daren't even mention this to the guys at work.' She patted her expanding abdomen. 'They'll think it's complete madness.'

'But,' he prompted.

'We-ell. My missing man is worthless. We've established that no one would pay to get him back but I don't see how else he would have escaped and evaded discovery.' She managed a smile but it was accompanied by a deeply troubled frown. Sometimes it was hard to detach yourself from a case even when you were in such a cosy environment. 'Oh, God,' she said. 'Stop me if I'm sounding insane.' His eyes were gleaming as he moved from the chair to her side in one easy movement. 'Jo?'

'What if it wasn't the old man who was the target?'

Now he was frowning too. 'Sorry?'

'But the teddy bear?' She held up a finger to prevent him interrupting. 'That was what went first.'

And her husband asked the obvious question. 'If what they wanted was the teddy bear, why abduct the old man at all? I take it that's your suggestion – that he was abducted.'

She shrugged. 'It's the only explanation.'

'I take it then you're pointing the finger at a member of staff.'

She nodded.

'That's a serious allegation, Jo.'

'I know it is. It's also pretty far-fetched, but I can't think of any other way or reason all this happened. He couldn't have gone very far on his own and he's definitely not within the search area.'

'Well . . . there are old toys that are worth a fortune like, presumably, the original Pooh Bear – the original.' He couldn't resist teasing her. 'I don't suppose your old man's name was Christopher Robin?'

She was tempted to throw a cushion at him, but her back was comfortably resting on it so she simply shook her head and Matthew gave the matter further thought.

'I suggest that really valuable old toys are few and far between and I can't imagine something worth a lot ending up with an old man with no particular connection to wealth who'd lived in Leek all his life.'

She nodded. 'It might be far-fetched but it's not impossible. At least not as impossible as a vanishing act.'

'Hmm. Well, if I were you I'd go back to the residential home and do a bit more digging around.'

'Residential home,' she corrected.

'Residential home, and see if you can verify your theory.'

Her raised eyebrows asked the question.

'By finding out what you can about the missing teddy bear.'

She nodded. 'Thank you.' And having registered that his eyes were drifting back towards the magazine, she smiled mischievously. 'And now you can return to your studies.'

Her reward for perception was a wide, warm, Matthew grin and she settled back. At least now she had a focus for an enquiry. But this time she would work alone.

TWENTY-SIX

Thursday 18 October, 9 p.m.

'Do you remember when I was in prison?'

Chi nodded, failing to see where this was heading but sensing trouble ahead.

'Remember that girl I shared a cell with?'

'Lakshmi,' Chi managed through dry lips.

'She told me lots of stories.'

Chi nodded, waiting.

'Do you remember the story about catching a tiger?'

'Yeah,' she managed. 'I remember.'

Kath continued, 'If the Indians needed to catch a tiger because it had turned man-eater, they used to tether a goat to the bottom of the tree.'

And suddenly Chi could see just where this was leading.

Kath aimed a dart at the picture on the back of the door. But this time she missed completely and almost hit Fifi who squealed, earning herself a sour look. 'I'd been wondering about this. I needed a goat.'

She leered at her, one of Kath's rare displays of pleasure. 'And now you, my *friend* . . .' Chi winced at the savagery in the word, 'have provided me with an answer. Thank you *very much* for helping me.'

Chi's response was blunt. 'How?'

Kath leaned forward, eyes glinting. 'I said I needed a goat. And you and your new friend are going to help me acquire one, aren't you?'

Chi paused, on the brink of making a promise she *knew* she did not want to keep. Her mind was racing around with question after question. What happened to the goat tethered to a tree in order to catch a tiger? She pictured it, bleating and panicking, terrified as the predator approached. Presumably the Indians would shoot the tiger *before* it actually attacked the goat? Wasn't that the idea? Surely the goat was simply there as a lure? Not really to be hurt? But in her mind she saw it all too clearly. The goat savaged by the tiger, the tiger shot too late to save the goat being mauled to death because in this story no one really cared about it. It was expendable, a means to an end. The goat had no value at all. She tried to blink the image away but it was stuck stubbornly to the inside of her eyelids.

Kath was waiting for her response and Chi knew she had no choice. 'What do I have to do?'

'I'll tell you.' Minutes later Chi's fingers were tapping out a text message.

I have a friend I'd like you to meet.

TWENTY-SEVEN

Wednesday 31 October, 8.30 a.m.

Joanna turned up at Ryland's unannounced and found Sister Matilda Warrender in her office working through the night's reports. When Joanna's knock registered, she looked up, hope flaring briefly in her eyes, but quickly dying at Joanna's shake of the head.

'Nothing?'

'No. I'm sorry. There's no sign of him.'

There was no mistaking her chagrin. But she picked herself up. 'So?' The tacit question was, what are you doing here?

'May I come in?'

'Yes, of course. Sorry.' She cleared some papers from the chair. 'What can I do for you?'

And suddenly Joanna was lost for words. Matilda Warrender watched her expectantly; she had to say something but she couldn't find the right phrase.

So she plunged in, as though to a hot tub or a chill pool. 'The toy that went missing. Was there anything special about it?'

Matilda looked even more bemused. 'I don't think so.' She was frowning slightly, her fingers weaving, her whole attitude troubled.

Joanna sensed her thoughts were either focusing on the last time she'd seen her patient, perhaps mourning the missing toy and his distress when he'd realized it was gone. Or maybe she was wondering whether to call the station and find out whether the DI in charge of the case was in her right mind.

After a brief pause, the matron related events as she'd seen them.

'It was the morning of Thursday the eighteenth,' she began, slowly at first. 'It was late in the morning when the day nurses told me that Mr Foster appeared agitated because his teddy bear was missing.'

'Had that happened before?'

'No.' Honesty prevailed. 'At least not to my knowledge.' She continued, 'He'd grabbed Shawna by the arm, leaving her with quite a bruise. He was quite strong, you know. Ned Sheringham said he lashed out at him when he went to give him a bath. Accused *him* of stealing it. Naturally Ned summoned me.'

'So you spoke to Mr Foster.'

'Yes, I did. He was adamant someone had stolen his teddy. He was very upset. I sat with him for a while, got the staff to search under the bed, in the bathroom, the wardrobe. Everywhere.'

'But it didn't turn up.'

'No.'

'And it hasn't turned up since?'

'No.'

'When did the substitute bear arrive?'

'I don't know.' She looked flustered by the question. 'It was just there. I'm not sure when it appeared but Zac was having none of it. I think it was there that day, but when, I'm not sure. One of the staff must have found it and out of kindness gave it to him.' And then she stopped speaking, her eyes wide open. 'I think,' she said slowly. 'I think it was there *that* morning. I seem to remember it on the floor – where he'd thrown it. I handed it back to him.'

Joanna felt that she was at last getting somewhere. This was tangible fact. No coincidence then. The toy had been substituted. But she kept her tone calm and measured.

'How did he respond to that?'

Ms Warrender was back on track. 'Not well, I'm afraid,' she said with a smile. 'He threw it across the room and was . . .' She seemed to lose track of what she was saying before finishing, 'Frankly he was inconsolable.'

A pause while her brow furrowed and her clear eyes met Joanna's. 'You think there's a connection, don't you?'

Joanna was cautious. 'It would seem so.'

But then Ms Warrender called her bluff. 'How?' And when Joanna didn't answer she sat thoughtfully while Joanna appraised her.

A trained nurse, divorced since her twenties, with a business head that Rupert Murdoch would have envied. Underneath all that starch and professionalism, she actually had a kind heart and a conscience. Realizing she was being sized up, the matron waited patiently for some response from Joanna, her head on one side balanced on her thin neck. Matilda, or Tillie as she was called behind her back, always wore an old-fashioned nurse's uniform, a dark blue cotton dress. Had she been asked why she wore such an outdated uniform, which she never had, she would have had her answer ready. Self-righteous and prim. A professional uniform indicates a professional attitude.

'So,' Joanna said slowly. 'Where did that new teddy come from?'

Matilda looked confused. 'I don't know.' Now she was looking troubled. 'I haven't asked. With Zac going a few days later, I suppose at the time it didn't seem important. I just forgot about it.'

'Has anyone actually admitted they put the new teddy bear there?'

The response was a slow shake of the head.

'Do you know when Mr Foster's bear was last seen?'

Matilda shook her head.

The nurse's grey eyes flickered and Joanna knew their thoughts were moving along the same track. 'You think someone deliberately substituted the other teddy? You think there's a connection to his disappearance? How?'

Joanna didn't even attempt to answer but tried to keep the subject neutral. 'Let's put it to the test, shall we? We can ask some of the staff if they have any idea who substituted the teddy bears.'

But the trouble with trying to pin down the last sighting of an object most of them had seen all the time and commonly ignored was that no one could give an exact response.

Ned Sheringham proffered the most reasonable account. Presumably Zac's original bear had been there when he'd gone to sleep on the Wednesday night before he disappeared – otherwise he would not have settled. Which shone a light on the staff who'd been on duty on the Wednesday evening, through the night, and on the Thursday morning before Zac had left.

And as luck would have it Jubilee Watkins, Ned Sheringham and Shawna Wilson had all been working a late shift on the Wednesday and an early shift on the Thursday. The night staff had also been the same: Joan Arkwright, Susie Trent and Amelia Boden.

Joanna began with Ned.

He was a cocky guy in his mid-thirties, with bright blond hair and a slight lisp which emphasized a broad Potteries accent. He swaggered in, hands in pockets.

Joanna tried to keep the conversation casual rather than an interrogation. She didn't want to alert the staff to the fact that she was focusing not so much on Mr Foster but his missing toy.

'Ned,' she said, 'I want you to think back to the Wednesday night before Mr Foster went missing.' Sheringham raised his eyebrows at the mention of Wednesday but made no comment.

'I understand you and the other two members of staff on duty that evening put him to bed and gave him his night sedation?'

His response was predictable. 'Yeah,' he said. 'Sometimes if we've got time, if we're quiet, we help out the night staff and do some of their stuff for them.'

'Did you *personally* put Mr Foster to bed that night?'

'Yeah, me and Jubilee.'

'Was there anything different about that particular night that sticks out?'

Sheringham thought for a moment then shook his head. 'No,' he said. 'No. He went to bed like a lamb. Cuddling his old teddy. He was quiet and settled down. I thought they'd have a quiet night with him.'

He looked enquiringly at Joanna, as if wondering at the turn her questioning was taking. Then his gaze dropped to her bulging abdomen and seemed to find an explanation there. Joanna could have stood up and aimed a punch at his nose.

She tried to keep the next question equally casual. 'So he was cuddling his teddy and went to sleep.'

'Yeah. So we settled everyone down and then the night staff—'

Joanna interrupted. 'What time was this?'

'Just before nine. Shawna said she'd do the report so me and Jubilee could sneak off early.'

'And that's what you did?'

'Yeah, well *I* did. Jubilee disappeared off into the ladies.' He made a face which looked comical – a shrug of his shoulders, an eye roll and a mischievous grin. 'Getting changed and putting her make-up on, I expect. I think she was going out somewhere.'

Joanna nodded. 'OK. And then you were on duty in the morning?'

'Yeah. No rest for the wicked, me mam used to say,' he said.

Joanna's too, but it had been accompanied by a glare which had confirmed her status in her mother's eyes. That's the trouble with being a daddy's girl – particularly when that daddy has scarpered off with a newer, younger woman. Her mother had never quite forgiven her for still loving her father after he had abandoned them. But what else can you do?

'And in the morning . . .' she prompted.

'He was awful. Lashing out, accusing us of stealing his beloved toy. Uncontrollable. I had to call Tillie.' Another naughty grin. 'Sister Warrender.'

'And the teddy?' she prompted delicately.

'It was a different one. Brown instead of black.'

'Any idea how it got there – the other teddy, I mean?'

Ned shook his head.

'You didn't ask the other members of staff?'

The question didn't even ruffle his feathers and, sensing she had extracted everything useful from him, she moved on.

She spoke to Shawna Wilson second, a petite, bubbly young character with red hair, who looked about seventeen. Her smile was friendly and open and her story more or less followed her colleague's.

Jubilee Watkins was a different character completely. Jamaican in origins, though another candidate with a Potteries accent, this time overlaid with Caribbean patois. She was nicely rounded, an imposing presence, but held a wary, suspicious air. She was patently on her guard. Whether that was to do with a natural wariness of the police, perhaps because of her colour, Joanna wasn't sure. She was uneasy from the first but her black eyes stared at Joanna with a bold expression.

'He go to bed like a little lamb that night,' she said with an abstracted smile, and Joanna sensed that Jubilee was fond of the old man. More than the other members of staff. She let her reflect for a moment before asking the next question.

'Cuddling his teddy bear?'

That was when she saw a note of panic. And Jubilee's response was halted. 'Of course.'

And then she smiled again at the memory. 'He always go to bed like that, his arm around Pooh Bear.'

'You had a name for it?' Joanna asked softly

The girl nodded. Guilt seeping out of her pores. She could hardly lift her eyelids, that guilt was so heavy.

Joanna picked up her question. 'But in the morning?'

The girl looked at her with a stricken look. 'It wasn't there.' Her shoulders dropped.

'So what do you think happened to it?'

From somewhere Jubilee dragged a hint of strength. In her eyes was a gleam of panic. 'I don't know,' she said. 'It must have got lost somehow.'

Joanna didn't need to be a trained detective to pinpoint the fact that between an old man falling asleep, helped by the home's policy of sleeping tablets, his arm around a beloved toy that he had clung on to since a child and waking up in the morning, his arms encircling a substitute soft toy indicated intervention.

'So what do *you* think happened to Pooh Bear?'

Jubilee had a practised answer ready. 'I think,' she said, 'that it must have dropped on to the floor and somehow ended up in the waste-paper basket. And then it got thrown out with the rubbish.'

She was word perfect, this explanation vaguely possible if improbable.

'And the other bear?'

'Oh, there's always stuff lying around.'

Joanna fixed the girl with a stare. 'Is there anything else you wish to tell me, Jubilee?'

Jubilee shook her head, holding her breath, waiting, no doubt, for Joanna to swallow the lies she had been feeding her.

'So what do you think has happened to your patient?'

Joanna saw, from the drooping of the girl's shoulders and a soft exhalation of air, that she was relieved Joanna had shifted her focus from the teddy bear to Mr Foster.

And again she had an explanation – of sorts – up her sleeve. 'I think,' she said, eyes fixed on the detective, 'that someone must have taken him in.'

'And missed out on all the searches and appeals?'

The girl waved her arms around. 'That's what I think, Inspector Piercy. I am sure he is alive and safe.' She hesitated before adding, 'He's a lovely man. One of my favourites.'

'Thank you very much.'

Joanna waited until the girl was halfway through the door before she asked her final question. 'Was there anything special about Mr Foster's little teddy bear?'

Jubilee didn't even turn around. 'Oh, no,' she said, comfortable now. 'It was a tatty old toy.'

'Thank you.'

Matilda Warrender was waiting for her outside the door. 'Any luck?'

'Sort of.'

Ms Warrender was holding something which she handed to Joanna. 'This,' she said, 'is the bear that Mr Foster threw on the floor when his own toy went missing.'

Joanna took the bear and studied it, her mind a mixture of emotion. Her child would, no doubt, have something like this snuggled in his cot. Matthew had already bought a Steiff teddy, tan in colour with a rather sweet face. It sat in the corner of the nursery he'd already decorated. Joanna was no expert in children's soft toys, but this one looked poor quality, its fur matted nylon, one ear chewed. Much of its body was threadbare and an eye was attached with a loose loop of black cotton, sewn on amateurishly with large, uneven stitches. She stared at it. Dumb and uninspiring as it was, this was the first clue which would lead her to the fate of the missing man.

'May I take this?'

Bemused, Ms Warrender nodded.

TWENTY-EIGHT

Holding the bear and already knowing it would be the subject of nods, winks, derision all round, Joanna returned to the station.

Back at Ryland's, Matilda Warrender's thoughts were also focused on teddy bears.

She wandered into the corridor and spoke to Shawna Wilson. 'I know this sounds mad,' she said apologetically, 'but the detective seemed very interested in Mr Foster's missing teddy bear. Almost as interested as in his disappearance.'

'What, the old black thing?'

'Apparently.'

'Well, it was horrible. Wanted chucking away. Filthy. But would he let me wash it? No, he wouldn't.'

'What happened to it?'

'I don't know. Is it important?'

Matilda Warrender simply said, 'The detective appeared to think so.' She shook her head, as though wanting to break the thought free. 'And the other one – the substitute that he didn't like? Where did that come from?'

Shawna shrugged. 'I don't know. I hadn't seen that one before.'

'So you don't know where it came from? Or who found it and gave it to him?'

'No. Maybe he missed his bear and the night staff found that other one and gave it to him hoping he'd settle off.'

'No one's said anything. But maybe. I'll have a word with them.' She paused before continuing. 'Have you had another good look for *his* bear?'

'Oh, yeah. We've looked everywhere. It's nowhere, Matilda. We've asked the others to look out for it too but it hasn't turned up. I wonder if he found it and *then* went missing.'

'It's a possibility.' She smiled at the HCA. 'In which case, if we find one we find the other.'

Thursday 18 October, 8 p.m.

It had fallen to Chi to convince Jubilee to cooperate.

Predictably at first, Jubilee was adamant. 'I will not do it. He is just an old man.'

This was the tricky part. 'We don't have much choice.'

Jubilee's black eyes studied her. 'What do you mean we don't have a choice? We always have a choice.'

'Not if we want to ever see Spanish Town.'

That silenced Jubilee so Chi pressed her advantage. 'She's already got wind of the fact that we've stolen something from him. All you have to do is . . . He'll be all right.'

Exploiting both Jubilee's complete incomprehension of the situation and any insight into Kath's character, Chi tried to feed her friend a story. But somehow it got tangled up in Kath's version and she mumbled something about tethering a goat to a tree at which point Jubilee snapped, eyes blazing. 'He is not a goat. He is just an old man with a muddled mind. And you are asking me to tie him to a tree?'

'Not literally.'

Jubilee simply raised her eyebrows.

It was up to Chi to try and reassure her. Persuade her that there was only one way through this. She put a hand on her friend's arm. 'He'll be all right.'

'You know that, do you?'

She had to convince her. 'I'm *sure* he will. She'll have no reason to hurt him.'

Kath? Who hurt everyone?

And then Chi had to spell it out. 'If we don't cooperate, we won't get anywhere. She's quite capable of ruining the whole thing. She can be violent, you know.'

That finally silenced Jubilee. She looked trapped and then she nodded.

Chi returned to the house in Mill Street. As she stood outside the front door, already spotted by the ever-vigilant Debs, her phone buzzed with a text.

OK. Speak to that lady and see about getting the money tomorrow and I will do as you ask. J X

Jubilee, she thought, what am I dragging you into? Not knowing anything about Kath Whalley, her friend wouldn't get it. But with Kath's involvement, this minor theft – which would have been disregarded by the Ryland's staff as a symptom of their patient's dementia – had escalated. Knowing Kath as she did, Chi knew that she would have planned this revenge right through her prison sentence. She tried to salve her conscience by telling herself that Kath would have had her revenge one way or another. All she'd done was to provide her with one small detail. She wasn't responsible for what would happen next. But however hard she tried to imprint this version on her mind, she didn't feel any less guilty.

As Debs opened the door to her she tried to override her fears and hum along to the little ditty her heart was thumping out in a syncopated reggae beat. '*This is it. This is it. Spanish Town? Here I come.*' She accompanied the words with a hip-wiggle all of her own while Kath and her two cronies looked on.

She tried to feel the heat of the sun, smell the coconut, drink the rum, but it tasted sour now. Never mind, she and Jubilee would soon be there for real.

Kath was watching her, taking thoughtful, deep drags on what was either a fag or a spliff. Even she wasn't sure which.

'All right, Chi? Your mate coming on board, is she?'

Chi nodded and Kath glanced at her watch. One o'clock.

Nearly dinner time.

Friday 19 October, 4 p.m.

Chi had a brief break between lunches and the evening dinners so had arranged to meet Diana Sutcliffe in the coffee bar on the market square. She knew how much was at stake. But she also knew that Kath was nearing her final plan. Time was running out. They already had their passports lined up. Her only hope was that if she could pull this off and get the cash *before* Kath had a chance to carry out her rotten plan, she and Jubilee could be halfway to Spanish Town and a crime would be avoided. Without Jubilee's cooperation, Zac Foster would remain at Ryland's but without his beloved bear.

Optimistic or what?

She watched as Diana approached, tottering on six-inch heels, finding it difficult to balance on the uneven cobbles. Then the door was pushed open. And already Chi was wondering. Did their future really depend on this?

Skintight black jeans and a faux leopard-skin jacket completed the outfit which, more used to locals in fleeces and wellies, caused all heads in the coffee shop to spin around and a few mouths to drop. Chi kept tight hold of the plastic carrier bag containing the precious bear.

She had her story off pat. Ready and waiting. Well practised, but she still felt sick with apprehension. If this didn't work – and quickly – there was no other way out. They'd have to fall in with Kath's plan. And there would be no beach bars, no Spanish Town. More likely they'd be sharing cells in HMP.

This *had* to work.

And for that she had to play her part.

'Hi.' She stood up, smile on face. Diana gave her a sharp, suspicious look. Not a good start.

'Hello,' she said back, quickly adding, 'I hope you're not wasting my time, Miss . . .?'

'Lawson,' Chi supplied. No intention of giving her real name.

Diana Sutcliffe continued in a brisk, cross voice. 'I've had to miss a sale in Macclesfield to meet you here. Had to leave bids and I *hate* leaving bids. You never know what you'll get run up to.'

Chi smiled sweetly. 'Can I get you a coffee, Miss Sutcliffe?'

'Cappuccino. Thanks.' Her response was grudging but at least she'd remembered her manners.

Chi went up to the counter taking the carrier bag with her. She didn't quite trust this woman.

Coffees always take longer than they should, and Chi was fidgety watching the bubbling, steaming, noisy espresso machine. Minutes later, after turning round a few times to check the dealer hadn't run out on her, Chi returned with a cappuccino and a latte. Diana Sutcliffe took a sip, eyeing her over the rim of the cup before prompting her. 'Come on then, let's take a look.'

Chi drew the bear out of the bag. Here, in the dingy interior of the coffee bar, it looked sadder and more worn than before. Diana Sutcliffe put some glasses on and held her hands out. Reluctantly Chi handed it over. Diana said nothing as she studied it from head to foot, paying particular attention to the button in the ear, the eyes, the stitched mouth, the fur, the ears. It seemed ages before she looked up. 'Just remind me,' she said, 'of the provenance.'

So again Chi trotted the story out word perfect, with a few little extra touches this time round: 'It was a great-great-aunt of mine, *terribly* affected by the tragedy. I think she lost someone when the ship went down but I'm not sure of the detail. Anyway, she bought it for my great-great grandmother.' She frowned. Even to her it sounded thin, suspicious, amateurish and totally unconvincing. She looked across the table. Ms Sutcliffe was watching her with rapt attention, hardly blinking. 'Go on.'

And Chi's confidence started to ebb. Her little tale wasn't going to fool this canny, sour, greedy businesswoman for a minute. Even if they were right about the bear and Ms Sutcliffe ran with the story, now she'd produced the tatty little toy the dealer was going to run rings round her. Spanish Town was fading faster than a TV screen switched off.

Diana was silent, eyes unblinking, sizing her up. Chi's mouth was dry with anxiety. They'd pinned everything on this. And it was about to get a whole lot worse.

She wished Ms Sutcliffe would stop picking at the seams and bloody well say something.

She wished Jubilee was handling this. Of course, they'd been worried the dealer would try and cheat them, or that Zac had been wrong about the toy. Mistaken. After all, he was a muddled old man. Even though Jubilee was fond of him, it didn't mean to say he didn't elaborate on the truth. The whole plan had hinged on his story and they'd counted on the dealer giving them ready cash. Enough to pay their air fare at least. And they didn't have much time now Kath was involved. Kath had waited long enough to achieve her objective. She wasn't one to hang around now she'd worked out the plan.

Chi took a sip of her latte and eyed Diana Sutcliffe across the table. The dealer was using an eyeglass now, her face almost touching the bear. She was scrutinizing poor old Ted. She lifted her gaze a couple of times before resuming her examination. It wasn't going to take her long to realize that Chi knew nothing about antique toys and their value. Chi glanced at the bear. To be honest, it didn't look worth much. One eye was hanging off and in places the fur was rubbed bald. Her spirits were sinking faster than a lead weight on a fishing line. And yet, as Diana took her study to the back of the bear, she could see why the old man had held such affection for him. He did have a raffish look about him. She tilted her head. If he *was* the special bear, he should at least represent a plane ticket out of here.

Ms Sutcliffe lowered her magnifying glass. 'What makes you think he's a *Titanic* bear?'

'This.' She laid the newspaper article flat on the table, the picture of a ship so famous that it was instantly recognizable.

'It sold back in . . .' She squinted. 'Two thousand.' She paused for effect before adding, 'It fetched £91,000.' She met the woman's eyes, calculating.

'It was probably in better condition than yours.' Diana Sutcliffe sighed. 'I'm pretty sure *I* won't be offering you *that* sort of money, or anywhere near it.' She raised her glance, trying to penetrate Chi's response. 'An auction is a chance, you see.' She met her eyes. 'You can be lucky or unlucky.'

Chi had anticipated this. 'I understand that,' she responded steadily.

'Have you approached any other dealers?'

Chi had thought about this. Should she play for more money? Pretend she already had an offer that she was considering? No. They didn't have the time for that. They needed the money. *Now.*

'No. Just you. But I will need cash.' Best not to mention that there were two of them in this deal. That would muddy the waters – she and Jubilee couldn't have had the same fictitious grandmother.

She felt she needed to add more detail, sound a bit more intelligent, tip the scales. She straightened up. 'The one that made all that money was the same size as my teddy.' Strange how already that phrase slid off her lips as easily as Vaseline. *My teddy.* 'Twenty inches.' And then to sound more professional, she added, 'Fifty centimetres.'

Diana's response was a long appraising stare at her. Chi met her gaze unflinchingly.

'And of course . . .' Now Chi was glad she'd done a bit of homework, 'there is the Potteries connection.'

That earned her a harder stare over the rim of Ms Sutcliffe's glasses, and just one word of agreement. 'Quite.'

Ms Sutcliffe moved her gaze down to the bear. 'Without a more detailed provenance I might not get top price.'

'I realize that.'

'OK. I'll be in touch.'

Chi shook her head. 'I need to know now.'

'I'll be in touch,' Diana Sutcliffe repeated, her voice uncompromising.

Chi tried to gauge her response but Ms Sutcliffe was used to keeping her cards close to her chest. Her face gave away nothing. She drained her cup and clip-clopped out of the coffee bar. And Chi was as unsure as ever that she would get those tickets to Spanish Town.

TWENTY-NINE

Saturday 20 October, 4 p.m.

Chi and Jubilee were having a huge quarrel. Jubilee was fearful. 'I wish I'd never involved you.'

'Well, it was your idea to nick the bloody thing in the first place and turn it into cash.'

'Which I could have done without you.'

'Who was it who told you about that antique dealer?'

'And a lot of good it's done. Where is she now?'

It hadn't helped that Ms Sutcliffe had so far failed to phone. Right on cue, Chi's ringtone played a Caribbean calypso, 'Island in the Sun'. It wasn't quite Harry Belafonte but still . . .

Chi read the number and winked at Jubilee, ignoring the fact that her friend was wafting her hand away in a dismissive gesture.

'Hi.'

Diana Sutcliffe was very guarded in her response. 'I'm really not too sure about this,' she said.

'Oh?'

'Well, first of all you have no absolute proof of ownership.'

The wisest thing was to say nothing.

'And you want cash for it,' Ms Sutcliffe went on. 'Which then puts *me* in a very difficult position if and when *I* sell it.'

'Would it help if I signed something guaranteeing it was mine to sell?'

'Not really. But I do have contacts, particularly in the States, who would be interested in your teddy and not too worried about the lack of provenance.'

Chi knew then that greed was about to win over morals. Yay!

She was proved right. 'I can't get the money now until Monday.'

Chi held her breath.

'But having checked over the little bear, I'm convinced he is an authentic Steiff *Titanic* bear. I can give you £20,000. Cash.'

Chi waited, schooling herself. She must not seem too eager. Finally she managed a casual, 'OK. We can meet up. Monday?'

'Ye-es. Not that coffee bar, though. Somewhere a little more private. Secluded.'

Which worried Chi. Was she about to be mugged for the bear?

'How about The Roaches? Just at the foot of The Winking Man? There's a layby. Say midday?'

And the deal was clinched. Or was it, Chi wondered as she ended the call. Was she about to be double-crossed?

Jubilee was still glaring at her.

The best form of defence is . . . 'Twenty grand,' she said. 'So how would *you* have got the money?'

The ringtone playing again worried them both. What if Diana Sutcliffe was changing her mind?

But it wasn't. It was Kath. 'I want to meet your mate. Bring her over here so we can finalize plans.'

As Chi had anticipated, Jubilee took an instant dislike to Kath. And Kath, in turn, regarded her with suspicion and a certain amount of distaste. True to form, Kath Whalley mistrusted anyone black. They tried staring each other out but neither backed down. Chi, who was watching without moving or even saying anything, regarded the standoff without contribution. But give Kath her due – she knew how to pull strings. With a sharp tug. She did try. It just didn't work with Jubilee.

'So you're the famous Jubilee Watkins, newest friend of my best mate Chi.' Her words sounded like a taunt and Jubilee stared back with the briefest of nods, still regarding her warily.

'That's right.' Chi admired the way Jubilee responded with such confidence. Jubilee wasn't frightened of Kath. But that was only because she didn't know Kath like she did. She hadn't seen her happy face when putting the boot in, hadn't witnessed her sheer love of inflicting pain. Chi stayed silent in the background. This was between Kath and Jubilee.

Kath kicked off with, 'I need the old man. I have a purpose for him. You can have his fucking teddy bear. I'm not bothered about that. But I need *him*.'

'What for? For what can you possibly want a confused old gent? He doesn't even know what day it is, what year it is.'

'Never you mind. You're committing a theft anyway. Pinching

from the poor old geezer. I just want you to bring him along. I'll look after him.'

Chi flinched. She knew Kath's *looking after*. She tried to console herself with the fact that he was an old man with limited mental faculties and was probably on his way out anyway. He wouldn't understand what was going on, please God. Her thoughts moved on. The real object of Kath's exercise was DI Piercy. Not Mr Foster. He was just the goat.

Jubilee didn't respond for a moment but continued to study Kath. Chi could almost see her thought processes move along.

'When are you planning for?' And Chi could tell that Jubilee was trying to work this one out. Was there any chance she could get the money and scarper before Kath pounced?

Kath was stony-faced. 'Soon,' she said. 'Very soon. Maybe even tomorrow. When I say I need him, you just get him out of there. OK? You and Chi here can have your little toy.'

Chi didn't believe that one for a minute. Kath, turn down the chance of money? She was stringing them both along. But they only had to stall until Monday. She tried to convey some sort of message to Jubilee by moving her eyes to the side without Kath realizing.

But the next bit was true. 'I want the old man. I need the old man. He's going to help me do something.'

'What?'

That was when Kath got snappy. 'That's my business. Nothing to do with you.'

Jubilee gave Chi a helpless glance. They were both equally powerless. But Kath would expect Chi to prove her loyalty by persuading her friend to fall in with her plans and to her shame she spoke up. 'It's the only way we have any chance, Jubilee. She'll split otherwise.' Chi touched Jubilee's arm and spoke right into her ear. '*And you don't know what she's like when she's crossed.*'

Kath heard and looked pleased at that. Jubilee scratched her head and looked accusingly at Chi. 'You fall in with some mighty peculiar people, my friend.' But she nodded. Kath looked triumphant, Chi fearful. Again she tried to Morse out a message with her eyebrows and, she thought, this time Jubilee picked up.

We need to get the money, get the tickets, get out of here before all hell breaks loose.

Chi tried to justify her stance. It had been such a little crime. Taking candy from a baby. And she hadn't even done that. She hadn't done anything wrong except act as a fence. Jubilee had assured her that no one would notice except him. And he would soon forget. That was the way his mind worked now. She'd banked on it without realizing that this toy represented a memory buried so deep it predated his dementia. All Jubilee worked on was that Mr Foster forgot whether he'd had his tablets or his lunch or his cup of tea. He forgot which was his room or the way downstairs to the day room. Who would take any notice of him when he reported something everyone regarded as worthless was missing? He didn't really count.

Kath was rubbing the stump of her tooth. 'Are you working tomorrow, Jubilee?'

Jubilee nodded.

'What shift?' Kath asked smoothly.

'The evening one.'

Kath smiled. 'Lovely. Perfect.'

Then she turned to Chi. 'I hope you're not plotting to double-cross me. Get the thing, take the money and run. All the way to God knows where?'

Chi shook her head.

'And you really think someone's going to give you some money for an old toy that's over one hundred years old?'

Chi simply shrugged without even looking at Jubilee. She felt her face freeze. Their goal was so near and yet still out of reach.

Kath had the intuition of a medium. She knew this was a race.

'Get out, all of you,' she said. 'I want to speak to Missee Jubilee on her own.'

They piled out of the house, all grumbling. Leek has a micro-climate all of its own. Cold, damp rain sweeps in from the moors and chills. On the blast of wind comes the scent of lost sheep, heather, marsh and peat. And riding on that come the screams of birds of prey or fallen climbers: they all sound the same.

Minutes later the door opened and Jubilee came out.

Jubilee's colour was almost yellow. She stumbled through the door, her eyes wide with shock or horror. She clutched Chi's arm. 'You gotta get that money. And soon.' Chi was silent. She hated what she was doing and only diluted that hatred by telling herself that this had initially been Jubilee's idea. *Steal the old man's teddy bear*, she'd said. *It will set us up for life. No more than taking candy from a baby.*

But this was a different ball game. Peering over the precipice, foreseeing events as they would unravel, she felt sick.

One thing had simply led to another. She and Jubilee stared at each other. Jubilee spoke first, in a whisper. 'Make that call. Please?'

'OK, as soon as we're out of . . .'

Jubilee's grip on her arm tightened.

Chi already knew that Diana Sutcliffe would stick to the planned meeting on Monday. If she tried to force the meeting earlier it would simply make the dealer more suspicious and the sale would be lost. And along with that, all their plans.

So she stood still, shaking her head. 'It's not the right thing to do. We should stick to Monday. If she thinks we're desperate we might not get the money at all.' Chi knew there was no way Diana Sutcliffe was going to come up with the money before Monday. Slowly she shook her head and watched as a single fat tear rolled down Jubilee's face. 'I don't want to do this.'

'We don't have much choice. It's only a couple of days.'

Jubilee stared at her. 'You don't know what she wants me to do.'

'I can guess.'

'Really?' After giving her a hard stare, Jubilee then turned and walked slowly back down the road, towards the town, shoulders bent. Her attitude was one of abject despair.

Chi watched. Who could have known that their clever, neat and tidy plan would become infected by Kath Whalley?

As soon as Debs and Fifi had filed back in, Kath made her first mistake when she'd shared her plan a little too graphically. To be fair she had no option. She needed Debs to drive, the only one who could and had access to a car – her mother's which she 'borrowed' fairly frequently. And Kath had a role for Fifi too. Someone had to be around for the old guy. Keep an eye on him.

The trouble was she also shared another part of the plan, the bit about making sure Piercy came without her almost ever-present bodyguard. And the little trail of 'breadcrumbs' she planned to scatter along the way to distract any officers accompanying her prey. She knew Piercy was tenacious and she knew also that she was impatient. Lost in her plans, Kath failed to pick up on the doubtful glances exchanged by two of her foot soldiers.

Missing out on this vital clue she ploughed on, issuing instructions like a general going into battle. 'So, this is what we're going to do. All right?'

Debs started to speak, something about money. She'd picked up on whispered phone conversations between Jubilee and her one-time mate, Chi. And there had been mention of money. Debs was a greedy sort. And, like all her friends, in constant need of cash.

But she was shouted down by Kath, who had ideas and plans of her own. She grinned cheerfully and steamrollered across the subject, dishing out one of her mantras, 'In for a penny, in for a pound. That's what I say.'

Chi needed to know everything Kath was planning and immediately picked up on Fifi and Debs's reservation.

Perhaps Kath did too because she started yelling. 'I want him, tethered like a goat. And she'll come running.'

'Yeah,' Chi said, dipping her toe in, trying to suss out what exactly Kath's plans were, 'with that big detective sergeant who never leaves her side.'

Kath pinned her with a look. 'Let *me* worry about him.'

Chi glanced at the other two. Were they picking up on this? She wasn't sure. But both looked slightly shell-shocked. Maybe they already had?

Kath was away with the fairies now, spinning out her yarn. 'And what better place to catch our little lady than somewhere where a bloke had his head chopped off?'

Chi flicked her eyes from person to person. They knew a lot more than she did. 'It's just legend,' Debs put in, her own eyes flickering between Kath, Chi and Fifi, unsure who was going to come out of this least scathed. Fifi sniffed. She'd recently had a nose ring put in. It had got infected, maybe because she'd had a cold at the time but had insisted the guy proceed. But the pain, swelling and constant streaming nose had made her even more tetchy than usual. It didn't exactly enhance her looks either. What with that and the haircut she was bordering on repulsive.

As soon as she could, Chi slipped away.

THIRTY

When she was out of earshot, Chi rang Jubilee, trying to console her. 'Look, by Monday lunchtime we'll have twenty grand. That's ten grand each. We can get down to Heathrow and book our tickets. Get on the next available plane.'

But Jubilee was inconsolable. 'Monday will be too late,' she said. 'She wants me to . . .' The words stuck in her throat. 'And I don't like her,' she finished. 'She has a nasty streak in her.'

'She's not really my friend and I know all about her nasty streak.'

'Why did you tell her, Chi?'

'I didn't. She found out. Kath has a sort of instinct.'

'Is it the money she wants?'

Chi shook her head.

'So what is she intending to do with my poor man?'

It was up to Chi to convince her. 'She just wants to get even with the detective who put her behind bars,' she said. 'She won't want to do anything to your man. He's just there to tempt the detective somewhere remote.'

'So what will she do to the detective?'

Chi knew she had to sanitize this or everything would go awry. 'Just rough her up a bit. Nothing'll happen to your guy. He'll be safe.'

'You promise?'

'I promise.'

'I am very frightened,' was Jubilee's response, and Chi had to spend the next few minutes extolling Jamaica, adding in facts she'd learned from the internet. 'It's only just over nine hours away and then we'll be in the bars listening to reggae music and . . .'

On the end of the line, Jubilee was silent. Chi sensed her doubt. 'Listen, Jubilee, you don't want to cross Kath, I promise you.'

'Sometimes I wish I'd never met you.'

'But if it wasn't for me, you wouldn't have had that lead to the dealer, would you?'

'That is true.'

Chi didn't like it that Jubilee was taking a lot of persuading.

'There's only one way out of this. Fall in with Kath or you're dead meat.'

'I will regret this for the rest of my born days. I just want out.'

'OK, OK, calm down. It won't help if you get panicky. Just do it.'

'It's OK for you. You're not going to be asked to take an old man from his bed and hand him over to some psycho lady who will use him to get revenge on a police person, are you? I'm the one who will be implicated. Not you. I am the one who will betray someone who has trusted me.'

Chi was silent.

Fee-fi-fo-fum. I smell the blood of an Englishman.

Kath had spent hours thinking about this part of the plan. All she needed to do was remove Korpanski. But Korpanski had a family. If any one of his little brood was injured, he would take time off work, wouldn't he?

So . . . Eenie meenie miney mo. It was time to choose, fine-tune the plan.

Eenie was the obvious one. AKA Detective Sergeant Mike Korpanski. He of the bulging biceps. Take him from Piercy's side and she would be without her right-hand man. Her protector, behind whom she'd hidden probably on many occasions, but one time in particular which had reached the newspapers, when the DS had taken a bullet meant for his inspector. Although he would be the obvious target, the downside was that not only was the DS a big, burly man and thus harder to disable, but he was also a police officer. He would have instincts of self-protection.

So Meenie? The gangly boy he'd had his arm around as they had set off for their run. The boy? An easier target and much more vulnerable. He would be cycling or walking to school. How easy to stage an 'accident'. But there was a downside to this too. If he just had a couple of broken ribs, maybe Korpanski would still go to work. Doing his job. Kath's plan was to hang on to the old man for a week or so before instigating the next stage.

Part of the punishment would be the ridicule that the police, and in particular DI Piercy, would be subjected to when they failed to find the missing geriatric. She wanted Piercy to look a pregnant fool. And then some.

Miney? The girl, the Mummy-clone – she would be even easier to hit, but the same problem as her brother.

So Mo? The wife? Kath stubbed her cigarette out. The trouble with Mrs Korpanski was that she appeared to work irregular hours. That would mean staking out and waiting for a suitable opportunity.

It had to be Eeenie. She couldn't take too many chances. She wanted him out of the way. With injuries severe enough, even DS Korpanski couldn't drag half a leg into work.

Everything was falling into place very nicely.

Sunday 21 October, 9 p.m.
Ryland's Residential Home, Room 11

Jubilee was on the late shift and had worked out how to do this. She could hide in the linen store and wait. She had her mobile phone on Silent. She just had to keep telling herself. Tomorrow they would have the money. By Tuesday she could be on the plane. Nine hours later they would land in her country.

All she had to do was . . .

She swept conscience aside and popped the extra tablet out of its plastic bubble.

Zachary Foster looked up at her and smiled. And that smile touched her heart. It was childlike, trusting, innocent. Jubilee had been brought up a devout Christian. Did Christ look at Judas in that same trusting way when he had kissed him? Yes. Now she knew how Judas had felt too, how sour and deceitful that kiss, how he had known it would have been more honest had he slashed the Master with a sword.

Zachary Foster had the mind of a small child. He swallowed both tablets obediently, without question or demur, and she handed him his cocoa which he drank greedily. When he'd finished he had a rim of dark cocoa around his mouth and she wiped it clean. 'Can you help me find my . . .' His head was already on the pillow.

She leaned over him, speaking very softly so that nosey old

Alf Dean couldn't hear. 'I'll find him for you,' she whispered. 'We'll find him together.'

Zac Foster gave a sleepy smile, wrapped his arm around the teddy she'd bought from the charity shop and gave a soft snore. Jubilee touched the top of his head, feeling his hair, sparse and soft. 'Goodnight, Zachary,' she said. 'Goodnight.' He never would remember her name, how many tablets he'd taken. Anything that had happened. She thought back to previous nights when he'd curled his arm round the ancient teddy bear and lain back on the pillow, his face calm in repose, looking not old but wise and relaxed. Jubilee watched him, feeling the guilt creep up her body until it reached her brain. Trying to convince herself. It was *his* fault. He never should have told her the story, shown her the article. That had been the start of it all. The sheer enormous value of that tatty little toy he dragged around all day and cuddled all night. She'd been surprised he'd made such a fuss when it had vanished. She'd thought he would forget quicker. But he hadn't. His distress had remained. But when she was getting used to the guilt she realized. This was something she could use in readiness.

She practised saying it in all innocence. *He must have gone to search for his teddy bear.*

It sounded convincing. But she could hear the wobble in her voice, the words streaked with guilt.

THIRTY-ONE

Wednesday 31 October, 5 p.m.

Joanna was sitting in her office with Mike, fiddling with her biro, clicking it. Mike shot a glance across at her. 'Are you going to stop doing that, Jo? Or am I going to have to take it off you?'

'Sorry.' She put the pen back on her desk. 'This case is going nowhere. He's been missing for ten days and there's no sign of him. I've interviewed all the staff who were working on the

Sunday evening but they're not talking.' She frowned, lost in a thought. 'There's something behind this, Mike, but I can't make sense of it all. It's as though two minds are at work. Stealing an old man's teddy bear is one thing. Abducting him and possibly keeping him prisoner is another. The one is a simple theft. The other an apparently pointless crime. Any time soon, Rush will tell me to scale down the search. It's probably one of my last cases before this . . .' she patted her bulge, 'makes an entrance. Matthew thinks it'll be sooner than January and we're nearly into November. This case will stick with me, Mike. Annoy me. Infuriate me and always puzzle me if I don't work out what's happening and why.' She turned round to face him. Waddling into work made her blame the pregnancy on her complete absence of bright ideas. The child, she told herself, was robbing her of her spark, her brain. And a less than flattering photo of her, side on, had appeared under the headline of: *So this is our police force.*

She'd seen it and ground her teeth. 'I want to see this through, Mike,' she said softly.

Korpanski wasn't great at words of comfort. He gave his throat a noisy scrape and made another noncommittal sound before making an effort.

'Have you got any leads, Jo?'

She shook her head, picked up the biro again and knew something was niggling at her.

'I'll get there,' she said. 'I will. I won't let this case defeat me. Tomorrow I'm back to Ryland's. At least some of the answer is hiding there along with the "devoted" nurses and the elderly residents. One of those people knows exactly where Mr Foster is, why he needed to be abducted and the true story behind the theft of his toy, because I firmly believe it was a deliberate theft. And my money is on Jubilee Watkins.'

'OK,' he said.

'Mike, you may as well go home now. I'll see you in the morning.'

'Yeah.' He shut his computer down and tried to change the subject. 'As usual Ricky and I are going for a run. Then I'll head for the gym, and after that we might just do a bit of Trick-or-Treating.'

'Sounds fun,' she said abstractedly.

'See you tomorrow, Jo.'

'Yeah.'

7 p.m.

She was still there, still clicking the biro, still trying to put her thoughts into some sort of order. Most crimes, apart from drunken brawls, stupid lash-outs and idiotic driving, have some sort of logic behind them. In general the police try to link various crimes together and match them to known criminals, search for similar MOs. Criminals are, in general, unimaginative. They commit the same crime over and over again. Ninety per cent of crimes are committed by less than five per cent of people. Most of the general public are law-abiding. She was now certain in her own mind that Zac had been deliberately abducted. He hadn't simply stepped outside and got lost. Someone inside Ryland's had helped him and now kept him prisoner. The next step would be to look into the home addresses of Ryland's staff.

She should go home, shower, put her feet up, rest, have some tea, but something was biting at her, like a gnat. She stood up, slipped her coat on. She had an idea how to test her theory. And she wouldn't have any peace of mind until she'd tested it out.

Evenings at Ryland's appeared to consist of television and more television. And as many of the residents were apparently deaf, Joanna could hear the sound of canned laughter punctuating her steps up the corridor. Matilda Warrender had let her in, looking puzzled. 'Inspector?'

'I wondered if I might speak to one of your old ladies,' she said. 'The one who's always knitting.'

'Oh, you mean Shirley?'

'Is that her name?'

What strange places these homes were, she thought, as she followed the matron along the corridor. Places to take care of those who could no longer take care of themselves. Not happy, not particularly sad. This then was Limbo Land, but at least they were cared for.

Shirley Barnstaple was still knitting; the other lady was still bad-temperedly trying to fit pieces into the jigsaw puzzle. Pieces were scattered over the floor and the old man was still walking around muttering to himself. Nothing, it seemed, had changed.

Shirley looked up. 'Hello, Inspector,' she said. 'Do you know I'm almost a hundred?'

'No, you're not . . .' One of the nurses who had been attending to another patient looked across. 'You're only eighty-seven.'

Shirley looked affronted. 'Well, I'm a lot nearer a hundred than you are, my dear.' She put her knitting down on her lap and folded her arms.

Joanna sat down beside her as the nurse burst out laughing good-naturedly. 'I won't argue with that, Shirley,' she said. Then addressing Joanna, added, 'They get you like that in here, you know.' And she continued brushing the other patient's hair.

'Shirley,' Joanna began, 'you remember the teddy bear that Zac used to drag around with him?'

'Yes.' Her head turned, eyes bright as a robin's. Curious too – intelligent and still possessing of a sharp intellect.

'Did Zac tell you anything about the teddy?'

'Yes,' she said slowly. 'He said his mother gave it to him. On account of . . . Now what was it on account of? Something to do with Hanley, I think.' She looked dubious, glanced down at her knitting, as though she wanted to continue clacking away, not be bothered struggling with memory.

A nurse came in with a cup of tea and Joanna recognized Jubilee Watkins, whose eyes were flickering, her face haunted. Her hand, as she held out the cup, shook, the cup rattling on the saucer. Joanna watched the cup, then the splash of liquid. Then she looked up into Jubilee's dark eyes with their curling lashes. Jubilee made an attempt at a smile but something had happened to change the girl. She had appeared happy at the first interview, ebullient even. Now she looked shamed. Joanna stood up. 'Jubilee,' she said softly, so no one else in the room could hear. 'Is there anything you want to tell me?'

The nurse shook her head.

8 p.m.
Mill Street

Kath was waiting for a call and was annoyed to hear the noise from upstairs. The old boy was kicking out.

She released herself from the sticky couch and stuck her head out through the door. 'Shut the fuck up there,' she yelled. 'I'm waiting for a call.'

Fifi stood at the top of the stairs. 'Sorry, Kath. He's a bit . . .'

'Well, give him some of those pills that black woman sent with him.'

Fifi looked confused. 'How many?'

'I don't bloody well know. I'm not a pharmacist, you know.'

'Yeah, but if I give him too many he might . . .'

She needed him alive, bleating.

'Just one then. One can't hurt him.'

She slammed the door, bounced back on to the couch and glanced at her phone. She was nearly there.

Maybe soon, she thought, it would be time to rope another family favour.

When Eenie was out of the way it would be time for stage two. Which (she was rather pleased with this) consisted of a sighting of the 'missing' man from an (anonymous) member of the general public. Hayley, her stupid sister, could make the call, citing the place where she had seen him. A very unlikely place with a bad history. And then? Kath stuck her index finger in her mouth and felt the familiar sharpness of her broken tooth. Anticipating the drama ahead she smiled. God, she was enjoying this.

Her phone rang.

THIRTY-TWO

Wednesday 31 October, 8.20 p.m.

Joanna used her phone to google the two words and she sat back and read the story.

In her office, Matilda Warrender had also googled 'the *Titanic* bear' and now was recalling some of Zac's words.

His Auntie Elinor had been his mother's aunt. She had drowned or died of the cold in that freezing sea. Her body had never been recovered. They had had compensation, which was as tainted an amount of money as had ever been minted. In Auntie Elinor's memory they had spent it on one of the Steiff memorial teddy bears and his mother had given it to him, making Zac give a sacred vow that he would keep it for ever and ever.

Should she ring the police now? Or in the morning?

8.35 p.m.

DS Mike Korpanski was a creature of habit. On Wednesdays he went for a brief run with his son, Ricky, and then he headed for the gym. And this Wednesday was no exception. He dropped Ricky back at the house. He still had some homework to do. And then DS Mike Korpanski started a brisk jog towards the gym, The Fit Factory. Only he never got there.

As he was heading down the road, a car accelerated behind him. He heard the noise. And then he felt the impact.

9.30 p.m.

Joanna received the call at 9.30 p.m., having finally made it home. She reached across for her mobile phone and read the number. And knew immediately something bad had happened.

'Ma'am.' She stiffened. No one at their peril ever called her *ma'am* or *boss* or *guv* or anything else that spoke of rank. To all she was Joanna, except in particular circumstances.

'It's DC Alan King, ma'am.'

She waited, heart hammering.

'DS Korpanski, ma'am.'

'Mike? What about him?'

Out of the corner of her eye she was aware that Matthew was watching with concern. He had this idiotic belief that she should constantly be kept calm. And this wasn't calm.

'He's been involved in an accident, ma'am.' DC Alan King ploughed on. 'Looks like a hit-and-run.'

She struggled to keep her voice level. 'What sort of state is he in?'

'We don't have an update on his condition.'

She waited for more. It was the silence that finally broke her. 'Where is he?'

More silence. Then, 'Where *is* he?'

Matthew had risen to his feet, hand up.

'Where *is* he?'

'They've taken him to the University Hospital of . . .'

Now both Matthew's hands were held up and he was mouthing, 'No. Joanna.'

It was as though she hadn't seen him. She hung up, grabbed her car keys, and was out of the door before he could react. For a moment Matthew Levin stood motionless.

Then he too was out of the door. He reached the car just as she was starting to reverse down the drive. He yanked the door open and sat down in the passenger seat. He'd play this a different way.

'I think I might be of some help, Jo.'

And she dropped her head on to his shoulder. 'Thank you.'

As she drove her mind was racing through all the possibilities. Dead. Brain damaged, spinal injury, amputation. The roads were quiet, the journey quick, and afterwards she would remember none of it.

Matthew had a permit to park at the hospital and at this time of night the car park had plenty of spaces.

Fran Korpanski had not been so lucky. Not having the right change, she was minutes behind Joanna and Matthew. They met

outside the entrance to the Major Injuries Unit and greeted each
other frostily. Fran was a nurse herself but not at this hospital.
Joanna managed, 'How is he?'

'I don't know, Joanna. I only know—' She broke off to greet
Matthew with a bit more of a smile. Fran Korpanski was only
too aware of her husband's close relationship with the DI and
had never (would never, she had said) forgiven the inspector for
putting her husband in harm's way. Or, as she put it, risking his
life. 'If this is anything to do with you,' she said, and Joanna
shrank from the hatred in Korpanski's wife. All she could do
was shake her head. But Mrs Korpanski hadn't finished. 'If this
is your fucking fault . . .' The profanity was all the more shocking
coming from Mike's diminutive, normally polite, controlled wife.
'He wasn't working,' Joanna said, stung into defence. 'He was
heading for the gym, wasn't he?'

Fran simply pressed her lips together as though holding back
another avalanche of profanities and accusations.

They entered together and approached the desk. Joanna hung
back. However close her working relationship was with Mike,
Fran was his wife. 'I think you have my husband here?'

The woman behind the desk looked up. 'Name?'

'Michael Korpanski.'

The woman looked flustered. 'Yes. We do have your husband
here. You're Mrs Korpanski?' Fran nodded, tears pooling in her
eyes.

'Would you like to take a seat? A doctor will be with you
in a minute.'

Fran Korpanski sank into a chair on the front row, Joanna and
Matthew a few chairs behind. The sounds and activities of the
unit a mere background.

The doctor, wearing green scrubs, was marked by a lanyard
and a stethoscope looped around his neck. The receptionist
pointed out Fran and he came straight over to her, introducing
himself as Dr Stefan. He had brown hair and sympathetic eyes
and spoke with a slightly Eastern European accent. He ushered
Mrs Korpanski away from the crowds and towards a door which
he closed behind them.

Joanna looked at Matthew. 'What does this mean?'

'I don't know, Jo.' Even Matthew looked worried. 'Maybe not good news. They tend to want a quiet room to . . . Maybe . . .' He covered her hand with his own. 'There's no point trying to second-guess.'

Joanna felt sick. Not helped by the baby bouncing around as though it was joyful. Matthew saw the activity underneath her top and smiled. Put his hands there, reassuring his son – or daughter.

Don't say it, she thought. *Not that lives come and go. Not . . . The Circle of Life. Korpanski cannot be dead. Or maimed. The memory flooded back of his strong shoulders and powerful arms, of the wry smile when he listened to her rantings, the warmth of those dark eyes and the unending, unquestioning loyalty and friendship. Without him she would be diminished.*

The door opened and Fran came out. Looking smaller than when she had gone in. She stumbled back towards them, tears spilling down her cheeks, the doctor a pace behind, his arms held out as though he was worried she might fall.

Fran stood in front of Joanna and met her eyes with a fierce hatred that shocked even her. 'They're trying to save his leg,' she said and sank down into the chair. 'He's in the operating theatre now.'

Joanna looked at Matthew and started to speak. 'Is there anything . . .'

But Fran Korpanski got there first. She pointed her index finger at Joanna. 'This had better not be *anything* connected with you.'

Joanna bit her lip. *How could it be?* she thought. *How could it be?*

Matthew managed to fill in the gap. 'Is there anything you want us to do, Fran?'

At which point Fran stuck her small chin in the air and addressed him. 'Yes,' she said. 'There is. Let them know at the station,' she managed steadily, 'and tell them all to stay away. He's my husband and we want some privacy.'

And Matthew nodded.

THIRTY-THREE

Sunday 21 October, 9.30 p.m.

I t isn't hard to pretend you've left. No one watches you. No one checks. They just assume when you open and close a door that you have gone.

Eleven o'clock, Kath had said. Just over an hour to wait. Jubilee sat and waited for her phone screen to light up.

11 p.m.

She heard the car creep over the gravel. Quiet as a ghost walk but she was listening out for it. The staff were in the kitchen, washing up the cups from the evening drinks. They would be helping themselves to Horlicks, cocoa, tea, coffee. It was a nightly ritual. They would have a drink and soon they would retire to the coffee room. She crept upstairs. Zac was hunched up in bed, lying in the foetal position, snoring softly. Something was puncturing his dreams. He was twitching and muttering something unintelligible. She bent down and whispered in his ear. 'I can help you find Teddy.' He sat up, recognized her face, slipped his hand in hers, confident *she* would help him. She raised her finger to her lips.

'Sssh. You mustn't make a sound.' And he smiled, trusting. She slid his slippers on, opened the wardrobe door. 'You'll need a coat. It's cold outside.'

She sat with him while the night staff retired to their room and soon the entire home was silent. Then she smiled. 'Now remember. Not . . . a . . . sound. I'll help you down the stairs.'

It was slow going, one step at a time, but finally they had reached the bottom. She led him along the corridor. He waited while she unlocked the French windows, watched her replace the chair against the wall and then followed her through.

She took his hand, closed the door softly behind her, and led him down the steps towards the waiting car.

She didn't feel cruel, she didn't feel a traitor. Not then. She felt, like him, that this was an adventure.

It wasn't until she'd closed the car door on Zachary Foster and had seen his face, completely bewildered, hands stretched out towards her. He didn't understand. *It won't be for long,* she'd mouthed. But then she'd heard Kath speak to him. 'Shut it, you fucking aged saddo. You can stop whining about your stupid . . .' She affected a silly childish voice. 'Teddy bear.'

The words were accompanied by an eye-watering slap on Zachary's thin shoulders and he'd dropped his face into his hands in an attitude of despair and complete bewilderment.

And then the car had whisked off and Jubilee stood still on the drive. What had she done?

She felt terrible.

She'd walked back to her flat, seeing his face everywhere. And even trying to replace Zac's terrified eyes with an image of her and Chi sprawling on a beach – rum in hand, white sand, blue water – all she could see were the sharks circling. And one of those looked just like Kath.

Perhaps it would have been some consolation to know that Chi was feeling just as bad. Sitting in the back of the car, Zac between her and Kath, she could feel the old man's bones, his hand shaking, sensed his confusion. Though the car was warm – almost stuffy – and he was wearing a warm coat over his pyjamas, the old man was shivering. She hadn't actually met him before. This reality was a shock; the tethered goat to keep Kath at bay. She'd never considered him as a person – simply the owner of an object which would fly her out of here. Now, as she looked at his face, Chi felt curious. How much of this was sinking in? How much of this would he remember? Would he be able to identify faces? In which case Kath wouldn't risk it. Which would make her and Jubilee an accessory to murder. Did he realize he was in danger?

How much could he feel fright?

Could he sense that he was about to be used as bait? It didn't help that he was now looking at her, his face screwed up like a child's, the appeal mute but perfectly clear. *Help me.*

Kath shot her a warning look and she settled back, returning to the uncomfortable thoughts. This was not how she'd imagined it. She hadn't realized she'd feel so awful, so guilty, so full of pity for the vulnerable. She tried to ignore him but Zac Foster slipped his hand into hers and she knew he'd transferred the trust he'd had for Jubilee to her.

Bad choice.

Monday 22 October, midday
The Roaches near Leek

It seemed as though The Winking Man was watching over her as she pulled over to the verge.

Diana Sutcliffe was already there in a blue Mercedes. Chi had persuaded a friend to drive her out there. There was no way she would have trusted Debs. If Debs had caught a glimpse of this much money she would have wanted a cut. And that didn't fit in with their plans. Chi got out of her car and walked over to Diana, who leaned across and threw open the passenger door. They smiled at one another, neither quite trusting the other. Chi's eyes dropped to the brown envelope which she hoped contained the money. Slowly she drew the teddy bear out of the bag and held it up. She could read the lust in the dealer's eyes and knew she would be making plenty out of this. Diana Sutcliffe gave the bear a quick once-over then handed over the money: £20,000 in £50 notes in £5,000 bundles with the bank's paper band still intact. Chi checked it. All there. She made Chi sign a piece of paper confirming ownership and the sale and watched as Chi filled in a false name and false address. She had the feeling the dealer didn't really care. When asked to provide provenance she would be equally inventive and dishonest. Chi put the money in the carrier bag while Ms Sutcliffe took possession of the bear, wrapping him in some tissue paper she'd obviously brought. Her fingers felt the wad of notes. Surely now they could get the hell out of here? The plan was to catch the bus from Hanley down to Heathrow Airport and get the first available flight out. They might only be able to be there for thirty days initially, but they'd deal with that when they were there. There were plenty of illegals in most countries. They'd just be joining the worldwide throng. The main thing was to get out of Leek. Get away from Kath.

She had the money. The friend drove her back to the town. Chi gave her a twenty-pound note she had in her pocket and the mate was well happy with that. Chi wandered across to Jubilee's bedsit.

Which was where she hit a snag.

Jubilee refused to fly. From somewhere or other she'd grown a conscience.

'I can't go until I know he's safe.'

Once she'd got over the shock, Chi tried every argument she could think of. From, 'He'll be all right. Kath'll let him go,' to, 'it won't make any difference' and 'it's too risky for us to stay'. But Jubilee flatly refused to leave Leek until she was sure Zachary Foster was safe.

Chi had no intention of leaving without Jubilee, so if Jubilee refused to leave Chi was stuck in Leek. For the time being. It wouldn't be for long, she told herself. Kath would soon make her move.

But Kath was taking her time, perfecting her plan. She couldn't afford for this to go wrong. She'd spent too many years plotting. And there was something she hadn't expected – savouring the anticipation of the moment, which meant she lived it over and over again in her mind.

Wednesday 24 October, 8.15 a.m.
Mill Street

The 'goat' was proving a problem. Kath hadn't bargained for this. She hadn't really thought of the old man as a person, only as a means to an end. The sprat to catch the mackerel. The goat to catch the tiger. But the fucking goat was misbehaving. She'd gone up to give him a drink as Fifi had headed off to the doctor's for some antibiotics to treat her infected nose, which had become swollen, red and very painful. Debs was out getting some shopping in and Chi was at work. So it was left to Kath to keep an eye on the goat. Not a natural nursemaid.

She put the cup of tea down on a chest of drawers, which was a good job as he lunged at her. She fended off his weak assault with a sharp slap of her own which didn't appear to teach him anything. He just glared at her. But she didn't want him too obviously damaged. He needed to look as though he'd just wandered out of the home and got lost for just over a week. That was the little story she was telling herself. Not that he'd been abducted and tied to a bed by a team of psychos, which was what people sometimes called her and her mates. Only the once.

Truth was she hadn't thought what to do with the old man once he'd fulfilled his function of luring Piercy to Lud's Church. And she didn't much care. She could let him go but he wouldn't get very far. However, trailing him back to civilization would prove tedious to her. Elated, she planned to spend the evening celebrating Piercy's demise with a pub crawl. The place would soon have its quota of coppers. *They* could find him.

But now, when she looked at him, she realized she might have to deal with him too because she didn't know how much of this was sinking in. She wasn't sure whether there was any point in making up some cock-and-bull story to explain his plight to him. Would he remember it anyway? But it was just possible that the old guy did have a working brain cell after all, and whatever she told him he'd remember and spit it out *when* or rather *if*, by some holy miracle, he was rescued alive. Debs had provided an explanation to him of sorts, patting his hand. 'Think of it as a bit of a holiday, mate,' which had shut him up for a bit but now he'd got disruptive again. They'd tried locking him in the bedroom but he'd banged on the window so hard she'd worried he might break it. And then there'd be trouble. There were thin walls either side and plenty of nosey neighbours round here always on the lookout to complain. And the last thing she wanted was the police hammering on her door. So far, sensing the potential for trouble, apart from the guy next door, most of the neighbours had given Kath a wide berth. But if they heard an old man yelling and shouting or even worse banging on the window they'd soon start dialling 999 with their nosey, inter- fering little fingers. This was not the right setting for her little drama. So she had no option but to tie him to the bed and feed him with some of the tablets Chi had got from Jubilee. It didn't take long for them to work. Ten minutes later he was quiet. In fact, looking down at him now, Kath wondered whether they'd overdone it a bit. He looked zonked and was breathing funnily. She kicked the bed and Zac's eyes fluttered. Not dead yet then. And she left the room. Not long now. Leave it a couple more days. She had another job to do.

THIRTY-FOUR

Thursday 1 November, 7 a.m.

'Darling.' Matthew was shaking her shoulder.

There was a brief second before she put events in order. 'Mike?'

'I've rung the hospital and had a word with the medics.' He sat down on the edge of the bed.

She couldn't bear to ask but appealed mutely.

'The operation went well apparently but it was a bad break. Tibia and fibula both with compound fractures. They're notoriously difficult and slow to heal. They just have to see whether the blood supply is sufficient.'

'And if it isn't?'

Matthew looked away and didn't even try to answer her query. 'Hopefully it will. He's a fit guy, Jo, but it's going to be a long time before he's back at work.'

'That doesn't matter. Oh, Matt,' she said, clinging to him. 'This is awful. Is Fran still with him?'

'Yeah.'

'Who's with Ricky and Joss?'

'Her mum.'

He hesitated before continuing. 'You'll know more about this than I, but there was a message on your phone from the station. You were asleep. From CCTV footage it appears it was a deliberate hit-and-run.'

'Deliberate?'

He nodded and she sat up. 'I need to get into work.'

'Yeah. Me too.'

'I wonder if they'll let me see him.'

'Jo.' Matthew put his hand on her arm. 'Darling. I wouldn't if I were you. I'd just leave him with Fran. She won't appreciate your turning up.'

As she climbed out of bed she knew she couldn't explain to her husband how excluded, how shut out and how frightened she felt.

But she had her compensations.

Matthew held her to him, kissed her hair, put his arm around her shoulders. She looked up into his face.

By eight o'clock she was at the station searching through CCTV footage. Everyone knew, of course. There was an air of gloom, as though the building and all its personnel had been swathed in dark gauze. In every corner theories were being swapped. It was deliberate, it was an accident. A revenge for someone Mike had exposed. A couple of joyriders out of control. But most of all it exposed their vulnerability. Everyone felt exposed. It could have been them.

From Fran Korpanski there was not one word, and when Joanna rang the hospital at 8.30 she was given little detail except to be told he was currently in a stable condition. What did that mean? Desperate to find out more, she texted Matthew.

Any chance you could get a bit more of an update on Mike? Please? Love you X

The accident had been recorded from two angles with well-appointed CCTV cameras mounted on shops. Just over a year ago, the police had liaised with the town council on the siting of CCTV cameras and this collaboration had paid off. A white van coming towards Mike, veering on to the pavement. There was little doubt DS Korpanski had been deliberately targeted. Joanna winced as she watched the impact and saw Mike lying still, blood pumping from his lower right leg and the van speeding off. He could have died.

DC Alan King was watching over her shoulder. 'Can you enhance it?'

'Already done, Joanna,' he said. 'We got the number plate. The van was nicked from outside a builder's yard two nights ago.'

'So this was premeditated.'

Alan King nodded.

'And it's been kept somewhere overnight?'

He nodded and she swivelled around to meet his eyes. 'Don't tell me,' she said wearily, 'it's been torched.'

'Yeah.'

'So will we get anything from it?'

'Probably not.'

11 a.m.

Telling her fellow officers had been hard, watching their faces and sharing the news that DS Mike Korpanski, her (beloved) colleague had sustained a serious injury and it was touch and go whether his leg might have to be amputated. All she read in their expressions was shock.

No one said anything personal but she felt bound to add, 'Fran's with him at the moment.' And though the news had already spread she finished with, 'It looks like it was a hit-and-run and that DS Korpanski was deliberately targeted.'

She didn't add a Why? A Why him? or Who? All these questions would be unravelled later when they had some hard evidence, although everyone knows that to torch a vehicle after it's been involved in a serious incident is the best way to destroy forensic debris.

By midday the burnt-out shell of the van was on a low-loader heading for the police pound. It had been found near a small trading estate off Ball Haye Road, only half a mile from where it had been stolen. It was an old vehicle without a sophisticated burglar alarm or anti-theft device. Which again pointed to someone with criminal knowledge.

She'd finished the briefing with a statement. 'I'll be taking the case along with a couple of uniformed, Jason, Dawn and Bridget, together with DC King and DC Gino Salvi.' DC Salvi was a newcomer to the team and Leek. An Italian father and Staffordshire mother had produced a black-haired, blue-eyed son, the apple of his mother's eye. He'd endured the ragging of the team when his father arrived, smacking a sound kiss on his cheek and presenting him with boxes of delicacies at regular intervals. His parents owned a small Italian restaurant on the Stone Road. So far, as a detective, he hadn't exactly excelled, but he listened intently and, Joanna felt, was prepared to learn. He also had an engaging grin which was hard to ignore.

It was DC Salvi who asked a question. 'What about Mr Foster's case?'

'DC Phil Scott will continue to pursue Mr Foster's disappearance. I've kept him up to speed and he'll report back to me if there are any developments. So . . .' She waited but no one commented. Everyone knew how close the two were. It was natural she should investigate what looked like a deliberate assault.

'Our first job is to visit the scene and see what we can get from that.'

Their nods were enough. Some of the officers' eyes were warm with sympathy.

She wished she could delegate her next job, which was to inform CS Gabriel Rush of the circumstances of Mike's accident. Relations between her and the senior officer who had replaced her beloved Chief Superintendent Arthur Colclough (now retired) had never been good. After the paternalistic Colclough, Rush had come across as a cold fish. Hostile to his predecessor's 'pet'. With the result that they had not gelled. Her failure to locate the missing geriatric and the resultant negative headlines were hardly going to put her in his good books. And now Korpanski had sustained serious injuries in a hit-and-run. The only silver lining was that Chief Superintendent Gabriel Rush was not based in Leek but in Hanley, so a phone call should suffice.

She still dreaded it.

'Sir.'

He interrupted, his voice sharp. 'I heard about DS Korpanski. How is he?'

She'd not heard back from Matthew and, as anticipated, Fran had not been in touch. Hardly a surprise for a wife who considered her husband's career and colleagues a serious threat to happy family life.

'I have no update, sir, except that he's come through the operation and they're waiting to see if he can keep the leg.'

The image that shot through her mind was too painful. She

swallowed and luckily Rush took up the conversation. 'It was a hit-and-run, I understand.'

'Yes, sir.'

'I take it you have several officers on the case?'

'Yes, sir. We've located the van, which was torched. It's been sealed and towed.'

'Stolen?' Rush was a man of few words.

'Yes, sir.'

He paused and she sensed a frown. 'You haven't had much taking without consent in Leek?'

'No, sir. Not since we put the Riley brothers into the Young Offenders.'

A deep sigh. 'Let's hope there isn't another couple of yobs heading down that road.'

'Yes, sir.'

'You think a local or a couple of guys from the Potteries or even farther afield?'

'We're keeping an open mind, sir.'

A pause. 'You'll be visiting him?'

'Family only at the moment, sir.'

'Right.'

He paused. 'Are you treating this as a chance hit-and-run, or do you think it was a deliberate assault on Korpanski as a serving officer?'

She could only repeat, 'We're keeping an open mind, but looking into various cases he's been involved in. Looking at the CCTV it does appear that DS Korpanski was deliberately targeted.'

'I see. Well, keep me informed.'

'Yes, sir.'

A long sigh before he took up another unwelcome subject. 'I take it there's been no sign of your missing man, Piercy?'

'No, sir.'

A deeper sigh this time.

'Tell me, Piercy, do you have *any* leads?'

She didn't dare tell him about the teddy bear, the anomaly about the doors or the suspicion that a member of staff had been involved. She was looking bad enough as it was.

'I have a few ideas, sir.'

He wasn't going to let her off the hook. 'Which are?'

'I wonder if he was abducted.'

'Abducted! Why?'

'It's just a theory I'm working on.'

The pause seemed to contain astonishment. Had circumstances been less dreadful, Joanna would have smiled. She was actually managing to surprise the chief superintendent? But he hadn't quite let go. He changed his question to, 'How? You think it was an inside job?'

Knowing he wouldn't see, Joanna nodded instead of answering.

At which point her mobile pinged with a message.

Korpanski's awake and talking. He's asked to speak to you.

And it gave her the perfect excuse to end the conversation.

'I've just had a message from the hospital that DS Korpanski is awake and asking to speak to me.'

'Well, you'd better go then.'

Thank you, Mike.

THIRTY-FIVE

Thursday 1 November, midday
Royal Stoke University Hospital Orthopaedic Ward

She hardly recognized him. Lying in bed, one leg suspended from a hook, pieces of metal sticking out, a bandage round his head, two black eyes. Had it not been for Fran sitting bolt upright by his side she might have walked right past his bed.

'I didn't expect this,' she said.

Fran simply stared at her while Mike did his best to smile. He raised his hand. 'Hi, Jo,' he said.

'Mike.'

She wanted to lean across and kiss his forehead, but not with his wife watching. Instead she sat down by Fran's side, who was doing an excellent job of pretending she wasn't there.

He had a blood drip running into his arm. His dark eyes fixed on her. He was trying to tell her something. Again he tried to smile, with no more success. Korpanski arched his back as though in pain and Fran instantly stood up. 'I'll fetch the nurse.'

As soon as she'd gone, Korpanski fixed his eyes on her. 'It was deliberate,' he managed. 'You know you said something about routine?'

She nodded. 'It was waiting for me. I saw it pulled up on the side street. When I jogged down St Edward's Street, it came towards me.'

'Did you see the driver?'

He shook his head, frowning. 'Just a glance. Two men, I think. They came straight at me, Jo. I thought I was going to die.'

And then she did bend over and kiss his forehead. 'Jeez, Mike,' she said. 'Why?'

He tried to shrug but at a guess his collarbone was broken too. It was a disjointed effort. 'I don't know,' he said. Then just as his wife re-entered the room, he spoke again. 'Be careful, Jo.'

She nodded, not really understanding, instead focusing on the information she had. 'We've bagged up the van, sealed off the area.'

'Stolen?'

She nodded.

Fran was like a little ball of fire. 'That's enough,' she said, practically stamping her feet. 'If he hadn't asked to see you, I would have kept him quiet.'

The nurse she'd summoned watched before speaking to her patient. 'Are you in pain, Michael?'

He nodded and she checked his drugs chart while Joanna turned to Fran. 'It's OK,' she said. 'I'm going.' She tried to cool her anger. 'He just wanted to set the investigation going. We'll take a fuller statement at some later date but, as you know, the sooner the better.'

It did nothing to improve Fran's fury. She simply scowled at Joanna and Joanna left.

THIRTY-SIX

Sometimes, Joanna thought, when you visit the scene of an accident, you are surprised at the lack of physical clues. People could die and leave little trace. Joanna had visited the scenes of fatal stabbings and seen hardly a blood-stain. She'd entered houses where there had been a fatal domestic dispute and seen all in order. People could be abducted, as in the case of Zachary Foster, or murdered, or suffer life-changing injuries and leave no evidence. But the point where Mike had been knocked down was well marked. Not only by police tape. A shop window was cracked; there was blood on the pavement, broken glass, a piece of black plastic – at a guess some of the bumper. And a couple of long rubber tyre marks. Two personnel in white forensic suits were gathering evidence and the entire width of the pavement was marked off with police tape and indicator arrows. She approached the team. 'Anything?'

One of them shook his head. 'Nothing new,' he said. 'Nothing we didn't already know as we have the vehicle. Looks like the vehicle came from the side street.'

'That's what Korpanski said.'

'You've seen him?'

'He asked to see me.'

'How is he?'

'Not great.'

'How's his leg?'

'Looks like time will tell,' she said. 'Apparently it's too early to say.'

The two guys couldn't find any words except to look at each other, their faces grave.

'Deliberate targeting, Joanna. Hit-and-run. Stolen vehicle.'

And she could do little but ask they be thorough in their

search for any evidence as to who had tried to murder her best colleague.

Then she left the scene.

Friday 2 November, 10.05 a.m.

In the house in Mill Street, Zachary was sitting on the bed, looking around, when Fifi entered the room. 'Hey, old man,' she said. 'You want a cup of tea?'

'I . . .' and Zachary stopped as he looked at her. Which sent the creeps up Fifi. What if he recognized her when all this was over? She was pretty recognizable with her swollen, red nose. She'd kill the guy who'd suggested she have a bloody nose ring.

Maybe she should wear a face mask like she'd seen in the movies?

Zac frowned and shook his head, puzzled, unable to work any of it out.

11 a.m.

Kath was pleased with herself. Her little plan was going like clockwork. So far. Thanks to her magic pills, Zac spent most of the time sleeping. The rest of the time he wasn't eating much. Fifi had given him a slice of pizza but she'd said he'd had trouble eating it, partly because he was so sleepy and partly because he did not have a full set of teeth. She and Debs took it in turns to keep an eye on the old guy while Kath laid her plans for the next stage. Apart from the fact that he pissed (sometimes in his pyjama trousers), and when he was awake he whinged, they weren't complaining, although Fifi said he hardly shut up about his missing teddy. She said she'd tried giving him a teddy she'd nicked off her little sister, but he kept throwing it back at her so she took it off him. 'You'd have thought,' Fifi said when she was telling Kath her woes, 'that one bloody teddy's the same as any other to a dement.'

Kath didn't respond. She was in her own little world where Piercy was begging for mercy and she kicked her right in the teeth. Then in her big, pregnant belly. Then in her head, then in her . . . She looked up. 'What'd you say?'

Fifi harrumphed and Kath returned to her world. It was all a matter of timing, she thought. Early afternoon would be the best. Get him out there, make the call. By four thirty it would be dusk. Just the right time for sending her out to the moors. And to delay her little team she would scatter breadcrumbs. The old guy's slippers. Maybe a bit of white hair caught on a twig. Make it convincing.

She almost rubbed her hands together. This was better than a snort of cocaine.

Feeling ignored, Fifi stomped back upstairs. With the result that the next time Zac complained it was the wrong teddy, he got short shrift from his jailer. 'I know that, you stupid fucker,' she snarled, 'but it's the only one we've got so you'd better get used to it.'

But Zac didn't. He threw it to the floor with a defiant glare and the sad little toy lay there, twisted, unwanted, unloved and neglected.

Debs was even shorter tempered with him than Fifi. When he was actually awake enough to start complaining, she was tempted to smack him, but she held back. This mad old man was vital to Kath's plans. If she so much as touched him, Kath would vent her anger right on her head. She'd seen it happen before – Kath lose her temper with one of her mates. Being a mate of Kath's didn't protect you from her violence or her anger. So she kept the old man as quiet as possible by feeding him the sleeping tablets. Jubilee had warned her via Chi they were strong and he couldn't have more than one in twenty-four hours. But Kath took no notice of that and so neither did Debs or Fifi. Chi was giving them a wide berth and when they did see her she was on edge, but Jubilee had turned up a couple of times to check they were looking after him properly. 'Where'd you get a conscience from?' Kath jeered and twisted the knife. 'If it wasn't for you, your patient wouldn't even be here. It's all your fault. And don't think the police won't put two and two together. They'll know it was an inside job. Anyway . . .' Kath's eyes narrowed. 'I thought once you'd got the money, you and Chi was going to do a runner.'

But Jubilee was one of the few people in the world who was not intimidated by Kath. She'd found some strength from somewhere. So she responded carefully. 'Chi and I might take a small holiday. When Mr Foster is back in his bed in Ryland's Residential Home. Now let me see him.'

All three of the captors looked guilty when Jubilee entered Zac's room. Her eyes took in the bindings that kept him on the bed, his stertorous breathing, and her nose recognized the smell. She turned on Debs, who was nearest. 'Why are you not looking after him properly?'

Debs had her answer ready, up her sleeve. 'Because I'm not a fucking nurse.'

'You are giving him too much sedation and you need to wash him.'

Debs stared her out but Kath looked at her, sensing the potential for trouble.

'OK,' she said.

Jubilee bent over the bed. 'You will soon be back, Mr Foster.' And she kissed his forehead.

Kath was glad to see her go.

When she'd seen her out, she sat rubbing her finger over the broken tooth.

She was nearly there.

As Jubilee walked back down the road, she was sick with guilt and worry. She had been forced to do this and right now she was regretting it bitterly. Even conjuring up her dream of Jamaica wasn't helping. The images of white sand, blue sea, green palms didn't look quite so attractive now and, besides, she'd heard in the news yesterday that there was a big problem of gun crime over there and tourists were being advised to steer clear of Kingston. And then the newscaster had added, 'And the gun violence is spreading to other towns too.'

And when Chi rang her they had both worried. 'Straight from the devil right into the deep blue sea. The world is full of villains.'

Chi's response had been, 'At least Kath doesn't carry a gun.'

'Because she doesn't need to. That person can do it all with fists and a knife.'

Jubilee's sense of guilt was eating away at her. She had put Zac into the jaws of the crocodile. After stealing his beloved toy and selling it. So now who's the psycho? she asked herself. But, she reasoned, she hadn't planned on his abduction. No one could blame her for that.

Oh, yes, they could, her conscience said. *It was your hand he slipped his into. When you put your finger to your lips and said 'Sssh,' he obliged. He trusted you.*

'I'll help you find it,' you whispered. 'I'll take you to your teddy. Come on.'

She'd held out her hand and, childlike, unsuspecting and innocent, he'd taken it. She'd lured him so he hadn't demurred or made a sound but had kept silent, tiptoeing out of his room, waiting for her to check no one was around, not even waking his vigilant roommate who would have raised the alarm. He had walked beside her, which reminded her of a song her granny used to sing when she was a little girl, 'I'll walk beside you . . .' She couldn't remember any more of it, only her grandma, singing it to her. But now, unwelcome, it simply conjured up the image of Zac. Less like taking candy from a baby, more like leading a lamb to the slaughter, she realized. And now, too late, she realized how deeply involved she was. She had been the catalyst. Without her cooperation, Zac Foster would still be lying in his bed. The police had already started asking uncomfortable questions. It was only a matter of time.

What she didn't know was why Kath had needed him.

She wished heartily that she'd never read that bloody article and recognized the toy for what it was, wished that Zac hadn't confirmed its value. They had the money now but it was bringing her no joy.

She hated herself. Not even the thought of a shedload of money, landing in Kingston, going home to Spanish Town, something she'd wanted so badly all her life, could replace the feeling of self-disgust. And when she'd delivered him to the car where Chi had been waiting, her new friend's face had mirrored her own expression. Self-loathing.

Then there was the question of the sleeping tablets. Jubilee might not be a trained nurse but she did know that old people and large doses of sleeping tablets don't mix too well. Chi had apologized for asking for more. 'Just in case he's a bit upset.' Which hadn't fooled her for a minute. So she'd stolen them, which had been the easy part. The medicine trolley was not checked frequently and there was always the occasional inmate who refused them. Checks were loose so she'd pocketed plenty. But as she'd handed them over she'd warned Chi. 'Don't give too many at once. He could die. He's an old man and isn't used to more than one in twenty-four hours. At most two.'

As if anyone was going to stick to that advice.

Theft of drugs. Another crime to add to her name.

How long did she have before the police connected her with Zac's disappearance and made the connection between whatever terrible event it was that Kath was planning? What was she going to be charged with? Murder? If Zac died.

She could almost feel the hand on her collar. Could she and Chi make their getaway before she was arrested? How fast could they run? Did Jamaica have an extradition treaty with the UK? She looked it up on the internet. No. Well, that was one little ray of sunshine.

As she neared the town centre, she tried to shift the blame to him. It would all have been all right had Zachary not kept that one article with its tempting headline. That one fucking article that he'd saved and showed her: *Teddy bear made as mourning bear following sinking of* Titanic *sells for £91,500.*

Zac had watched her read it, smiling, proud of his little treasure.

'Mummy gave it to me. Her mummy bought it for her with the compensation after Auntie Elinor drowned.' He'd been stroking the teddy as he'd talked. And she'd listened. 'Compensation,' he repeated, 'but Mummy said nothing could make up for what happened. It was a big ship and it didn't have enough lifeboats and the other ships saw their distress flares and they thought it was fireworks. But an iceberg had struck and ripped it open . . .' He'd displayed this with a tearing gesture of his hands. 'Ripped,' he repeated, 'a big hole in the ship and it broke in half and then it sank. Right to the bottom of the sea. And my Auntie Elinor who worked as a kitchen maid went with it to the bottom of the sea. She's still there. And this is all I've got left to remind me of her.'

He'd wrapped his arms around it and closed his eyes, smiling, gone to sleep. And she'd looked at the teddy, read the headline for herself and had the idea. Surely, she'd reasoned, Zachary's tatty little teddy wouldn't be missed? He wouldn't notice a substitute. He was too demented. But he had. The value meant nothing to him. It was just a childhood toy with a memory and a past, but it was something familiar, something reassuring. She was realizing that now. Too bloody late.

She'd done her homework, studied the bear, checked everything she could against the article, the size – fifty centimetres. The little button in the left ear and the magical name *Steiff.* Looked again at the astonishing amount of money. And the little seed of greed had been planted. And then she'd met Chi with her contacts.

> *Antiques and Objets d'Art*
> *Bought and Sold*

She could pinpoint exactly when she had first tasted reservations and the fear.

It had been when she'd met Kath.

And now? She would go when she knew Zac was safe. Not before. Going to work was hard. She felt her colleagues' suspicions. Real or imagined?

And every time the police visited, she sensed them inching towards the truth.

And then the sergeant was involved in a hit-and-run. And suddenly the heat was off. They were too busy searching for the person who had driven the stolen white van.

THIRTY-SEVEN

Friday 2 November, 7 a.m.

DS Mike Korpanski's day started with the curtains being drawn around his bed. Two doctors, one of whom was the surgeon who'd operated on him, were examining his right leg. The consultant was instructing the very pretty Asian doctor standing behind him.

He put his hand on Korpanski's groin. 'OK,' he said, to the Asian doctor. 'Tick for femoral.'

She wrote something in his notes.

The consultant groped again, this time behind the knee. 'Popliteal. Yes.'

Korpanski watched, concerned. This man was the one who would be deciding whether he was going to lose his leg or not.

He looked from one to the other. The surgeon was frowning and touching lower down the leg. He didn't look happy.

All of the Asian doctor's attention was on the consultant. Neither of them was looking at him. He was starting to panic.

The doctor groped again further down the leg. 'Anterior posterior tibial.' He nodded, smiled to himself.

He touched the top of his foot next. 'Dorsalis pedis.' He looked at the Asian doctor.

He touched Korpanski's foot again, a different part this time. 'Medial lateral planters.' He was frowning now, shaking his head. He moved his fingers lightly. Korpanski had always been ticklish, particularly on his feet. But he wasn't tempted to laugh now. He could hardly feel the doctor's fingers.

He tried to get his attention. 'And in English?'

The consultant met his eyes. 'Well, Sergeant,' he began. Korpanski held his breath, knowing the medical profession were notoriously pessimistic.

'Let's just say . . .' The consultant managed a tight smile and exhaled deeply. 'It is too soon to say.' He was speaking very slowly and deliberately and couldn't seem to manage a smile. At which point he departed, but not before the pretty Asian doctor finished writing in his notes, and flashed him a wide, friendly smile.

Korpanski stared after them, his heart rocking in his chest.

8 a.m.

It was lucky she'd headed in to work early, because Friday morning brought an unwelcome and unannounced visit from Chief Superintendent Gabriel Rush. 'Sir?'

He stood in the doorway and she looked up, met the pale eyes, the thin mouth, and what could only be interpreted as a scowl.

'Piercy,' he said and closed the door behind him. Sat down in 'Korpanski's' chair. Would he ever sit there again?

Without any preamble he invited her to, 'Fill me in.'

'You mean about DS Korpanski?'

'That and the progress you've made in finding out what has happened to the elderly man who went missing from a residential home almost two weeks ago.'

And when she hesitated he prompted her. 'You said that you had a line of enquiry?'

She chose her words carefully, picking them out like fish bones, speaking slowly, considering each word before she spoke. Over the course of the couple of years they'd worked together, she'd learnt something about Chief Superintendent Gabriel Rush. There was only one way to play him. Dead straight. No messing around, no flowery language and definitely no jokes.

'Even though it appears a physical and mental impossibility that Mr Foster would have been able to travel far, we haven't, so far, found him.'

Rush's mouth tightened. 'CCTV?'

'Negative. No sightings.'

'Go on.'

'We've done a thorough search of the town and its surrounds.'

'Dogs?'

She couldn't suppress her smile. 'We let Holmes and Watson loose after sniffing on his clothes, but they just went round in circles.'

'So?'

'I'm working on the theory that he was picked up by car.'

Rush frowned. 'Doesn't that seem a little unlikely?'

'It is unlikely, sir,' she agreed, 'but it is the more likely theory. It isn't possible he's wandering the moors after such cold weather and, as you say, after almost two weeks.'

'What about looking for a body?'

'We've taken the helicopter over the remoter areas of moorland with a heat-seeking device.'

Rush was still frowning. 'So you think someone is harbouring him?'

'It's the only logical theory, sir.'

'Why?'

She shrugged. 'As to that, sir, I have absolutely no idea.'

'You mentioned an inside job.'

'I won't go into the entrances and exits to the home but, suffice it to say, we were working on the premise that if the night sister was telling the truth when she assured me she had locked and bolted the day-room door, Mr Foster could not have let himself out. It's impossible to gain access from the outside unless a member of staff lets you in, and all three members of staff working that night say they had no visitors. I can only infer that someone on the inside led him out.'

As she'd expected, he questioned the word: 'Led?'

'He was elderly, frail. I think it unlikely he left Ryland's of his own volition.'

'You've searched the moorland?'

Joanna nodded, picturing the steep hill that led up to Ramshaw Rocks, overlooked by The Winking Man, a craggy rock formation in the shape of a man's profile. A hole in the rock behind gave the appearance as you passed of the man appearing to wink, something which amused passers-by. For a second, Joanna permitted herself a regretful smile. That was a stiff climb on a bike but she'd done it a few times, panting at the top but exhilarated too, loving the majestic panorama and watched by the stone man who, to her, appeared to smile as well as wink as she passed. The question that depressed her now as she rested a hand on her belly, which was appearing to expand by the minute, was: would she ever do that climb again? Not if Matthew had anything to do with it. Ouch. She felt the child move, kick her right under the ribs, and hastily resumed her report.

'As well as the helicopter I've alerted PCs Timmis and McBrine, the Moorlands patrol, but they've seen nothing of a wandering man. They've interviewed the general population of the area.' She smiled. 'Hikers, bikers and climbers and residents but, so far, nothing there.'

'I've had frogmen down both Tittesworth Reservoir and Rudyard Lake, but nothing there either. Which leaves me with the most likely narrative being that he was abducted and is either dead or being sheltered somewhere possibly against his will.'

'Still doesn't answer why.'

She allowed herself a smile. 'No.'

'I take it he wouldn't have wanted to escape the residential home?'

'Ryland's appears quite pleasant, sir.'

'Do you have suspicions of any particular member of staff?'

'I'm keeping an eye on all of them.'

'You don't sound as though you've got very far, Piercy.'

He'd picked up on that then. 'I am . . . confused,' she said. 'Initially I expected us to find Mr Foster wandering, muddled, somewhere in the town, spotted by a member of the public within twelve hours of his going missing. Instead – we seem to have hit a brick wall.'

'OK. OK,' he said impatiently. 'Yes. I agree.' Another pause while he thought it out before making a brisk response. 'If you want to extend the search at Tittesworth and Rudyard that's OK. For now I suggest you keep your powder dry and keep the search up.' Another brief, thoughtful pause before, 'Put more stuff in the media. See if you can draw a response from Joe Public. Someone, somewhere *must* have seen him.'

'Yes, sir.'

'I want him found whether he's dead or alive.'

She nodded.

She didn't even mention taking the police helicopter up again. There was no way Chief Superintendent Gabriel Rush, her senior officer, recently moved to Hanley to cover the entire Potteries area, which included Leek, was going to sanction further use of that. But she'd got her way with the police divers. She should be grateful for that. Thanks to budget cuts and assessments, they all knew how much everything cost these days and could anticipate decisions made on cost-effective interventions, which often meant no interventions at all. She should be content with the team of divers and could always involve the local civilian divers' club.

'Did they say Mr Foster has dementia?'

She wanted to say, *I am no doctor. I never met the missing man. I have no clue as to his mental state except* . . . She began, keeping her tone carefully neutral, 'He is diagnosed with dementia but I know little and understand less about his mental state, except that he was attached to a childhood toy which had apparently gone missing.'

Chief Superintendent Gabriel Rush gave no clue that he had heard this, except a minute raising of the eyebrows. She could read his expletive. And the sarcasm made his voice sour. 'If I'm not mistaken, one line of enquiry you're following is to do with this "toy"?'

And she had no option but to jump in with both feet. 'I have a theory about that, sir. From things that were said by another resident of Ryland's, I think there's a possibility that the teddy bear Mr Foster was so fond of carrying around might be valuable.'

She tried to ignore the fact that Rush was looking at her with incredulity and tried to avoid his eyes, staring, instead, at the floor.

He beetled his ginger eyebrows together. 'Are you saying that the teddy bear was, you think, stolen, and that has some relevance to Mr Foster's disappearance?'

'It's one line of enquiry we're pursuing, sir.'

Rush tried his hand at a joke. 'And you think the old man is also valuable?'

Not even tempted to smile, Joanna shook her head.

Rush continued. 'You think the old man was abducted?'

'Yes, sir.'

'Possibly by the same person who stole his teddy bear?'

Joanna was cautious. 'I think it's at least a workable theory.'

And he destroyed her entire hypothesis with one word. 'Why? They could have simply nicked the bear.'

And that was the point when Joanna shrugged and gave up.

But not CS Rush.

'So what do you intend doing next?'

'I've appointed a team to continue looking into Mr Foster's disappearance while I look into the hit-and-run accident involving DS Korpanski.'

'Ah, yes. DS Korpanski. First of all, do you have an update from the hospital?'

'His wife rang this morning. She says the doctors still have concerns. They're worried he could still lose his leg, particularly if he picks up an infection.'

'I see.' He was silent for a moment, his response difficult to interpret apart from one long sigh. 'And your investigation into the hit-and-run?'

'It'll take a few days to get any prints or DNA from the van, if any survived the fire. Apart from confirming that the collision was deliberate, we've not picked up anything helpful from the CCTV footage.' She corrected her statement. 'At least, we see the car travelling up Russell Street with two people in. We're trying to get the images enhanced but we're not hopeful we'll be able to identify them.'

That kept him quiet for a moment. His expression was grave. He shook his head. 'This is bad.'

And this time it was she who was trying to cheer him up. 'Sir, it's early days yet. I'm hopeful we will get the driver.' She didn't dare broach the subject of Korpanski being a potential amputee. Her voice would have let her down. And she didn't want that. Not in front of Rush.

For the briefest of moments, their eyes met. Neither said a word. Then Rush nodded. 'Do you need more manpower? A couple of officers on secondment?'

'Not at the moment.'

He stood up and, surprisingly, touched her on the shoulder. 'When do you go on your maternity leave?'

'The end of the month, sir.'

'And when do you intend to return to active duty?'

'As soon as possible. The baby is due early January, though my husband thinks it will come early – before Christmas. I hope to be back by February.'

His eyebrows would have met his hairline, but CS Gabriel Rush's hairline had receded too far back.

'Motherhood not your thing, Piercy?'

And she gave an honest answer. 'I don't think so, sir, though I've yet to try it.'

At which she read a new expression on the chief superintendent's face. Surprise.

Then he turned towards the door. 'Keep me up to date, won't you?'

'I will, sir.'

'On both counts. And Piercy . . .' Now he was frowning. 'That Whalley girl?'

'Quiet as a mouse, sir.'

His response was predictable. 'Let's hope it stays that way.'

It was only after he'd left that she had time to reflect on his attitude. Not judgmental, not critical. In fact, with his offer of backup officers, CS Rush had been positively helpful.

12.50 p.m.

Kath was on a last recce. She wanted this to go right and she couldn't afford any problems so she was going to have a trial run. Monitor times, allowing for the old man slowing her down. She gave him an extra dose of the sleeping stuff, left Fifi in charge and 'persuaded' Debs to drive her over to Gradbach and park up while she hiked the mile or so over open moorland to Lud's Church. She was drawn to the place by its dark past.

She didn't care what was fact and what fiction. She was going to make her own fiction into bloody fact.

Kath rubbed her jagged tooth and remembered the ship's figurehead in the form of a woman which had been placed at the entrance to the ravine. 'I wonder,' she mused, as she strode towards the entrance, 'if one day they'll put a little statue or a plaque or something saying:

Here lies Detective Inspector Joanna Piercy and child. Murdered by . . . Martyred by . . .

So she, Kath, would have her own permanent tribute here too. So fitting. But at least she'd be alive, whereas Piercy . . .

Kath was a stocky girl and, in spite of a life so far filled with fags and plenty of cider, she was well able to cover the hike through bracken-lined paths, sloping across mud and bare trees. With a satisfied smile, as she threaded through bracken, she realized she hadn't seen another soul for almost an hour. Perfect. The area was scrub, a few trees but mainly open moorland. Of course, dragging the old man along would have its challenges. But she'd manage it.

Even though she knew the area well, it was still easy to miss the entrance. But there it was, slippery moss-covered steps steeply descending right down into the narrow cleft in the rock which had hidden the Lollards so effectively from their fate. Kath smothered her mouth with her hand, the chuckle still escaping. 'No such luck for you, Piercy,' she said.

But the remoteness of the area posed a problem. They were going to have trouble bringing him here. The old man didn't have much juice in him any more. If they dragged him he would struggle. Even without the bellyful of sleeping stuff they were habitually feeding him. And so would they. It was quite a hike from the nearest place a car could drop them off, and the ground was rough and uneven. It would be very difficult to get him here. But it did have to be here.

Nowhere else would do. Kath wasn't stupid; she was a strategist these days, thanks to the teachings of Lakshmi. She closed her eyes for a moment, saw the old man pushed down the steps, Joanna Piercy *charging in for the rescue*. But she had a plan for the bitch. No one was going to rescue her. Kath fingered her knife, sharpened in readiness. By the time the rest of the team got here, having been delayed by her scattered clues, Piercy would have been dealt with, the sproglet no longer kicking around in her womb. She rubbed the jagged tooth with her finger. Two for the price of one.

She felt so happy she laughed out loud. Kath's laugh was an odd sound, more of a cackle. And it served as a warning to those who knew her well. Kath didn't laugh at the usual things, the jokes and tricks. She laughed at misfortune, accidents, particularly bad ones. The worse the tragedy, the harder Kath laughed.

She descended the steps, slipping on the damp rocks covered in moss; she tried to grab a handhold on the dripping and cold walls of the gulley, but they were too slippery. She looked up. The walls were as high as a house. Well concealed from prying eyes. In the week, at this time of year, in this dull and uninviting place, it was empty.

She walked to the end of the chasm, emerging into the watery light at the bottom. Then she looped round the back and found some rocks on the top. She stroked them as a friendly ally. To add insult to injury she could bury Piercy and child under a cairn.

She leaned over. 'Look out, Piercy,' she sang out, her voice bouncing along the walls, calling back to her. *Look out, Piercy. Look out, Piercy.*

And then she left the dripping chasm, hardly able to wait before she added to its sinister folklore.

She covered the ground quickly, hiking back to the car, and Debs who was peering into her phone.

THIRTY-EIGHT

Kath was nearly ready for action. She just needed to prime her sister, Hayley, teach her the words, and just hope Hayley didn't make an absolute mess of it. Tomorrow, she told herself. Tomorrow.

Chi sensed that Kath was working up to her climax. Tomorrow would be the day. She was serving lunches in Rosemary's, thinking possibly it would be her last day as well. Tomorrow Zac would be rescued and they could be out of here. Jubilee had promised. 'As soon as he is safe and free, then we can head to London, board the plane and carry on with our *original* plan.'

There had been no shifting her but Jubilee was not one to break a promise.

4 p.m.

During the break between lunch and dinner, Chi thought it might be a good idea to check on Zac and reassure Jubilee that all would be well. By tomorrow they could be hitting the road. Reassuring Jubilee that all was well with her patient would help their escape to go smoothly. But as soon as she entered the room, the stink hit her. She almost needed to cover her mouth and nose. Stale urine and something else. She frowned, trying to identify it. It wasn't shit. Zac had hardly eaten anything since they'd abducted him. It was something else.

She was no nurse but something had changed in the old man. He was sleeping but flushed. 'Fifi,' she said, 'we're going to have to wash him.'

'Augh!' She expected nothing else from the girl. 'I can't do it,' she said, her face still expressing nothing but disgust. 'I'll be sick.'

Chi looked at her. *Useless*, she thought, before opening the door and shouting down to Debs. 'Bring a bowl of hot water and some soap.'

Needless to say, Debs was doing nothing without an argument. 'What for?'

'We're going to have to wash him. And open the window. It stinks in here. And I think he has an infection.'

'Oh, Gawd.'

But two minutes later Debs was on her way up and Chi could hear the water sloshing around in a plastic bowl.

Chi was worried now. If the old man died they would be up for an accessory to murder – manslaughter?

She wished Jubilee was here and then she could ask for her advice. But Jubilee was working what she hoped would be her last shift.

Debs stood in the doorway. 'What a stink.'

'We need clean sheets,' Chi said, 'and some antibiotics. Otherwise he could die.'

Fifi held out a red and black capsule. 'He can have a couple of mine.'

'Thanks.' Chi bent over the old man. 'Zac,' she said, 'swallow these. You're a bit ill at the moment. These will make you better.' She put them in his mouth and held a glass of water to his lips. Initially he gagged, but then he swallowed. 'Thank you,' he said, and Chi hoped with all her heart that he could be returned to Ryland's and live out the rest of his days in peace. But first she knew Kath had a plan for him.

She felt Debs start. As she placed the bowl of water and a towel on the floor, her eyes met Chi's. 'Die?'

'Well, you must have realized that might happen,' Chi hissed. 'He's old and we haven't exactly looked after him. All we've done is feed him sleeping pills. Now come on, help me clean him up.'

And with some satisfaction she read the fright in Debs's eyes. 'What we going to do?'

Downstairs, Kath was frowning. She had a logistics problem. How was she going to get him there? What about a wheelbarrow? Trouble was, if they met anyone, that would arouse suspicion. Wheeling an old man along in a bloody wheelbarrow over narrow muddy paths. That was when it hit her. Perhaps this was going to be harder than she'd thought.

Upstairs, Chi had stripped Zac, who was mumbling incoherently.

She and Debs washed him before turning him over and Chi saw what was causing the smell. On his bottom was a large, raw area from which seeped pus.

'What's that? What's happened?'

She took out her mobile phone, took a photograph and sent it to Jubilee. Her phone rang immediately. 'It's a pressure sore. He needs to lie on his side. Turn him every hour or so. And he'll need some antibiotics.'

'I've given him some of Fifi's. Can you get us some more?'

But instead of responding, Jubilee clucked her tongue on the roof of her mouth. 'When are you going to get him back to Ryland's?'

'I don't know. Soon.'

Chi heard Kath stomping up the stairs. She felt cold. There was something very hard about those steps. Kath was practically stamping. Did she mean to kill Piercy? The baby too? Being involved in the death of a policewoman meant the force would come after them with all the manpower and might at their disposal. And two officers? She'd heard the news that Korpanski had been involved in a hit-and-run. And don't tell me they won't connect that to Kath, she thought. Kath was making no real attempt to cover her tracks. And that wasn't all. The full force of the law would be as nothing compared to Piercy's husband's vengeance if they harmed his baby. His revenge would be terrible.

What had Kath unleashed?

And then Chi thought about her own future. Lately she had seen Kath looking at her and realized she was next in the firing line. Kath no longer trusted her. And then she was standing in the doorway. For a moment she watched, not reacting to the smell or the scene but looking at her, perhaps reading her mind, while Chi held her gaze. Kath jabbed her with an index finger. 'I'm going to need help to get him there,' she said. 'You'll help me, Chi, won't you?'

Chi knew there was only one answer to this. She nodded.

Kath peered down at the bed. 'It's going to be hard, though.'

'I know that.'

Kath turned around and stumped downstairs again. Chi studied the man in the bed. She might not have a medical degree, but it didn't take one to know that Kath needed to move things fast. The old man wasn't looking too well. He was sleepy most of the time. He wasn't eating and he was beginning to look a nasty yellow colour. Even Fifi had stopped fiddling with her infected nose and was beginning to make comments about abduction, death, stuff like that, words that Chi didn't even know were in her vocabulary. If Kath didn't sort it soon, the old geezer would snuff it.

She gave him a sip of water which he took greedily.

They tidied him up and went downstairs.

Kath met her at the bottom. 'You can keep any money you get for that thing,' she said. 'I don't care about that. You can fuck off to Jamaica if you like with your new friend before the heat comes on.'

Chi narrowed her eyes. Kath was not known for her generosity. She was up to something.

'I just want you to help me get him to Lud's Church.'

Chi was still suspicious. 'And then what?'

'Never you mind.' Kath grinned, her jagged tooth on full display. When Kath tried to look innocent, Chi had realized, that was when you really needed to watch out.

Kath was still sounding conciliatory. 'You can leave all the details to me. I've got what *I* want. I have my goat. And now we have to tie him to a tree and wait for the tiger.'

It was that tiny word, 'we', that told Chi what she needed to know. Kath was intending to land her right in it.

THIRTY-NINE

Saturday 3 November, 6.58 a.m.

That morning as the sun rose over The Roaches the far wall of Lud's Church had the briefest dusting of gold, though the glow only penetrated the top few inches. The rest remained sullen and dark, quiet as the grave except for the drips which tapped out a slow beat as they coursed down the walls, quenching the thirsty ferns and finally puddling on the floor making the stones slippery as an ice rink ready to make the unwary fall. A mouse skirted the edge but, peering over, was glad to scuttle back into the safety of his nest.

11 a.m.

Kath had already primed Hayley. After considering her three best 'mates', she had decided she needed Chi to help with the old man. Besides, she had plans for Chi. Fifi's voice, particularly with its current nasal overtone, would be recognizable. Besides Fifi was too stupid. Even stupider than Hayley. She'd mix her words up, make a mess of it all. And Debs? She needed Debs to drive. No. Family loyalty was the best plan.

In other words Hayley.

Now Hayley was her sister and as such could be expected to be loyal and want to help her. But sometimes she didn't seem to want to play ball. And this was one of those annoying times. The stocky little shit had stood her ground. 'I don't want to, Kath.' Her next statement had almost guaranteed a smack in the face even if she was her sister. 'I'm trying to go straight, you know.' Kath had stared at her, amazed. 'Go straight?' she jeered. 'Why would you want to go straight?'

Her sister's reply had stunned her. 'Because I don't want to end up like you.'

'But you're a Whalley. Of course you'll end up like me. Crime's in our blood – just like being Jewish or something. You can't change it.'

Kath was beginning to panic. She needed her sister's cooperation.

She'd rarely had to try persuasion on a family member. It wasn't her usual way of making certain people do as she wanted. Threats and fear, chuck in a bit of torture. That was more her style, but this was one of those rare moments when she needed to use another weapon. Loyalty? Balled fists held behind her back, she tried again. 'All you've got to do is read the fucking words on the sheet and don't answer any questions.'

'I'll get it wrong, Kath,' Hayley bleated. 'I know I will. Besides, what if they recognize my voice? They'll know it's me. They'll come after me and they know where I live.'

'You silly cow. They won't know it's you. Just make up a name. Don't use your own and disguise your voice.'

Hayley still looked reluctant, so Kath tried another card, even more foreign to her. 'Come on, Hay.' She accompanied this with a leer and a soft punch (softer than she wanted to administer) on the shoulder. 'You're my sister.'

Hayley simply stared back, uncertain, but now Kath was reading fear in her eyes. She would know the cost of crossing her big sister. Maybe persuasion hadn't been the best way of convincing Hayley to fall in with her plan. Maybe she should have relied on good old-fashioned threats. She could see in Hayley's eyes that she was wavering.

'I am never doing anything for you ever again.'

'You won't have to. This is a one-off.'

Midday

Being in hospital, confined to bed, with restricted visiting hours, DS Mike Korpanski had little to do except fiddle with his phone, play games, watch the nurses bustle around their work, observe the doctors, feel himself for his leg pulses, at least the ones he could reach, and think. Strung up like a chicken, his leg was throbbing. He rang for some painkillers and then attempted to settle and read on a Kindle that Fran had brought in but had filled up with detective stories. Detective stories? As if.

As boredom set in, Korpanski began to recall the accident that had put him there.

No accident. The more flashbacks he experienced, the more convinced he was that it had been deliberate. What he couldn't work out had been why?

Until a Eureka moment.

2 p.m.

Bundling him downstairs had been trickier than they'd anticipated. Hoiking him a mile across the moors was going to be a big challenge. Luckily she had Chi to give her a hand. At least Chi was strong. They were held up at traffic lights, which made all of them twitchy, except Zachary, whose eyes were wide open, his shoulders hunched. Traffic lights meant being stationary. And anyone could have looked in and seen three women with one frightened old man.

The lights turned green.

Leaving Debs to mind the car ready for escape, Kath and Chi staggered along the path under pine trees dragging Zac between them. A cold wind rattled through the pine needles, making the experience even more unpleasant, and Zachary was too drowsy to stand upright. Maybe they had overdone the sedation. His feet dragged along the path, picking up mud and pine needles. 'Please,' he managed, 'can't we stop? Why are we here?'

'We're looking for your teddy, Zac.' Chi was attempting to cheer him up.

But he looked at her with perceptive eyes. 'You won't find him out here,' he said. 'Teddy wouldn't have come out here. Not without me. We should go back.'

'Soon, old man,' Kath said, spitting out some chewing gum that had lost its flavour. 'You're helping us.'

'How?'

'Never you mind. I'll explain when we get there.'

They walked a few more steps before Kath turned back to him. 'Give me your slipper.'

'I'll be barefoot.'

'I said give me your slipper.'

Without further argument he removed his slipper and handed it to her. She left it at the side of the path. Just in sight, ready to be found.

He was silent for a few more steps but then, childlike, he spoke again. 'Is it much farther?'

'No. No. Not much.'

It was cold. Kath started muttering. 'Nearly ready, my dear. Come to Kath.'

Chi spoke up. 'Is this all really worth it?'

She practically blenched when Kath turned furious eyes on her. 'You don't get it, do you? This is the best time possible. Now she's carrying that sweet little infant. All blond hair and blue eyes.'

Debs was sitting in the car tempted to leave the scene. It wouldn't be long before the police cars would come screaming along the road, if Kath's plan came off and Hayley played her part. The terrain was such that you could hear police sirens all the way from Leek. What if they'd met someone on the path while they dragged the old man between them? She didn't want to be around when Kath finally had her way with DI Piercy. She didn't know Kath's exact plans for the detective, or for the old man, but she could guess. She'd do what she was going to do to Piercy – and just abandon the old man to his fate. And then more officers would pour into this remote location. And someone would have taken a note of her mother's car number plate. Worst of all, there was nothing in it for her. From her eavesdropping it sounded like Chi had money and Kath would have her revenge, but for Debs there was nothing at the end of the tunnel.

And right at the back of her mind was another uncomfortable thought. What exactly was Kath planning to do with her? She would be a witness, part of the whatever crime. They'd all heard of 'joint enterprise'. Whatever Kath did, she would be complicit, and she hadn't missed out on the paranoia Kath Whalley was displaying towards an increasing number of people.

They were halfway there when Kath demanded the second slipper, leaving it, like the first, just a little off the path, and Chi realized her plan. Little breadcrumbs strewn along the way would take up any officers apart from Piercy, who would head straight for Lud's Church. Considering the terrain and having to bring the old man, they weren't making bad progress. It wasn't far now. Chi spoke up. 'You want me to stay with you, Kath?'

Kath turned her head very, very slowly and fixed her eyes on Chi, who could read her plan. She was going to be the one to take the rap. Kath continued to stare and Chi had the uncomfortable feeling she was looking right through her, as though she couldn't see her. As though she didn't count. Was this what obsession was like? she wondered. A shutting down of the periphery, losing everything that was not connected to your focal point? It made her feel very uncomfortable and extremely apprehensive. She was realizing how little she really did count. No more than the old man, who was looking at her with those pathetic, bleary eyes begging her to help him. She was expendable, nothing but a means to an end. Her function was solely to help tether the goat.

She looked at Zac and knew she couldn't help him.

If she so much as gave him a glass of water, Kath would jump her.

She'd seen her take it out on too many people. And Kath was strong. Built like a weightlifter and even stronger and more solid since her jail sentence. Chi wasn't going to take her on. She had no option but to fall in with her plans.

But she moved slowly, placing one foot in front of the other, arm hooked under the old man's, dragging him along, trying to block out his pleading.

'Where are you taking me?' His voice was quavering. 'What have I done? Let me go. Please. I want to go back. I'm cold.'

Kath was taking no notice of him either. It was as though she couldn't even hear him. Her face showed a calm determination, eyes blazing ahead, skin pale. She was slightly ahead of Chi, tugging the old man hard, muttering to herself. Chi could guess what she was saying, uttering curses against Piercy, combined with malicious taunts interspersed with 'fuck this' and 'bastard' that, and other profanities. That was when she realized. Kath was mad. For now, her focus was purely on 'getting even. Getting Piercy'. It was her absolute obsession. But Chi wanted that freedom and sunshine. She didn't want to be here on this freezing dark moor where another dark deed was about to happen. But what could she do? Nothing. And so she trudged along the muddy path, strewn with pine needles and long-dropped beech leaves, wishing she could turn around and head in the opposite direction, taking the old bloke with her, depositing him on the doorstep of that nice, warm, comfortable residential home where he would be safe. It was her last chance. She knew this area well. They weren't far now. She was running out of time. Soon it would be too late. She skipped two steps ahead, dropping the old man's arm so he stumbled on to his knees with a groan.

Kath turned, eyes blazing. 'What did you do that for?'

Chi dropped her eyes.

They'd reached the entrance to the chasm. Kath pinned her with a stare. 'Don't even think of stepping out of line, Chi. I'll know.' She was already pulling her mobile phone out of her pocket ready to put Hayley into action.

Chi's last glimpse of the old man was him holding out his hands to her, beseeching. Then he seemed to crumple as Kath pushed him down the steps. 'You,' she said, 'stay right there.'

As they descended the steps, Chi could still hear his voice, weak but caught on the wind. 'Please don't hurt me. Help me. *Help me.*'

Chi was tempted to put her hands over her ears. Of all the appeals she had ever heard made to Kath, this was the least likely to provoke any response. She didn't want to hear it because she knew that voice, those words, would resonate inside her ears for ever.

'Good luck, old man,' she whispered, but her words were carried along in the wind.

3.05 p.m.

Time for Hayley to play her part in the phone box.

She'd pulled her hoody well up and completed the 'disguise' with a pair of outsized sunglasses which, if anything, only drew attention to her more. She clutched the sheet of paper, having practically memorized it, apart from a couple of little 'alterations' she'd made for effect and to show that she wasn't a hundred per cent under her sister's thumb.

As she walked along the High Street, she practised her lines as though she was an Oscar performer, even adding little flourishes to her words. She was going to make a good job of this. By Godfrey, she'd have them all running.

Debs had wanted to explain to Kath's deluded silly sister that this phone call would probably lure a police officer to her death, but she hadn't dared cross Kath. It would be *her* death that would be next in line if she so much as opened her mouth the wrong way. Debs didn't have much of a conscience, but buried deep was a sense that this was a step too far. She was frightened. She'd heard Hayley repeat her lines and had been able to tell by the way she was concentrating that she didn't have a clue what part these 'lines' would be playing. So Debs had made a couple of contributions of her own. Though she couldn't be certain anyone would pick up on the tiny trail of breadcrumbs she was scattering.

She'd left the front door of Mill Street wide open, knowing that their nosey neighbour would take note. She'd also left the door to the bedroom wide open and the sheets still on the bed. Maybe the smell would draw someone in.

That was as far as she dared go.

Some things are just too hard and dangerous.

3.10 p.m.

Hayley reached the phone box, as instructed, and dialled.

'Hello.'

PC Gilbert Young, in charge of the protected number, knew his lines. 'Your name, please?'

'Meredith Kercher.'

Young made a double palm-up sign to his colleagues, a what-the-f? But he scribbled the name down all the same and passed it to DC Alan King, who immediately typed it into the PNC with a confusing result. On a Post-it note he scribbled, *Girl murdered in Italy*. He passed the note to Joanna.

'OK, Miss "Kercher", you have some information about our missing man?' They were not only listening in but also recording.

'Yeah.'

It was a local accent.

'Go on, Miss . . .?' PC Young glanced down. 'Kercher.'

Silence on the end. So Ms 'Kercher' needed prompting.

'I think I saw him. I was out hiking,' Hayley read, nervous now. Even she had picked up on the fact that this guy didn't believe her. She hadn't convinced him. What had she done wrong? Kath had told her to use a false name. She'd only plucked one from the internet.

'Where do you think you saw him?'

DC King was frowning into his computer.

'It was near Lud's Church.'

'Lud's Church?'

'Yeah that's right.' PC Gilbert Young frowned. That didn't

make any sense. Lud's Church was nearly nine miles from Ryland's, a good mile from the nearest road and a hike across open moorland with paths through wooded areas. An old man with limited mobility who'd been missing for nearly two weeks?

'What makes you think it was the missing man rather than another hiker?'

'He was wearing pyjamas.'

Gilbert Young was shaking his head, meeting the faces of his fellow officers with bemusement. 'OK, Miss "Kercher", *when* did you see him?'

''Bout an hour ago. He was wandering. It's taken me this long to get back, you see. He looked a bit muddled to me.'

'So why didn't you bring him back with you?'

'He would have been too slow. I thought it'd be quicker if I headed back and phoned you. Besides, he wouldn't come. He said he had to find something.'

'Did he look in good health?'

'He looked all right to me.'

And she put the phone down. She'd done her bit. Kath would surely be pleased with her.

Gilbert Young looked at DC Alan King.

King already had his answer to the question he knew would be asked.

'Call box,' he said, 'Market Square.'

Which was both good and bad news. A public call box was so much less traceable than a landline or mobile. But the Market Square and in particular The Butter Market had a plethora of CCTVs since an outbreak of vandalism a few years back. Even better, like the cameras mounted on St Edward's Street, they did their job.

They all sensed this was not right, but Joanna was already on her feet. 'I don't have an option,' she said. 'Unlikely as this is – and it could be a red herring or a wild-goose chase. But I don't have an option. I've got to check it out.'

She had some hiking boots in the boot of her car. If she put the blues and twos on she could be there in less than twenty minutes. 'OK,' she said, already on her feet. 'King. You and Jason – let's go.'

If she did find Mr Foster, she could call for help and bring him to safety. It would soon be dusk. If he was out there he would be out in the cold for another night. She didn't have an option.

She knew the area well. She and Matthew had walked the trail many, many times, had enjoyed picnics overlooking the crevice in the rock, taken photographs, even slipped on the moss-covered steps as they'd descended into the chasm. Like many others, they had been imbued with the atmosphere so strange it was hard not to believe the legends. Once you had hiked across the moors, the place had a strange, haunted air; a sense of secrecy, violence and tragedy. But one fine summer's day a few years ago, both she and Matthew had had a rare glimpse of the escaped wallabies and that had cheered them up immensely.

Unfortunately, while Lud's Church survived, the wallabies, escaped from a private zoo, had not. Staffordshire winters were too harsh for them.

FORTY

Saturday 3 November, 3.59 p.m.

'My feet are cold. Please. Can I have my slippers back?'
Some hope, Chi thought.
Zac's voice wafted up from the bottom of the crevice. 'Bring them back. They are my slippers, you know.'

She looked around her. It was dusk already, the place acquiring a sickly gloom.

Debs heard the squad car come screaming up the road and back up, out of sight, nudging into the entrance to a field. She ducked out of sight as it passed.

Joanna saw the car and radioed the number in. And then the three of them pulled up in a layby, leaving Dawn Critchlow in the driver's seat.

They pulled on Day-Glo tabards and armed themselves with

a silver survival blanket, a thermos and waterproof boots before trudging along the track towards Lud's Church, flashing torches into the undergrowth as they went. They skirted the rim of trees and came out into the open countryside crossing a stretch of open moorland. DC Alan King flashed his light and picked up on the first slipper. 'Bag it up and take a look around,' Joanna said. 'I should head straight on to Lud's Church just in case he's there.'

So she and PC Jason Spark continued, calling as they walked.

There is a softness about the November countryside at dusk. Footsteps are muted; rain drips adding a rhythm to the scene. If you listen enough there are other sounds too: a mouse scuttling beneath the dying bracken or a buzzard calling overhead. Even its cries are less harsh, less predatory, less threatening. In the far distance a barn owl hooted.

Joanna had doubted there was any truth in the story. It was someone who wanted the sensation of having diverted the police, played a trick on them. But seeing the slipper raised some questions. Afterwards she might reason with herself and understand it all right from the beginning. Had the missing man been less vulnerable, had the time been an hour or two earlier, had the area been less remote, she might have made a different decision. Not to plunge in. She might have spent more time wondering. Why the false name? Just another attention-seeker? But this shabby brown slipper was the first tangible evidence that had turned up since Zac had disappeared. Not to have followed up this lead, had the caller been telling the truth, would have resulted in disciplinary action, accusations of negligence.

'There's the other one.'

'OK, Jason. Take a look around and get it bagged up.' This was strange. And concentrated her feeling that she was being led into a trap. Watchful now and alert in spite of her bulk, she increased her pace. There wasn't much daylight left and she didn't want to be out here after dark. Even with Jason and Alan King, who would soon catch her up.

She would rather have had Korpanski. Would have felt safer with Korpanski. They hardly needed to communicate when in a situation like this. Working with someone day in day out, each knew what was in the other's mind.

She quickened her pace again, anxious to be back at the car. She might have a torch but it was easy to lose your way, become disorientated and lost. Behind her she could hear the two officers rustling through the undergrowth, calling out his name.

As she was doing. 'Mr Foster. Hello. Are you there?'

She thought she heard a whimper and began to run. Or had it just been a sigh of the wind making its presence felt as it blew through the trees? She couldn't be sure. The rain was soft and sly now, sliding down the needles, pooling on the path to create slippery mud puddles.

She must not fall.

She stepped forward, out into the clearing where the top of the flight of steps led towards Lud's Church. And then, ahead of her, down, cowering in the crevice, she saw him. Collapsed, crying against the stones. Her natural instinct overran caution. She started down the steps. 'Mr Foster?' She could hardly believe it. Was this place, with its history, now playing tricks with her mind? She slithered down further steps. 'Mr Foster?'

He looked sick and terrified. Not at her but at something behind her, something hidden behind a rock. And in a flash it all made sense. Mike's accident, the abduction of an old man, the continued disappearance, the phone call so late in the day. Too slowly, Joanna turned around and recognized Kath Whalley. This, then, was the missing connection.

She didn't waste time asking any questions because Kath was holding a long knife against her throat.

All police officers are trained in self-defence. You duck. You slide away, you do the unexpected. You hit out at vulnerable, painful areas. Joanna knew all this. But she was bulky and slow now and Kath's knife was now pointing down towards her belly.

Kath spoke into her ear. 'I don't exactly have a degree in midwifery,' she said. 'Or obstetrics, but I reckon I can manage a caesarean section just as easy as the next guy.'

She pulled open Joanna's coat and stroked the knife down

her baby bulge. Pressed it into her sweater, eyes meeting hers. Joanna felt the prick of the knife, the baby kick as though to defend itself – if its mother could or would not.

Joanna's first thought was that Matthew would be furious.

Her second thought was sheer terror as she felt the knife pressed harder against her baby. And the child stopped moving. She actually looked down to see the ooze of blood.

Her third instinct searched desperately for the application of her self-defence training.

And then something else happened which Joanna couldn't understand at first. Something she had never felt before.

Yes, she was scared. Terrified, as Kath Whalley moved her face next to hers. She smelt stale cider and cigarettes and almost retched as Kath whispered in her ear, while behind her she caught the gasp of horror from the old man. Kath's yellow spittle landed on her neck. Joanna took some deep, gasping breaths and felt her heart rock inside her chest, panic making her dizzy. But in the next moment that paralysis of fright was swamped by a wave of fury and protectiveness towards the child she held in her womb. Her training flew in to help. She turned around and lashed out with extended fingers, straight into Kath's eyes. She felt their soft wetness at the same time as she screamed, 'You will not hurt this child!'

Kath's response was to press the knife harder and Joanna knew it was now or never. The baby would not survive this onslaught.

She roared and, in the same moment, almost in the same smooth action, she drew back her hand before holding it rigid and angling it upwards right underneath Kath's nose. *A surprisingly painful area*, the instructor had said. *So don't try it except on people you really want to hurt.*

And she really did want to hurt her. This criminal, this psychopath, this monster of a woman who wanted to murder her baby. The spurt of blood pouring from her nostrils on to the rocks was a welcome sight and only fed her hatred. She grabbed the knife and held it against Kath's throat. In that moment Joanna knew she could easily kill her. Kath was tough but not quite that tough. And she hadn't expected Joanna to fight back. Not with this intensity. She was like a mad thing. She staggered back and Joanna heard voices.

Jason Spark and Alan King had caught up and were already on their radios. Kath was neatly cuffed, Zachary Foster had a police-issue waterproof wrapped around his shoulders.

Chi slipped away, as slinky as a cat.

FORTY-ONE

Saturday 3 November, 9 p.m.
The antenatal ward, Royal Stoke Hospital

'I will fucking kill you.' Not Kath Whalley this time, but Matthew's furious response.

'I had a lead,' sounded feeble. 'I did take two other officers with me, Matt.'

They'd insisted she be 'checked over' in the hospital, and that was where her husband had finally caught up with her.

The midwife was rubbing her abdomen with clear gel, ready for the ultrasound. Matthew was staring at the screen. She could see the baby's heart beating strongly, tiny legs folded up. Large head. Of course everything was all right, but right now she wasn't absolutely certain she wouldn't rather face Kath Whalley with her long knife than Matthew who was practically shaking with anger.

He continued watching the ultrasound and the heart which was beating with a new intensity, and she recalled his words that he would never forgive her if she had done anything to harm their baby. (His son.) That had been when she had simply fallen off her bike. This was just a little bit different.

'Matt,' she managed.

He was avoiding her eyes, continuing to watch the screen and the child.

It was going to take Matthew Levin a while to decide whether he was more angry than worried or more worried than angry. Maybe in a few days he would get there.

Zachary Foster, wrapped in a blanket, his confusion absolute, even when the officer assured him he was safe, repeating the phrase over and over again. All he said was, 'Have you found my teddy?'

'I'm sorry, mate.'

It was obvious from the old man's eyes that he understood that. He looked sad. 'That's a shame,' he said.

Finally, Matthew, sensing she was penitent and perhaps sensing something else had changed in his wife, wrapped her in his arms. She felt his pulse banging away, his heart rocking in his chest. 'Jo,' he managed. 'Jo. Please – don't ever . . .' He couldn't finish the sentence.

'I'm sorry, Matt. I'm really sorry.' Her apology inched towards mollifying him, but his mouth was still tight when he wasn't kissing her hair, his hands feeling for the movements of the child. 'I can't believe that you put him at risk.'

She didn't even have the fight in her to make her usual protest – it might not be . . .

She had completely flopped, lost all muscle tone, all will, all strength.

Chi and her new friend were on the train to London, passports in hand, money safe. But when they looked at each other they could read their own shame mirrored in the other's eyes. They had already booked their tickets. By tomorrow they would be heading out of Heathrow Airport. Terminal Five. Next stop: Kingston, Jamaica.

To distract herself, Jubilee had brought her tablet. And there she read some text about a *Titanic* teddy bear that would soon be coming up for sale at a specialist toy sale, Christie's in London, with a guide price of £110,000. She read the article out loud. 'It says here the bears have a low survival rate because they were often destroyed after childhood epidemics of infectious diseases. Only a small number have survived. And that's why they fetch so much money. Oh . . .' She looked triumphant.

'What?'

'It says here in this article that the vendor remains anonymous.'

FORTY-TWO

Zachary was stretchered to hospital with one of the nurses from Ryland's accompanying him.

Even though Jubilee Watkins had failed to turn up for her shift, Ned Sheringham had volunteered to lose his day off to sit through the night with his old friend. Zac was checked over by a doctor and by midnight was discharged and was tucked up in his old bed at the side of his mate, Alf Dean.

The pressure sore was duly noted. 'We'll soon get that to heal,' Matilda Warrender assured the members of staff. Incredibly, Zac didn't seem too damaged by his experiences.

As she tucked him up in bed, Matilda reflected. Maybe sometimes short-term memory loss can do you favours. The teddy bear was not quite forgotten, but now Zac managed to cuddle a Jelly Cat rabbit which had been dropped by a young visitor. He sucked it and stroked it and it began to feel familiar. She bent over him. 'It's yours now, Zac.'

His response was childlike. 'For ever?'

'For ever.'

'And no one will take it away?'

'No. I promise.'

He lay back against the pillow and smiled, sensing he was safe, back where he belonged.

Joanna wasn't quite so fortunate. Matthew's fury might be lessening, but now she'd left the maternity hospital, she had to be debriefed, as well as make a call to Chief Superintendent Rush, who listened to her stumbling phrases without comment until she'd finished.

'So where are you now, Piercy?'

'Back at the station, sir, writing up the account.'

Maybe he could hear the wobble in her voice or maybe her upset at Matthew's anger was somehow transmitting itself down the phone.

'Are you fit to go home or do you need a medical check-over?'

'I've had a check-up, sir. I need to go home. Matthew will be there.' She flicked her gaze up towards her husband who was standing on guard.

'Then go home,' Rush said, 'and take a few days off.'

'Yes, sir.'

It was Matthew who ended the call, at which point she leaned in against him, exhausted, frightened and guilty.

He was too angry or – she stole another look at him – worried? to speak, but fetched his car, drew up outside the front steps of the station and moved round to open the passenger door.

Then he looked at her long and hard. 'God, Jo,' he said, 'I don't know how you could have been so stupid. You walked right into a trap.'

Perhaps it was that one word, 'trap', that made her put everything into place. Korpanski's injuries had been no accidental hit-and-run, no clumsy driving by so-called 'joyriders'. Fran Korpanski was right. It *was* all her fault. It had been a deliberate attempt to remove him from the scene. Korpanski would have stuck to her side like glue.

Matthew started the engine and headed off.

It wasn't until she was home, lying on the sofa, that she began to shake. And now Matthew's voice softened and he was looking at her with that familiar warm green light in his eyes.

He took her in his arms, pressing the child between them. 'Have you no idea?' He spoke softly, gently into her ear. 'No idea at all how much you mean to me? You're everything. You and him. You are my family, Jo.'

FORTY-THREE

Wednesday 7 November, 11 a.m.

It wasn't until Joanna stood in number 40 Mill Street that she realized how deep the hatred was that Kath Whalley had felt for her, and understood how being in prison she had harboured and nurtured that hatred; how she had spent her entire sentence planning and plotting her revenge.

When she entered the small square room and pushed the door behind her, she came face-to-face with the image of herself punctured with a thousand holes, one dart still stuck in the bull's-eye of the pupil of her left eye. As she waited for the police photographer to record the image, Joanna realized that each dart had been thrown with enough venom and hatred to scar the wood of the door behind. A couple had gone right through. Joanna looked at the punctured blue eyes and the hundreds of tiny holes in the swollen belly that held Matthew's precious child, be it son or daughter. So this had been behind it all. The abduction, the concealment of Mr Foster. All planned carefully. She knew her husband would never forget this, but it was also possible that Matthew would never really forgive her either.

His dealings since that night had been cool and she knew he was deeply damaged by how near he had come to losing both wife and child. His silence more eloquent than any words or finger-pointing.

Hoping he would never see it, the door was wrapped, sealed and removed as evidence.

She hadn't spoken to Fran Korpanski – neither had she explained her connection to Mike. She would tell him at some future date. Just not yet. Not until she knew whether he was going to lose his leg. The word from the hospital was still wrapped up in typically neutral language, and they were still waiting for forensic analysis of specimens recovered from the van which hadn't been completely destroyed in the fire. But Joanna would guess that whoever had been behind the wheel, it had been Kath Whalley who had organized it.

She had hoped that little of the dramatic events at Lud's Church had reached Fran Korpanski, who was too smart not to put two and two together. What she needed was a private word with Mike, so at five p.m. on the Wednesday she headed for the hospital.

As luck would have it, Fran was sitting by her husband's bed and, in spite of Joanna's girth, showed absolutely no sign of leaving them alone or giving up her seat. All Joanna had to communicate were her eyes. She plonked a bunch of grapes on to the locker and managed a grin. Korpanski looked back at her steadily. 'Jo?'

There wasn't another chair and there was no chance of Korpanski's wife giving hers up. She didn't even look at her but gave an angry snort down her nostrils. *Great*, Joanna thought. *That's two people who absolutely want me off the face of the earth.*

'How are you doing?'

His dark eyes fixed on hers. 'Not bad. And you?'

'Won't be long now.'

'I didn't mean that.'

His wife shifted on the chair.

'I meant . . .' He gave her a very Korpanski grin. 'Drama in the moorlands, eh?'

'It bloody well was,' she said.

'Shame I wasn't there.'

His wife's back stiffened.

'A set-up then?'

She nodded, then tried to change the subject before Fran cottoned on. 'How's your leg?'

He shook his head and his face crumpled. 'They won't say, Jo.' He tried to smile. 'At the moment I have to be just grateful I've still got two. For now.'

There was an awkward pause then Korpanski took in a sharp breath. 'Do you have any idea who was driving the van?'

'No. We've got a bit of blood splatter on the front and a fingerprint on the steering wheel, as well as some marks where they hot-wired it.'

'I thought they torched it.'

'They missed a bit.' And something suddenly burst out of her. 'You're going to be off for ages, Mike.'

'If he ever returns.' Fran's voice was an acid drop.

'And I'll be on . . .' A meaningful glance at her ever-active bulge.

The conversation was so stilted. Korpanski took up the subject. 'So who's going to keep Leek law and abiding?'

'I don't know.'

She felt swamped in despair and, looking at Mike, she could see he felt the same. At which, wife present or not, she bent and kissed his brow. 'Good luck,' she said. 'Keep in touch.' Turning to Mrs Korpanski, she said, 'I'm sorry,' and without waiting for response or questions, she left.

Heading down the hospital corridor, her mind was filled with memories. Korpanski's initial resentment at working beneath (as he'd seen it) a woman inspector; Korpanski when she had dragged him along on a stakeout which both had known was both dangerous and against rules. And he had taken a bullet meant for her. Korpanski's pride in his children, his mischievous leg-pulling, his advice and his friendship.

Her life would have been poorer without him.

FORTY-FOUR

Monday 12 November, 8 a.m.

The day began, unexpectedly, with a phone call from Chief Superintendent Gabriel Rush.

'You're sure you're fit to be back at work?'

'Yes, sir. I'm fine.'

They had insisted she have time off work, which had driven her to the very edge of madness. Sitting around, trying to fill up time, watching daytime TV, reading, pointless shopping trips depressed her as much as it delighted her husband. Matthew couldn't keep the smiles off his face at the sight of her home cooking or sitting on the sofa. The night before he had nestled up beside her. 'This is what you should be doing during the last weeks of pregnancy.'

'Really?'

At which point he had simply laughed out loud. 'Oh, Jo,' he said. 'I wish you could see yourself. I am teasing you and you have swallowed it hook, line and sinker. I know this isn't you, but we'll soon have a child to take care of. Mum and Dad will watch our baby and you can continue with your upholding of the law and restoring peace and order to the town of Leek, Staffordshire.'

Something gentle and understanding in his voice brought out a warm glow of love in her and for once she was silent.

There was nothing to say, but she had insisted on no more than a week off and had turned up this morning bright and early.

Rush cleared his throat. 'Erm,' he said, awkwardly. 'Piercy, it's . . .'

She guessed what he was being forced by protocol to say. 'I don't need counselling, sir.'

'Ah,' was his response. 'You've given your statements to the CPS?'

'Yes, sir. That was an interesting experience.'

'I don't think Madam Whalley will be bothering you again, or her hench-ladies. Unfortunately one of them, and a member of staff from Ryland's, are beyond our clutches.'

'So I understand, sir.'

'And the evidence of the van?'

'Interesting, sir – a link to a couple of known associates of the Whalley family.'

'Good.'

'Fingerprints, one hair, some blood spatter and a woollen hat with plenty of recoverable DNA. The van was not completely destroyed in the fire.' She swallowed. 'And Korpanski's blood too.'

She had never thought of herself as squeamish, but those words, *Korpanski's blood*, made her feel sick.

'We'll be charging them with attempted vehicular homicide.'

'Good.'

'And you leave in . . .?'

'Two weeks, sir.'

'Any idea how things are with Korpanski?'

'No, sir.' She didn't add that Korpanski's wife had erected a firewall round her husband so she didn't even know the basics of his medical situation. Did he still have two legs?

'Hmm. Well . . .'

Wednesday 12 December, 2 p.m.

On 12 December, at a specialist antique toy sale, a teddy bear catalogued as a rare Steiff *Titanic* bear, 1912, vendor and buyer anonymous, sold at Christie's Auction House in London for £110,000 plus, of course, buyer's premium. The bear was subsequently held in an alarmed cabinet at a famous New York Museum.

Diana Sutcliffe was happy. Every dealer needs one lucky break in their life, and this had been hers.

Kath Whalley was held in remand, while the case against her was carefully constructed, though sometimes she would explode with hatred.

And Chi believed she had had a lucky escape. She wasn't sure either she or the old man would have made the journey back from Lud's Church.

Monday 3 December, 8 a.m.

On her first day of maternity leave, Joanna was sitting up in bed. Matthew had brought her a cup of tea. However much she protested, he seemed to enjoy treating her like a pregnant sow, she thought, smiling. He sat on the edge of the bed, his hand on his child. 'I don't think it'll be long now.'

'I hope not,' Joanna responded fervently. 'I . . .' And then she stopped. How could she possibly complain? He kissed her. Not a sexy, passionate kiss, but something that felt as though it would last for ever. Soft, warm, gentle as velvet. Sometimes, she thought, she understood why it was that a mouth-to-mouth kiss is so committing. It is a bonding action like no other. She'd read somewhere that prostitutes rarely allowed their customers to kiss them on the mouth. They could fuck them, but a kiss was so much more personal, so much more intimate. It is kisses that stay within your heart, dripping honey into your soul. 'God, I love you, Jo,' he said and, in her womb, she felt the child's joy with a fierce but tiny kick.

'Ouch.' And then she touched his cheek. 'Hey,' she said. 'Are you going to tell me the name you've chosen for this child?'

'Bad luck to tell you.'

'You old romantic.'

He nestled beside her. 'And what makes a person romantic, Jo?'

She laughed, warm, comfortable. Later she would wonder. Had her very smugness been the catalyst? She would return often to that moment and wonder whether it was her last perfect joyful time. Without guilt, without apprehension, without foreknowledge? She had heard mothers describe the constant conflict of trying to balance work with a career, particularly policing, which was notoriously unpredictable. And at the back of her mind she worried. Was it possible that the recent traumas had harmed the child?

Surprisingly it was Matthew who referred to her work. 'What about the two that got away?'

'Beyond us,' she said. She tried to make a joke of it. 'In Never-Never Land.'

Matthew looked concerned. 'Which I believe has problems of its own? Pirates? Villains? Drugs?'

'Not in Never-Never Land, Matt.'

She threw back the covers. 'There it's always sunny and warm, the people friendly and the doors thrown open wide to welcome in strangers.'

He raised his eyebrows. 'If I didn't know you better, Jo, I'd say that you weren't taking this seriously enough.'

She was almost in the shower room before she responded. 'But you do know me better.'

Matthew's prediction turned out to be right. The child came early.

FORTY-FIVE

Sunday 16 December, 2 a.m.

Two weeks later, she woke with a 'show'. And then, with a soft gush, her waters broke. She woke Matthew straight away. 'I think I'm in labour.' The intense pain shooting through her back and tightening up her abdomen confirmed it. He took one panicked look at her. (For goodness' sake, he was a qualified doctor. He could have delivered the baby on the kitchen table – if that had been the only option.)

'I'll drive you to the hospital.' His hands were shaking. 'Hey, Matt.' She touched him. 'It'll be all right, I promise you.' *Surely life could not be so cruel that Kath Whalley could have harmed their child?*

He put his arms around her, buried his face in hers. But then a stronger contraction came and she gasped. 'Matt, can we get a move on?'

10 a.m.

She hadn't realized labour could take so long or be so tiring.

It was more than twelve hours later when the child finally showed its head. Matthew, white-faced, stood at her head, and in a rush of blood and liquor they laid the child on her deflated abdomen, a little cord stump with a clip on it. The connection severed, Matthew picked it up and nestled it against him.

'Welcome, my little darling.' And with a triumphant glance at Joanna, he announced his name. 'Jakob Rudyard Levin. And he's perfect.'

'How did you know it was a boy?'

He grinned. 'I saw the scan,' he said. 'Unmistakable.'

'But . . .'

He wagged his finger at her. 'You said you didn't want to know.'

The face he turned then to Joanna would stick in her mind for ever. The purest, most wonderful joy.

'Thank you,' he said.